FRANK FROM JERSEY

FRANK FROM JERSEY

DIOGENES KAUFMAN

Published by Trash Panda Press

ISBN 978-1-7362544-8-6

Typesetting services by BOOKOW.COM

To All Comrades Great and Small

Acknowledgments

I owe gratitude to numerous people for their support and guidance in the process of creating this book. In particular, thank you to Steve Passiouras from Bookow.com for formatting this book. Also, thank you to James from GoOnWrite.com for designing the book cover. Also, gratitude to Linda, Robin, Debbie, and the "Pod" people for beta reading and helping with your feedback along the way. And of course, thank you to Michael for listening to early drafts.

FRANK FROM JERSEY

PREFACE

The first thing you have to know is they wanted him dead. No bloodlust. They just wanted to get rid of him. He was a nuisance. Both in his words and his deeds. Problem is, he proved to be one not easily disposed of.

His predecessor, Joshua, had it better. He died. Mostly. And in being killed, his story remained true.

But Francesco kept returning to haunt them. So, they remade him in their image.

That's how you came to know him. Or rather, the fable of him. They had to tame him. Humble him. Break his will through legend.

Time passes. Few are old enough to know the truth. Elephant perhaps. A scaley turtle or two. But you won't find them in Assisi. They're old, but they didn't know him.

I did.

I'll tell you the story.

The *true* story.

It will make no difference if I bring you into my groves. If you gather around me and let the sun bake sweat onto your brow. A sun that, like Francesco, you only think you know. You don't know it until you see it dry the grasses, watch the donkeys take shelter at noon. See the Nonnina wipe the heads of babes with a damp cloth, working their fingers into a sign against the evils that come with too much heat.

I could tell you of the sprawling fig trees, how their leaves brought modest rebellion to Eden- another story contorted by the time you learned it- but you wouldn't know it. You wouldn't know the smells of rosemary, thyme, and poverty. The sound of church bells rings differently here.

You wouldn't recognize the land of my roots. So, I will come to yours.

The story of Francesco has already been painted with layers of tempera- rotten eggs- a fairy tale. What difference does it make if we place him in his native Assisi or New Jersey?

New Jersey it is, then.

PART 1 FORTUNATE SON

CHAPTER 1

Spring 2022

Francesco

The highway ahead is dark and glossy from the steady rainfall. Francesco doesn't see the flashing lights. Both hands gripping the wheel, he didn't mean to stay out this late. All he can think about is Bella, at home, waiting for him.

"I was about to bang Mila." Jonathan uses his sarcastic voice as he jokingly punches Francesco's shoulder. He hasn't stopped fidgeting in the passenger seat.

"For what it's worth, I banged her last week, you're not missing anything."

Jonathan runs a hand down his face, shaking his head. "I can't believe you're making us leave early so you can feed your damn dog," he whines.

"Talk about Bella that way again and I'll punch you." But Francesco won't and they both know it.

Jonathan cracks the window and throws a cigarette butt out into the rain as Francesco leans his foot harder on the gas.

Almost home.

"Hey, slow down, it's pouring out." Jonathan chastises as he scrolls through his phone, still sulking. Francesco ignores him. After a moment of silence, Jonathan changes the subject. "Hey, let me get one of your pills."

"Fuck off, I need to sell those." Even if Francesco wanted to share, the last thing Jonathan needs is Adderall.

"You don't *need* to sell shit. Your dad always has your ass covered."

It's then that Francesco hears the sirens, and sees the flashing lights.

"Shit! I told you to slow down!" Jonathan checks his pockets and looks around, frantic.

"They're not pulling me over," Francesco says as the police car in the rearview mirror closes in behind him.

"The fuck they aren't!"

"Just fucking calm down." Francesco pulls the car to the shoulder of the road. It's wide but there's no lighting.

"The fucking pills. And the weed, Francesco, tell them it's yours, 'k? Tell them the truth."

"Shut up." Francesco's heart races as the police car pulls up behind him.

"I'll lose my scholarship! My dad can't bail me out!"

"I said shut up!"

"Dammit! Think about someone other than yourself for once, please!"

"Shut up. Fine. Relax, just be quiet." Francesco lowers his voice to a hiss.

A beam of light shines through the rain. It sends pain shooting through his eyes and for a moment he can only see tracers of the piercing light.

Fuck my life.

Francesco rolls down the window and cold damp air fills the car. He can barely see the hairy arm floating behind the beam of light. Francesco turns his face away from the sharp light circling the car. It reminds him of the stage lights at an opera he saw with his parents years ago. The beams formed a figure eight on ruby curtains. It had been amusing then.

"Know why I pulled you over?" a deep voice inquires.

He wants to tell the cop to fuck off. To ask to see his badge. To threaten to call his father's lawyer. Instead, he says "I, uh, was I speeding? I need to get home to feed my dog. Lost track of time."

"You been drinking?"

"No, I'm only in high school, sir."

"I need to see your license and registration."

As Francesco reaches across Jonathan's bulky legs to dig through the glove box, his friend tries to whisper, "my scholarship, my fucking scholarship," but Francesco opens the glove box hard and it slams into Jonathan's knees.

"Ah! Dammit!" his friend grips his leg, rubbing his knee with both hands.

Francesco grabs his wrinkled registration papers and then digs his license out of his back pocket, he hands both out the window to the cop. The Flashlight is no longer aimed in his face; the cop looks pissed. His square chin is dotted with a dimple, his jaw is set in a stern look that passes for anger. He looks Francesco up and down then turns his attention to the documents. Francesco thinks he looks like a cartoon cop. As if his exceptionally square jaw and prominent, dimpled chin had fated him to a life in law enforcement. Like Buzz Lightyear or the guy from the show his parents watched, Dudley Do-Right.

Jonathan starts to jitter. His foot taps the floor repeatedly. Francesco wants to smack his arm and tell him to chill the fuck out, but he sits still instead.

A shadow passes over the steering wheel. Francesco turns to see the cop, Officer Dimples, leaning both hairy forearms on the door of the car, peering his head close enough to the window that it's almost inside the car. He's wearing cheap aftershave. The stuff the guys that go to public school wear.

"Bernardoni?" the cop begins, "You a relation to Pat Bernardoni?" The cop's eyes are now interested. His face has lost the edge. Francesco is used to this reaction.

"Yes, sir, he's my dad."

A grin spreads across the cop's face, too far above his dimpled square chin. Francesco thinks he's about to let them go when the man's eyes fix on Jonathan. His expression changes. Francesco doesn't want to turn. Doesn't want to see. And he doesn't need to.

"Hey, what you got there? What's he doing?"

The cop doesn't wait for an answer.

"Out of the car, both of you, now!"

Couldn't just leave it alone.

Jonathan's eyes are bloodshot. When he stands up, the baggie of pills he had been trying to hide is now in plain sight.

"What the fuck! You brought pills into my dad's car?" Francesco doesn't hear himself say this until the words are already out, echoing farther in the darkness than he intended. Jonathan stands across from him, his face a mix of fear and betrayal.

He looks like I just kicked his mom.

His friend tries to speak but can't. Officer Dimples calls for backup.

The last thing he hears Jonathan say before two cops put his friend in the back seat of a patrol car is, "My scholarship!"

CHAPTER 2

Francesco wishes Jonathan would stop pounding on the wall.

"We're in jail, no one can hear you." Francesco turns his head away.

Jonathan pounds again, this time harder. He's crying. And now he's closer, hovering over Francesco, tears, and snot running down his face.

And into Francesco's mouth.

Another slam and Francesco is awake, bolt upright in bed. His face is wet not from Jonathan's tears, not from snot. He knows this now because Bella, his dog, is whining and licking his neck, pawing at his face. Before he has time to register the shift, in reality, he hears another slam.

"What the fuck is wrong with you?"

He hears his father's voice.

"I got a call from the police. The *police*! Are you trying to *ruin* me?" his father rants as he paces in front of Francesco's bed.

Francesco instinctively reaches for Bella, who leans into him, licking his arm as his father continues to shout.

Francesco thinks of Jonathan.

My scholarship!

Even if the judge drops it, Jonathan is finished at St. Vincent Preparatory Academy. Ruined.

And it's my fault.

"And under no circumstances is your mother to find out about this!" his father's voice breaks in. Francesco looks down, focusing on Bella as his father hovers above him.

The older man's eyes protrude, veins in his neck now visible. His face is red, and he raises an index finger, holding it inches from Francesco's face. Bella whines. Francesco tries to hold her, not wanting her to growl.

"Ok. Sorry. It was a mistake. I wasn't doing drugs, I was speeding, I needed to get home…"

His father continues pacing, ignoring the excuses.

"You're not like the other kids." He pounds a fist into his palm with each word for emphasis, speaking the words in a lower tone through gritted teeth. "You're a Bernardoni. I have a reputation to think about, and so do you!"

"I'm sorry."

His father ignores him.

"Not a word to your mother!"

The old man yells this loud enough to make Francesco wonder if his mother could hear it herself, but he doesn't talk back. His father leaves the room, slamming the door behind him.

Bella lifts her head and licks the side of Francesco's face. Her breath is fishy, but he doesn't mind. He pets her, distracted, thinking he fucked over the one friend he's had since childhood. Before anyone figured out who his father was let alone cared.

"I had to do it, Bella," he whispers to the dog.

She puts a paw over his lips, hunches up against his shoulders, and kisses his neck.

CHAPTER 3

Francesco walks to the dinner table on eggshells. His hand reaches into his pocket as he instinctively grabs for his phone, then releases it.

No phones at the table.

He's the last to take his seat, relieved that the long mahogany table puts distance between himself and his father, seated at the other end. The setup is designed for large families or parties. He has neither. His father glares at him, fork and knife in hand. Francesco feels as if he's on the menu. He looks down at his empty plate. Beneath the table, he feels a weight. Bella is taking her customary position lying across his feet, leaning into his legs.

His mother busies herself piling food from their housekeeper's serving tray. Margie isn't just a housekeeper, the older woman is also their cook and server, but he's only heard his parents call her the "housekeeper."

He remembers when she used to make small talk and joke with the family. Now, she just goes about her business, making only the bare minimum conversation.

"Dammit, Joann," his father barks, his voice harsh in a way the family has come to expect, "save some for the rest of us. Food isn't cheap."

His mother sets the tray down, silently obeying. If his father's tone affects his mother, she doesn't show it. They go about their business.

Francesco's sister Connie sits across from his mother. She's already begun eating. A good sign. If she heard his father yelling, if she or his mother knew about his recklessness the night before, he would know it. Connie's face would be pensive, tear-stained, and morose. She would be picking at her mashed potatoes and prime rib rather than shoveling forkfuls into her mouth. As for his mother, she would be in her private bedroom, door locked, Xanax bottle in her hand, sobbing while the meds kicked in.

But they're here. His father hasn't given up the secret. Steam hits his face as Margie approaches him, serving tray in hand, a plate filled with roast vegetables, prime rib, and mashed potatoes at eye level until she sets the plate in front of him.

"Enjoy," she remarks, making haste across the dining room as she heads back to the kitchen. The grandfather clock ticks like the countdown to an explosion. He dares to raise his eyes. His father's face hasn't softened.

"I need new riding boots before the competition, Daddy," Connie breaks the silence.

"Why?" He's surprised to hear a level tone in his father's voice.

"Because," she looks up at the ceiling, feigning naivete. It's beneath her. "Because mine has scuff marks on them. I need them replaced."

His father nods and returns his attention to the prime rib. He slices it with his knife and blood spreads across his plate. The routine always works. Francesco can't understand why. His father's no fool. But Connie is the youngest. And the only daughter left after the incident with Carmen.

But they never talk about that.

Francesco picks up his fork, realizing he's been distracted from eating. He's not hungry, but he doesn't want to draw attention to himself.

Not a word to your mother.

The prime rib tastes like sandpaper. He would drown it in ketchup if there was a bottle of it on the table. Jonathan hasn't updated his socials. He may have spent the night in jail. May still be in jail.

Fuck him. If he hadn't been trying so hard to get laid, I wouldn't have been in a hurry to get home. I wouldn't have been speeding. Never would have been pulled over. He shoves mashed potatoes into his mouth, sloshes them around with his tongue, and ruminates on the night before. It's true, he realizes now. The whole incident was Jonathan's fault.

And to think, he was trying to pin it all on Francesco, trying to make him feel guilty. What kind of a friend does that?

Francesco feels Bella's paw scratching at his calf. He doesn't have to peer under the tablecloth to know she's giving him the sad-dog-eyes. When his parents are distracted with chatter and his sister isn't looking, he slices a hefty chunk of meat and lowers it to the eager jaws waiting to pull it from his fork. As Bella chomps, she leans against his legs. He forgets the cops, the drugs, and Jonathan. Francesco reaches down and scratches Bella behind her ears.

CHAPTER 4

Through the third-floor window of St. Vincent Preparatory Academy, Francesco watches two squirrels chase each other across limbs of late budding trees. One twitches a grey tail streaked with brown, the other freezes, and the chase begins again. They spiral up the trunk of the tree. It makes him think of the spirals of DNA. Soon they are beyond his sight.

Sun shines through the branches. Through their bare spaces, he can see the school's courtyard and the fountain, water still off for the season, only to be turned on after May first. They'll have a half day then, and the students will be expected to help clean the campus before meeting in the main hall for a catered dinner. He's never touched a rake or trash bag. He's always spent the free afternoon hooking up in the park off school grounds or at whoever's house is vacant while their parents are at work.

All thoughts of Fountain Day vanish as an urgent buzzing pulls him from the daydream. He thought his phone was on mute. His teacher has stopped droning on about whatever the day's lessons were supposed to be about. Everyone is looking at him.

He grabs the phone as if trying to catch a mouse before it darts away.

"Sorry," he offers, but his voice is flat.

Class resumes. When he's sure no one is looking, he turns the phone over in his lap and checks the texts.

Why haven't you texted me?

Where have you been?

I heard you and Jon got pulled over

WTF

Why did you leave the party so early?

I'm starting to think you're not interested in me…

Well, Celia was right about that last one. He turns the phone over, shaking his head. You never know when a night of fun will turn into a nightmare. She's been blowing up his phone on and off all week.

Take the hint. It was fun, that's all.

He'll have to block her later.

With a louder intrusion, the alarm bell signals the end of class. He jumps in his seat, face reddening, hoping no one noticed. His classmates rise from their desks, heading for the door. A shadow over his desk draws his eyes upward. His teacher, Miss Duncan looks down at him.

Dammit.

"I'd like to speak to you privately." She stares at him through glasses suspended on her nose with what looks like a hand-made beaded chain.

"Um, yeah. Okay."

As the last student leaves, she eyes the door, pausing for a moment, then returns her gaze to Francesco.

"Finals are coming up, and I have big concerns about you."

"I've done all the homework," he didn't mean to sound defensive, but it was the truth.

"Yes, but your test average is a C+, which leads me to wonder if you're handing in your homework."

He freezes in his seat, running through a list of excuses in his mind. She's silent, waiting for him to admit Celia's been doing his homework all year.

Was doing your homework, he reminds himself. He should never have messed around with her.

He stammers a reply, making it up as the words leave his mouth, "I do better on homework. More time. I'm not a good test taker."

"I'm not going to hound you about grades, Mr. Bernardoni. I know senioritis when I see it. And clearly, you have a career waiting for you regardless of your grades, no?"

"Yeah, I guess."

"Is that what you want? Are you planning to at least go to college?"

Francesco shrugs.

"Give some thought to the life you want to make for yourself Francesco. Someday you may not want to be in your dad's business. You'll want to have options."

He looks down at his hands, letting her lecture uninterrupted. His eyes burn. Why does she have to nag him? She doesn't do this with the other kids. Probably jealous. Teachers make shit money. Probably hates successful men like his dad.

"Uh-huh." He shrugs and agrees when she poses a question. His father's voice, in his head, interrupts Miss Duncan.

Don't upset your mother.

She backs off.

People don't understand what it's like. His father has to protect his business from greedy people who try to steal what he's worked for. Francesco has to help. It's just the way things are.

"See you tomorrow."

He nods, then grabs his backpack and heads for the door.

CHAPTER 5

Bella runs circles around his feet, trapping Francesco in a shuffle over the park lawn. With every step he takes forward, she lunges at him, large paws bouncing off his chest, tongue logging from the side of her mouth. She pants and huffs breath only he can love. She doesn't realize how heavy she is. Francesco is no lightweight, but at sixty pounds, the chocolate lab mix is no longer the puppy she pretends to be.

To calm her down, he rubs her sides with both hands. She lands both paws on his shoulders, licks his face, and waits for him to lean down on one knee.

"Easy, Bell. We're on a mission, remember?"

She groans and rams her side into him, nearly knocking him over. They've been partners in crime since he was in junior high, but they didn't start playing this game until last year. Bella tolerates it. She gets to run alongside him through the park. He gets something else entirely.

Spotting a gnarly tree near the path, he stands and continues to try to trudge along, Bella jumping at him, begging for attention. After a series of pets, nudges, and repetition of the mantra *good girl*, the pair make their way to the shady area near the tree. He leans against it to catch his breath. Bella sits heavily on his foot, trapping him in place. She nips at his hand, eager for affection.

It's late afternoon. There should be more people here. Francesco checks his phone and then slumps down closer to the ground, careful not to get his new pants dirty. He smooths his hands over his dark hair, trying to tame the stray cowlicks into place. Bella follows along, trying to lick a path over his hair, but he subdues her.

Stroking the dog's fur and scratching around her head, she settles down beside him. Children rollerblade with their fathers. Francesco wonders what kind of dad has time to rollerblade around a park on a Saturday afternoon. Before he can ponder this for too long, Bella's ears perk. She turns her head, and he follows her gaze. A girl he would guess to be about his age wanders down the path, eyes fixed on her phone. She's hot enough, but nothing special. He'll have to see how this plays out.

He's surprised when she suddenly raises her eyes, catching sight first of him, and then of Bella. Her eyes rest on the dog, his phone is forgotten. She smiles, holds out a hand, and starts cooing at Bella.

Works every time.

"Is your dog friendly?" she asks.

Bella is great with people, but time is short. The answer he gives depends on his rating of the person asking. If she's hot, the answer is always "yeah, she loves people" and sometimes even "I'm training her to be a therapy dog."

They love that one.

If she's so-so, the answer is, "she's kinda shy, but thanks for asking."

But today, the answer is yes.

"She's very friendly."

Francesco hopes the blonde with the phone is also very friendly. Time will tell.

CHAPTER 6

Francesco's phone buzzes again. He's been lying in bed, staring up at the ceiling, Miss Duncan's words playing on repeat in his mind. He tries to distract himself by juggling text conversations. He doesn't usually care what teachers say. His future is already mapped out, pass or fail. Besides, he's smart. He could pass the tests if he gave a shit.

Bella licks his toes. It tickles and he pulls his foot back reflexively.

"Enough, come here," he beckons to the dog. She army crawls up the bed until her nose touches his. Bella lands a paw on his chest and leans over. Staring into his eyes, she pants.

His phone buzzes again. He lets it go a few moments longer so he can rub her belly. She sneezes and rubs her back on the bed. He scratches her with one hand while eyeing his latest messages.

Mila: Hey, what are you doing this weekend?

Celia: You're an asshole! Rot in hell! Why haven't you texted me back?

Derek: Party at your place this weekend?

Scott: Don't worry about Jonathan. He's a loser.

Derek: I got some people interested in buying some beans.

Michele: Cute dog. U going to the park tomorrow?

He ignores the others to answer the blonde who spent the afternoon flirting with him and petting Bella. He tries to flirt now. But all he can see is Miss Duncan's eyes, staring through her glasses- suspended with homemade beads- and judging him.

Fuck you.

Michele: WTF????

Realizing what he's done, he sits rod straight in bed, startling Bella who also jumps up on all fours.

"Relax girl, it's ok," he tries to placate both the dog and Michele, but to her, he writes:

No! Sorry! Wrong person.

Too late. She blocked him.

"Fuck!" He slams the phone down on the bed and bangs the heel of his hand against his forehead.

Bella starts to whine. She pushes her head past his hand, licking his eyes, the inside of one nostril, and his forehead.

"It's ok, I just fucked up. You know me."

She lays her head against his face and rests a paw on his shoulder. He hugs her, replaying Miss Duncan's lecture over in his mind still.

"I don't need a fucking test. And I don't need some bitch from the park."

Bella pulls her head away, a stern look in her eye. Moments like this make him swear she can understand English.

"No offense, you know what I mean."

She paws his shoulder again. All is forgiven.

CHAPTER 7

Bella sniffs the perimeter of the tiny office- more like a closet- that Francesco has been assigned at Bernardoni Realty. Her snout roots along the edges of a file cabinet. She has only enough room to pace in tight circles, whining her frustration.

"I know, girl, I want to go to the park too. But we're both stuck here," Francesco tells her, without looking up from a stack of papers. Bella's head slinks low as she pushes between Francesco and the old steel desk, settling on the floor at his feet. He lowers a hand to scratch her ear. A glance at his phone tells him it's only been a half hour, also, he's missed five texts from the guys. They've probably given up on him. Probably going to a party at Mark's house. He'll miss the fun, thanks to the busy season at his dad's business.

He rubs his eyes, blurry and dry from reading through tedious records, auditing the last six months.

"Why do you need to do all these audits?" he asked his dad last year when he first became an intern at the business.

"When you have money, everyone tries to steal it from you. The audit is where we catch them."

"It's babysitting. Why hire people if you have to babysit them? Why not just do the work yourself?"

"First," his father began, and Francesco knew he was in for a lecture, "no one is going to care about your success but you, Francesco. Remember that! Now, how do you get to be the top development and realty company in the tri-state area? By knowing when to delegate. But when lazy people see how successful you are, they want to take what's yours. Do they bother to put in the time to work for it themselves? No! Why should they? They may start out hard-working, but don't let them fool you. They're lazy. They'll take what they can get. That's why we have to watch them like hawks."

"How do you know they're all lazy?" Francesco had asked.

His father paused, brow furrowed, and considered this before replying, "because if they weren't lazy, they'd be the boss."

Francesco scans the forms in front of him now. Names of employees he can barely match with faces. Productivity reports. Timesheets.

Lazy. Or they'd be the boss.

He runs a finger over line after line, comparing one form to another. People are too lazy to do the work.

They just want to ride Dad's coattails.

But Francesco is next in line. An intern now, after graduation, he'll be an assistant.

"What about college?" he hears Miss Duncan ask in his imagination.

His shoulders tense. His hand clenches into a fist hard enough to snap the pencil he was holding. Bella yawns, rising from her rest, she whimpers, bringing him out of his daydream.

"It's ok, Bell," he scratches under her snout and lets her lick his hand.

What if he didn't become the assistant?

What if he went to college?

The questions creep forward from the recesses of his mind, and with them, the remnants of another life. He was small, but Bella was even smaller. He carried her through the house as she wriggled in his arms. He had set her down on the floor and looked up at his father, seated at the dining room table pouring over his paperwork.

"Dad, I want to be a vet. Like the doctor, we take Bella to."

His father slammed his fist on the table. Little Francesco's smile was erased in that instant, he tried to maintain a blank stare, to do anything but cry. He remembers the invisible punch he felt as if the wind had been knocked from him, from feet away.

"Cut the shit, Francesco. You're going to work for me until you can take over the business," his father shouted, before lowering his voice and adding, "unless you want to end up like Carmen. You saw what that did to your mother. Is that what you want?"

Francesco feels Bella, now full grown, try to crawl into his lap, sensing the change in his mood.

"It's okay, girl, it's okay. Down."

She leans into his side and licks his pant leg. He pets her head, memory once again behind the locked doors of his subconscious. Hovering among ignored mirages, above the forgotten things.

Like Carmen's face.

And what he said to his father on that day.

"Dad, Bella can talk, and I understand her, and I want to be a vet..."

Just like the forgotten memories of Bella speaking to him.

Outside the door of his makeshift office, he hears a familiar voice shouting from what must be the other side of the hallway.

"Insolent! Are you stupid, man? Who else thought this was a good idea? Who?" Followed by the quieter voices mumbling their excuses.

"Sounds like Dad caught someone trying to screw him over, Bell," Francesco pats her head and returns his tired eyes to the papers in front of him.

Babysitting. Because people are lazy. And if they weren't they'd be his dad.

CHAPTER 8

A late-night rain pelts steadily against his bedroom window as Francesco sleeps. Insulated from the cold downpour, Francesco rolls onto his side, lost in a dream, his arm around Bella's shoulder as she sleeps beside him. He doesn't hear Bella snoring in his ear. He doesn't feel her twitching paws lightly tapping at his legs.

In her dream, they're at the park. He watches women walking on the path. Bella doesn't wait for his permission, wandering off on her own. A squirrel catches her eye. His grey tail stiffens, a rust streak down the center. It twitches. She feels something tingle. The squirrel twitches his tail again, staring at her, frozen, eyes wide.

She pants, smiles, and hunches low. She should check on the boy, but it will only take a minute. The squirrel darts away from her and launches himself into a tree. Bella leaps through the air. She's never jumped this high. It's like flying. She almost makes it. Almost tastes his tail. With the wind passing by her tongue, her senses are alert. She can smell what the squirrel ate this morning. She just wants to get a closer look.

But he's gone. High in the tree. And she can't fly. She can only sit. And stay. At the base of the tree. Pawing at the bark, ignoring the splinters it leaves in her pads.

Awooof! She demands. But nobody listens.

She can no longer smell the boy.

The boy.

She jumps from side to side, turning her head.

He's gone.

In trouble. He must be in trouble. He gets in lots of trouble when she's not there. She races back to the spot where he stood. Gone. She lifts her nose and scents the air. Nothing.

She paws at her nose, but the scent is gone.

Bella howls in her dream, but only a whimper escapes into the waking world, eclipsed by the driving rain, unheard by the sleeping boy entrenched in his own dream.

In Francesco's dream, he's a boy again. Too young to even know the dog who now sleeps by his side, eight, nine, maybe ten? His mother's belly is round, but it will be years before Connie is the reason.

"A baby is coming," his mother reminds him. He doesn't understand how this promise relates to his mother's midsection or her sickness or fainting spells.

"Dammit, Joann, he doesn't have a clue what you're saying," his father cut in, adding, "your mother has a delicate condition, don't stress her out. Understand?"

He didn't understand his father's words, but the tone meant he was not to ask questions, only obey.

"Clean up your toys and go play. All this money your mother spends on junk for you to play with, and you leave it on the floor to trip me."

Francesco gathered his plastic construction trucks, his Lego pieces, and a battery powered robot with buttons that made blue and green lights flash. He piled the toys into his arms and hurried out of his father's way, depositing his toys on his bed before leaving the house for the day.

He knew by now that when his father said certain words and talked a certain way- not yelling, but not nice either-it meant he was better off outside. He already learned that 'dammit Joann' was not a proper title given to his mother, but a sign his father was angry. He found that out when a teacher asked him mother's name and looked at him horrified when he answered 'Dammit Joann.' He thought he was being formal, but a phone call from school and punishment that evening taught him otherwise.

He puts the memory away, with all the others, and focuses on the birds, the warm sun, and the smell of grass.

Stalking through the yard, following a squirrel. Just wants to catch, to pet, to touch. But he's too slow and now the squirrel is too high in a tree, scolding him with chattering teeth. He gives up and sits against the tree, digging in the dirt with long, thin, fingers. He turns over a stone and worms slide along the dirt beneath.

He watches with curiosity, then gently lifts one between his fingers and holds it up to see. The worm wraps its body around his finger, resisting the acrobatics of dangling in the air. He lets the worm slide along his palm before returning it to the ground. They've got his full attention. He almost doesn't hear his mother, in the house, crying.

It's only when her cries become loud, shrill screams that he looks up. Through the window, he can barely see the outline of his father. But he hears his father's voice. Ranting. Raging.

Francesco creeps close to the house, trying to hear from a safe distance.

"I work every day of my fucking life and it's not for you to destroy my reputation!"

"You're destroying the Earth, Dad. You don't have to do it!" his older sister, Carmen, shouts back.

No one shouts at his dad. But Carmen does. It must be because she's older. Fifteen. Not for nothing. He once saw his dad punch Carmen in the mouth for talking back. But she does it anyway. Just like now.

"Bullshit!" his father shouts back. Something inside the house crashes. He hears the sound of glass shattering as the shouting continues. He leans against the side of the house, peering around the edge to catch a glimpse as the front door slams. Carmen runs toward the road, a backpack slung over one shoulder.

The front door bursts open, and he instinctively retreats to the backyard again, but not before hearing his father's voice, hoarse from screaming, "You're out of the will!"

His father yells it again and again before returning to the house and slamming the door behind him. Francesco doesn't understand what it means. He'll ask his teacher in school tomorrow. All he can think of now are the trees. He runs into the woods behind the yard and continues to run until the stitch in his side forces him to collapse to the ground.

Heaving to catch his breath, he leans against an oak tree, gripping the bark to steady himself. He won't ask his teacher what his father's words meant. He'll forget. By the time he returns to the house for dinner, his mother will be locked in her room where she'll stay for what seemed like months.

"She has a condition," his father will repeat as Francesco sits down to dinner that night, just the two of them. "She has to stay in her room for now." His father will explain that he begged Carmen not to leave, but she refused. With dry eyes and a neutral face, his father will say, "she said she doesn't love any of us and she doesn't want to be part of this family anymore. She upset your mother. Made her condition worse." And then, as if nothing happened, his father proceeds to eat his dinner.

He watches his father at the table, licking soup out of his spoon.

"Dad? What happened?"

His father turns to face him and rises from the table. He puts both hands on his son's shoulders, leans down, and begins licking Francesco's face, like a zombie in a movie. Francesco screams.

He screams loud enough to wake himself, as he tries to take another breath, Bella's tongue fills his nostrils with the smell of shoes and fish.

He wraps his arms around her thick neck and leans his head on hers and she leans into him.

"Sorry, girl. Did I wake you?"

She doesn't answer.

CHAPTER 9

Bella pads along the trail beside Francesco, his stride not broken by her constant circling today. He lets her wander ahead knowing she'll stop to sniff the edges of the grass and he'll catch up with her. She never goes far from his side, even without the leash he stashed in his back pocket. A polite chime signals a bicyclist passing on his left. He steps aside onto the grass and turns as a woman rides by. She doesn't notice him, but he analyzes her before deciding she's both too old and also too far ahead of him on the path to be bothered with.

It's been almost a month since his last hook-up. Frank steps back onto the path, the sun is beating down, searing his eyes as he scans the park looking for Bella. He wipes a sweaty hand on the side of his shirt and shields his eyes. Across the lawn to his right are picnic tables occupied by a group of kids not yet in junior high but old enough to wander without adults. Their talking is animated and one, with a booming voice, keeps shouting over his friends. Just ahead, people fish in the pond, which is generously called a lake. Trees line the other side, their formation broken here and there with statues commemorating famous historic city leaders and war heroes whose names Francesco never bothered to remember.

There are plenty of dogs here today, most trotting beside oblivious people, lunging and pulling on leashes, eager to explore places their humans are oblivious to. He doesn't see Bella.

He turns in a circle, scanning the same areas again.

Nothing.

His back, previously sweating in the unseasonable heat, now feels chilled. She can't be far. She wouldn't have left him…

A wave of nausea hits him. He was supposed to be keeping an eye on her. He feels a sudden rush of adrenaline and his mind comes into focus. Walking on the path, he turns side to side, calling her name, trying to keep a panoramic view as he advances.

It's not like her to walk more than a few feet ahead of him. His heart pounds, hands sweat.

She can't be lost.

His mind begins racing. He'll put signs up and contact the shelters. Does she have a microchip? He can't recall. Two little boys play with squirt guns up ahead while their mother shields her tablet from the spray of water. A middle-aged woman speed walks, pumping one arm, phone in the opposite hand, oblivious to his distress. A group of skaters dares each other to ride off the steps leading up to a statue of some important person who has never mattered to him.

His vision blurs and he rubs his eyes, calling her name again. If his heart beats any faster, he's afraid he'll have a stroke. Or pass out. Or have a heart attack because Bella could be anywhere, and he was too busy checking out some woman on a bicycle to even keep track of…

"Is this your dog?"

He blinks, realizing he'd clutched a hand to his chest. His eyes focus again, meeting hazel eyes peering at him. There's a face, an entire body, accompanying these eyes, but he can't think of that right now. He's focused on the amber-streaked irises. Embarrassed, he shakes his head to break the stare and looks down.

Bella's eyes meet his now. She's sitting on the girl's foot, leaning against her leg. He can't remember her ever being that friendly with a stranger.

"Is this your dog?" she repeats.

"Yeah, yes. Thank you. Bella, where'd you go?" He does his best to sound casual. Concerned, but not panicked. Bella pants, her mouth extended in a smile, tongue lazily drooping over her jaw.

"Thanks for finding her," he continues, not sure what else to say. He talks to girls all the time. It shouldn't be complicated. But something is different. He doesn't want to flirt with her. Does he? He wouldn't mind. But she's not his type. He takes a closer look, feeling relieved that he's not attracted to her after all.

But why is that a relief?

She smiles. Her hand strokes Bella's head and the dog raises her mouth to lick the stranger's fingers. The sizable lab mix is now on her feet, turning to the stranger in a stance Francesco recognizes. Before he can warn her, Bella is almost face-to-face with the stranger, paws on her shoulders as if inviting her to dance.

"I'm sorry. Down girl, down," he tries to reach for the dog. She ignores him. The girl doesn't seem to mind. She's laughing.

"Here, I'll make it easier for you," she talks to Bella, also ignoring him. And then she does something even more stunning. She drops to the ground kneeling and turns her face so Bella can sniff and lick at her ear, cheek, and even her eyes.

Feeling like a third wheel, Francesco tries to make conversation.

"So, you like dogs?"

Way to state the obvious.

"I love dogs," she answers, trying to avoid speaking while Bella is covering her face with her wide furry snout. "I would love to have a dog, but we can't have pets at the apartment where I live."

"That sucks."

"Tell me about it."

The stranger remains attentive to Bella, who slumps to the ground, rolls on her back, and exposes her belly. Francesco has never seen her this affectionate with a stranger.

"Um, I'm Francesco."

The girl continues rubbing Bella's chest and leans down for the dog to lick her face. "And what's this beauty's name?" She finally asks, not making eye contact with Francesco.

He smiles, "You guessed it. Bella, which means beauty, so basically, yeah. You guessed it." He stumbles through the answer.

He glances from side to side, looking for an excuse to continue their walk. He's used to people stopping to pet Bella, or even to chat, but usually, they talk with him, not her.

"I never see you around at St. Vincent Prep. Do you go there?"

She laughs, and he feels like she may be laughing at him, though he's not sure why. "No, I go to Milton High."

He raises his eyebrows, then tries to hide the look of surprise. She wouldn't have noticed, too busy with Bella. He's never really met anyone from the public school. Maybe just to hook up, but not someone that he's wanted to talk to. Not someone like her.

The stranger shows no sign of losing interest in Bella, who basks in the attention, pawing at the girl's face and grinning. Francesco watches the girl. Her dark hair is wavy with fly-aways despite a ponytail. Her face is obscured by all the activity and Bella blocks his view to lean in for sloppy kisses. The girl wears a hoodie and jeans with holes in the knees that look like they came from wear and tear, not from the manufacturer.

His phone buzzes.

Should he pick it up?

They wouldn't even notice. Still, it's rude. And for reasons he can't explain, he doesn't want to stop watching her playing with Bella. He surveys the ground at his feet. It's not too bad, mostly grass, some bare patches of dirt. No mud or dogshit. He leans down and reluctantly sits, watching them play.

Bella is up on all fours and bounces around, tempting the girl to play a game of chase. She doesn't get the cue and remains seated. Bella runs to Francesco as if she's just remembered he's there. She licks his face and runs back and forth between Francesco and the stranger.

"I guess she wants us to walk together," Francesco says.

"Sounds good." The stranger stands up and wipes dirt from her legs. Francesco does the same. He sees now that a red A with a circle around it is printed on her sweatshirt. He's seen it before somewhere. Thinks it's a band symbol but can't remember the name of the band. They walk together, Bella between them, for what seems like hours. The awkwardness Francesco felt subsides. Suddenly, there are things to talk about and she's no longer just focused on Bella.

After their third lap around the park, the stranger leans down again to pet Bella before saying "The sun's going down. I better get home. My grandmother will get worried."

"Your grandmother lives with you?" He's intrigued by this; his grandparents live out of state. He hardly ever gets to see them.

"More like I live with her. Long story, but yeah, it's getting late."

"Well, wait, you never told me your name." He doesn't want her to leave.

"Mallory."

"Mallory," he repeats as if practicing.

"You pronounced it right the first time," she teases him.

He feels his face turning red and hopes the dimming light hides this. "Okay, how about your number?"

"Maybe next time," she smiles.

He can see her eyes sparkling. He doesn't want her to disappear.

I want to see you again, he wants to say, but a lump forms in his throat. What the fuck is going on?

"Well, it seems like Bella likes you. She probably wants to walk with you again," he stammers slightly. Bella comes to his rescue, choosing the perfect time to jump up on Mallory, her front paws on the girl's shoulders, and she stretches her legs.

Mallory laughs. It sounds like wind chimes. But that's ridiculous. *It's just a laugh*, he tells himself.

"Well, Bella found me today," she leans her face close to the dog's snout and lets Bella lick her nose and cheeks before continuing, "she'll find me again." Mallory kisses Bella's head and turns to leave. Bella starts to run after her.

"Bella," Francesco calls. The dog stops and turns to look at him, and Mallory does the same.

"I'll see you again," she reassures Bella and only then does the dog trot dutifully back to Francesco's side.

"Good night!" Francesco calls to Mallory, who is now walking farther away, hands in her pockets.

"Night!" she calls back without looking.

"Be careful!" he calls to her again after a moment. She gives him a thumbs up, barely looking back over her shoulder. Francesco remains frozen in place until he can no longer see Mallory in the darkness.

Bella nudges him, she's ready to go home

CHAPTER 10

The Next Day...

What are you doing here?

Francesco checks his phone again. It's been a half hour and no sign of Mallory. Not that they have a date.

She'll find me again...

Bella nudges his leg and jumps back, tempting him to play a game of chase.

"Not now, Bell, looking for Mallory."

She sits, stomping a paw on the ground and tilting her head to the side. A whine escapes from somewhere deep in her throat. Francesco has been pacing around the same few feet of grass in the park where he'd met Mallory the day before. On the one hand, she didn't say she'd be here today. But on the other hand, what if she is?

Bella starts to mouth his hand impatient for her walk to continue. A pang of guilt hits him. Wasn't he freaking out right in this spot yesterday when he thought Bella had run off?

"Okay, girl," he pats her head and continues to walk across the lawn, far enough from the lines of trees, the statues, and the picnic tables so he still has a clear view of the path. Just in case.

Bella pants as she trots beside him in the afternoon sun. Every so often, she darts in front of him. Once he almost stumbles over her. He indulges her and jumps side to side. She leaps and pushes off his torso with her paws, mouth in a wide smile, eyes alight.

He tries to focus on her but can't resist the urge to glance side to side, scanning the horizon for a girl with long, dark hair with flyaways, and an unseasonable long-sleeved sweatshirt.

He only sees the usual. Kids with parents. Groups of teens. A stray bicycler or rollerblader. Busy businesswomen walking designer dogs.

He tries to hide anxiety, anticipation, and ultimately, his disappointment. This isn't like him. Just like it isn't like him to look her up on Facebook, Insta, TikTok, and every other platform he could think of. He doesn't have her last name but tried different variations of her first name.

Nothing.

What kind of person isn't on social?

Carmen, for one, a voice from his subconscious reminds him.

By the time they've circled the park twice, the sun is retreating. Francesco's arms erupt in goosebumps, and he folds them into his shirt to try to stay warm.

He checks his phone again. There's a message from Mila, looking to hook up. Three messages from the guys at school, wanting to party next weekend. And one from Jonathan.

Hey. You there?

It's the first Francesco has heard from him since they got pulled over. He'll text him back later.

The sun is setting again and though he's not alone in the park, he suddenly feels as if the entire world is empty. Today is a disappointing contrast to the time spent walking beside Mallory yesterday. It was all a waste of time.

He feels a rough tongue on his hand and looks down at Bella, eyes wide in a worried look.

"Not a complete waste. We got to have fun, right?" He tries to convince himself. Bella whines softly, rubbing her head along his hand.

They walk home together.

CHAPTER 11

Jonathan slams a foot on the floor of his bedroom, Francesco is starting to close in on his lead in the video game. Francesco hardly notices.

It's been days since he's seen her. When he thinks about it, his face reddens. He can feel the heat in his cheeks, part embarrassment, part anger, as he thinks of the time he's spent walking around the park with Bella, looking everywhere for Mallory.

His father's voice interrupts his thoughts, *she doesn't wear the same shirt every day, dumbass.*

"Yes!"

Francesco snaps out of his daydream. Pining for Mallory just cost him another round. Jonathan pumps his fist, cheering for himself.

"I'm kicking your ass," he pushes Francesco's arm.

"That's because I'm not even trying," Francesco tries not to sound defensive. Jonathan just started speaking to him again and he doesn't want any drama.

His friend's long, bulky legs are spread out in front of him as they both sit on the floor of Jonathan's room, playing his PlayStation.

Old school.

Jonathan is good to have around on days like today. The guys are away at a party by the shore. He had to work at his dad's office this morning and couldn't go. But Jonathan is always around.

And so is Bella. Lying on the floor, a front paw and her face nestled against Francesco's foot. He tosses his game remote aside.

"This game got boring in the 90s."

"You weren't even playing it in the 90s," Jonathan snaps back.

"Whatever, it's boring. Enough of this shit."

Francesco leans back on his elbows and stretches his neck. His head is throbbing from doing his dad's damn audits and he hasn't gotten laid in days. Not that he's been trying. He can't get Mallory out of his mind.

"What's wrong? You're being a bigger douche than usual." Jonathan observes.

Francesco hasn't told anyone about her. The guys would laugh at him. Jonathan would too. Then again, Jonathan's a pretty big pussy, so it doesn't matter.

Francesco turns to his friend. Jonathan looks concerned, his brow furrowed, side-eyeing him.

"You on something new and not sharing?" Jonathan asks.

"Is that all you think about is getting high?"

Jonathan jerks his head back as if he's been slapped. Francesco stretches an arm forward and pets Bella. She opens an amber eye and rolls on her back so he can pet her.

"I met someone." He dares to glance at his friend. Jonathan is silent, a skeptical look on his face for a moment before he bursts out laughing.

"Yeah, you had me for a minute." He mocks falling over on his side, exaggerated laughter more annoying than insulting.

"No, for real, asshole," Francesco tries again. "Man, fuck you. No wonder I don't tell you anything."

"You tell me everything," Jonathan sits up. His grin is playful, not malicious. "And I'm the only one you tell real shit to." His voice is suddenly serious.

Was that true? Francesco wonders.

"So, who is she? When can I meet her?"

"Good questions." Francesco turns to Bella. She watches him raising one eyebrow, then the other. He traces waves through her brown fur with his fingers and she shakes as if she's been sprayed with water.

"Wait, you're not stalking a celebrity on Insta, are you? Because you remember what happened to Dan a few years ago."

Francesco cuts him off. "Really? What do you take me for?" Then without the edge in his voice, "No, I just met her. She didn't give me her number. Said she would find me again."

Bella turns her head to the side. She stretches a paw and grabs for his leg, whining.

"Okay," he corrects himself, "she technically said Bella would find her again. It was the craziest thing. I thought Bella ran off, but she was hanging with this girl, I guess? And she didn't want to leave her."

"First of all, I'm only telling you this as your friend," Jonathan begins, his voice somber. He leans in, runs a hand through his hair, and continues, "it's really weird how you and your dog have these little conversations."

He can tell Jonathan is only kidding but something in the pit of his stomach turns sour. The words chill him, but he doesn't know why.

Just a stupid joke.

"And secondly," Jonathan adds, "you can be an asshole, so maybe it's better for you that this girl met your dog first."

Francesco fixes his jaw, pretending to be angry long enough to find something to toss at his friend. A pair of black Nike shorts are strewn across the floor amidst piles of laundry. He doesn't think about whether it's clean or dirty, just rolls it into a ball and chucks it at Jonathan's face.

Bella is roused to her paws by the game. She jumps as Jonathan throws a pillow at Francesco in return, catching it in her mouth and landing between them.

"Drop it," Francesco tries to grab the pillow.

"Nah, she can chew it. No worries. She's helping to hook you up." Jonathan intervenes.

"No, it's not like that. It sounds fucked up, but I can't stop thinking about her."

"A crush?" His eyebrows raise. No longer mocking. "How long has it been? Since Tiffanie?"

Francesco pauses, eyes rolling up as he calculates the time in his mind. He shrugs. "Maybe, I guess. And that was what?"

"That was like fourth grade. You didn't even know what to do with your dick back then."

"Whatever. I'll probably never see her again." Francesco tries not to sound as devastated as he is. The emptiness in his chest, this feeling of longing, he's felt it for things. He felt it when he thought Bella was gone. He doesn't even remember feeling it when Carmen ran off. But he feels it now.

"Don't say that. Really. I'm sure you will. I talk shit about your dog, but she's got some Wishbone shit going on so I'm sure she's got you."

CHAPTER 12

After days of Ark-worthy rains, the park is swampy. Francesco's hands, balled into fists, rub the inner lining of his jacket's pockets, as he tries to stave off the damp chill. Only the most die-hard joggers pass him by. Their faces were dutiful, not happy.

Bella runs her snout along the wet grass, lapping up rainwater from the puddles. She doesn't care that mud has streaked her legs almost up to her trunk.

"Okay, you got to have your fun, let's just go home now," Francesco pats his thigh.

"Leaving so soon?"

He turns at the sound of the familiar voice. Mallory, hands in the pockets of baggy jeans, strides toward him, smiling.

"This is the kind of day you spend in the park?" He tries not to sound annoyed.

"Just passing through on the way to volunteer." She stoops to pet Bella, who smears her jeans and hoody with mud as she covers her with kisses.

Mallory doesn't flinch. Francesco blinks, he starts to apologize but lets it go.

"Volunteer? Like at a nursing home?"

Mallory laughs, pulling her face away from Bella's overzealous snout.

"Food Not Bombs."

She continues walking. Bella follows her. Francesco hesitates for a moment and then falls into step behind them, trying to catch up.

"Food Not Bombs? What, you throw food down on people from rooftops and watch it explode?"

She gives him an indulgent look, but her voice is patient. "No. We make food for the community."

"What community? Like a soup kitchen? For poor people?"

Mallory halts in her tracks and explains as if she's reciting from memory. "Those types of things are a charity. We get together and give food to whoever shows up. It's not about patronizing people, it's about building community."

"You like that word a lot," Francesco still isn't sure what she is talking about, but he doesn't want to ask more questions. It will make him look stupid.

"Well, we're setting up right down the block so why don't you stick around, and see for yourself?" She points to a section of the park Francesco avoids. There were always homeless people sleeping on benches. Drug dealers. Scott even got mugged there once. Someone stole his iPhone after his mom waited in line for hours to get it for him.

"You walk down here by yourself?" He instantly regrets the question. Mallory rolls her eyes.

"Yep, and sometimes," she looks side to side, conspiratorially, leaning closer and lowering her voice, "sometimes I even wear pants that show my ankles!"

His face reddens, "I didn't mean it like that," he tries to defend himself, but she's too busy laughing and striding ahead with Bella to continue the argument.

Up ahead, people are dragging picnic tables together. A man with his hair in locks unwraps a tablecloth and sets it over the surfaces. An older woman wearing a pullover raincoat picks up trash from the ground and drops it into a bag.

Someone with long hair dyed like a rainbow arranges foil trays.

"It's like a picnic."

"Yeah, pretty much, that's a good way to think about it." Mallory smiles.

He's used to women flirting with him, but she acts like he's just another guy. He walks faster to keep up with her. Bella is already running toward the food.

"Bella, leave it," he calls after her.

The woman with the raincoat stops to pet Bella, who promptly sits on the woman's foot and then flops belly-up, oblivious to the mud.

The man with the locs laughs. "Are you bringing along stray dogs now too, Mallory?" he calls out, his voice is friendly.

Francesco feels a rush of adrenaline as his fists clench. Bella is not a stray!

"This is my new friend, Frank. And that's Bella." She reaches out and puts an arm around Francesco as she says this.

Butterflies erupt in his stomach. Mallory retrieves her arm. Time is moving too fast. He wants to preserve the feeling he had just a moment ago. He's never liked the nickname Frank, always thought it sounded like a car mechanic. But he loves how it sounds when she says it. His moment of anger diffused; he feels as if he is among friends.

"Put on some gloves, they're right over there," Raincoat directs him. He nods, not quite sure he wants to get involved but also wanting to impress Mallory.

He starts to reach for a plate, anticipating a bite of the lasagna, salad, baked beans, and what looks like a giant burrito bowl, when Mallory calls to him.

"You can stand over here, by me. I'll show you how this works."

Bella follows him as he takes a place beside Mallory. Francesco learns the picnic is not for him, Mallory, and her friends. They're here to serve strangers, though she knows them by name.

For the next three hours, they hand out plates and packaged meals and brown paper bags with what a person wearing painted jeans tells him are "hygiene supplies."

By the end of the evening, he's exhausted, but Mallory is glowing.

"Okay, see you all here next week!" Raincoat announces as she helps a few others whose names Francesco forgot pack supplies into a van that's beginning to rust around the doors.

"See you then!" Mallory calls back to them. Rather than heading back the way they came, she walks toward an intersection leading to what the kids at school called the Stones.

This part of downtown got its nickname because unlike the streets on the opposite side of the park, lined with shops, boutiques, bistros, and office buildings, this block is filled with potholes.

He stifles a look of surprise.

"Where you off to now?" He walks alongside her. Bella sniffs the ground close to her feet.

"Home. You?"

"Uh, I'm walking you home." He tries to sound casual.

He expects her to thank him for helping her hand out food, but she doesn't. As if she thinks it's just a normal thing that people do. He doesn't bring it up.

"So, you go there every week? How do you know those people are actually poor?" he asks.

For the first time, Mallory looks annoyed, "What do you mean?"

"Well, like, what if those people have food, but they're just showing up to get more because it's free?"

"Well, so what?" she asks casually.

This puzzles him. "So, you don't care if people are ripping you off? Taking your time and energy when they really don't need it?"

She crosses her arms. "That's the thing. The people who show up, they show up for a reason. Maybe they have food at home. Who cares? They may stop by to see a familiar face. To know people care about them. Maybe they have more than I do? Doesn't matter."

He stops, brow furrowed, trying to process her words.

"The problem," she continues, "is that we've been convinced that everyone is out to get something for nothing."

He thinks of his father's words.

"Aren't they?"

She laughs now and this confuses him even more. "Usually, the people who think like that are the people out to take the most. But seriously, we're not about competing. We're about helping to bring people together. Food tends to do that. It's not about proving yourself worthy. People just come together and get food. Whether one person needs it more than the next isn't really an issue we worry about. Only a fool would care."

"Maybe I'm a fool. For you at least," he smiles, looking into her eyes. He thinks this is the time to lean in for a kiss but before he can get close enough, she rolls her eyes, laughs, and walks away.

"Well, maybe you are a fool. You make me laugh, at least."

They walk for a while in silence. Francesco is more than a little embarrassed. The quiet is too much for him.

"It's dark down this way," he begins making small talk.

"That's because the city doesn't think we're worthy of street lighting."

"Oh, good point," he tries another tack. "So, what kind of things do you like? I mean, music, or books, or what do you like to do?"

She smiles, her eyes sparkling even in the dim light, "Well, this. What we just did. Food Not Bombs, I help with some of the other stuff that goes on around here, you know, we have a lot of community events, it's pretty fun."

"Yeah? Like what?"

"Well, next weekend, my building is having this big fundraiser. It's going to be like a flea market but also some local musicians and artists will be there, everything is donation based but the funds are going to go to helping Mrs. Votti, that's an elderly woman who lives in the building, we're going to help her get a new electric wheelchair."

"Why do you have to do that? Isn't it up to her insurance company?"

"You've never dealt with Medicare."

"No, I haven't. But why should that be your problem?"

"Well, it's not that it's my problem," she stops to pet Bella, "but if someone needs something, and there's something that we all can do about it, and fixing the problem brings people together and we get to eat, and drink, and listen to music, and party, why not?"

He nods slowly trying to follow her logic.

"So, anyway, you should come down with Bella. I think Votti will love her. Most of the people in the building will. It's Saturday at noon."

She's slowing down now. Francesco agrees, then hesitates, "I have to help my dad Saturday for a bit, but I can stop by after, maybe later in the afternoon?"

"Sounds like a date."

She turns to point at one of several older buildings, a three-story multi-unit apartment complex that looks like it was built in the seventies and was likely in rough shape even when it was new.

"Well, this is it."

"This is what?" Francesco asks.

"Home sweet home."

Francesco wants to smack himself on the forehead but resists the urge. Bella jumps on Mallory's legs, reaching to lick her face.

"Oh. Well, uh, it was nice dropping… uh… food instead of bombs… with you."

Mallory breaks out into genuine laughter and for the first time, he's sure she's not mocking him.

"I'll see you on Saturday, my Fool," she waves, turning to head into the building. He watches her leave and stands there still, imagining which row of windows is hers.

Bella finally nudges his hand.

"You found her again, good girl," he pets her and leads her back the way they came.

CHAPTER 13

Francesco was already an hour late to Mrs. Votti's party when he spritzed himself with cologne and grabbed Bella's leash. He starts to head for the car, then reconsiders. Mallory isn't like the rest of the people in that neighborhood. He can trust her. But not them. He puts the key fob back in his pocket.

"Guess we're going to walk to the park, Bella," he confides in the dog, who is pulling him to walk faster. It's a long way to downtown, and the park, and then further from there to get to Mallory's apartment.

After two blocks, he picks up his pace. When he gets closer to the park, a bus passes him, choking fumes hitting him as it cruises through the intersection.

I could take the bus.

He plays the scene through in his mind. Does the bus take credit or Apple Pay? What bus do I take?

He imagines a heavy-set bus driver looking him up and down, rolling his eyes, and answering Francesco's questions. He imagines a bus crowded with people who smell like cigarettes and alcohol. Do they even let dogs ride the bus?

Forget it.

He walks faster.

For once, Bella doesn't pull him left and right, trying to play and sniff at everything extending more than a few feet from the ground. She keeps on task. His feet hurt. As the greenery fades and the streets fill with pedestrians rather than cars. He's thirsty. His phone keeps buzzing but he doesn't stop to check his notifications.

His heart pounds and he curses his dad for making him work this afternoon. Remembering his dad's words, he curses the lazy people who try to cheat his father's business.

Then he sees Mallory's face, in his mind.

"Are you sure?" Imaginary Mallory asks. "You think that's true?"

As if she's said it to his face, he squints, flinching, her imaginary words a slap.

The fantasy distracts him, and he stumbles over a piece of sidewalk jutting out at an odd angle, he falls face first, landing on both palms and just missing his knee coming down hard on a jagged piece of concrete.

"Dammit!"

Bella stops short, retreats to his side, and licks his face. He regains composure. Thank God Mallory didn't see that.

Frank has admitted to himself and Bella that he's in love with Mallory.

He hears the crowd before he can see them in any detail. *This is a picnic?*

It looks more like a small concert. A familiar feeling of anxiety tightens his chest. A group of young people with torn shirts and partially dyed and shaved hair jump in time with the music. The smell of barbecue sauce and something else- savory and exciting- makes his mouth water. Bella smells it too and pulls him harder on the leash. He rushes to follow her.

The crowd is a sea of bodies, some dancing, some talking and laughing, carrying plates stacked with salads and casseroles and things he can't identify. He doesn't recognize anyone from school.

Most of the people are older and some have small children. A few have hairstyles and tattoos that remind him of the Food Not Bombs crowd.

Bella begins jumping from side to side and Francesco follows the dog's gaze. She's found Mallory, sitting on the ground beside a couple in lawn chairs.

She sees Bella, then him.

"Hey! You made it!"

"Yeah," he tries to play cool, to forget the pain in his feet and now in his hands and wrists from breaking his fall, "I wanted to text you I was on the way, but I forgot to get your number."

"No, you didn't." She smiles when she says this, and he can't tell if she's fucking with him.

His cheeks burn. He looks from side to side. No one seems to have heard, or maybe they don't care.

"Hey, I'll be back," Mallory tells the couple in the lawn chairs, patting a woman on the shoulder before jumping to her feet. She approaches them, ducking down to meet Bella halfway for a sloppy dog kiss.

Francesco smiles, imagining her greeting him with this much excitement.

"I'm glad you made it."

She looks into his eyes. Maybe today he'll tell her that he's realized he's actually in love with her and she has to feel the same way and then he can get her number and…

"You must be hungry, come on." She grabs his wrist, and he tries not to flinch from the pain still throbbing. The touch of her hand is all he wants to think about.

Bella trotting at his side, he follows Mallory as she gently pulls him to a lineup of folding tables. He's been to some elaborate parties with his parents, but he's never seen this much food set up all at once. Ever.

"This is a lot of food," he remarks.

"Well, there's a lot of people here. Everybody brought a little something."

He feels a lump in his throat. His eyes burn, as he suddenly realizes he never even considered bringing something.

"I, um, I didn't bring…I'm sorry,"

"No worries, it's not required. Just something a bunch of people decided to do. Besides, you had a long walk. And you brought Bella," when she says the dog's name, her voice takes an excited, playful tone and she leans down to rub the dog's head.

"There's plenty of food," she pushes a paper plate toward him, "eat up, it's good stuff, try the curry lentils."

He doesn't want to admit he has no idea what curry lentils are and is more than a little afraid of the contents of the bowl. But it's bad enough he didn't think to bring anything, and he was late, and she already probably thinks he's a snob. He takes her advice and plops a serving spoonful onto his plate. He adds some garden salad, potato salad, and a hotdog and grabs an extra hotdog for Bella.

"Now, eat up, because there are some people I want you to meet."

If she told him to jump off the roof of the building, he would have. He begins to pick around at the food and after a few forks full, decides that whatever curry lentils are, they're amazing, and not too bad with bits of potato salad mixed in. He tries not to eat fast, hoping to avoid burping or dropping food down his chin, or generally looking like a glutton, but everything is delicious.

When he and Bella have cleared the plate, Mallory pulls him again, this time by wrapping her arm around his, toward a group of people.

"This is my neighbor, George, he plays wicked guitar, sometimes way late at night, though," she laughs as she says this, and George tips a beret at Francesco. George is older than them, in his thirties perhaps. He has a mustache like the man on the Pringles logo. He wears a shirt with three arrows at a slant.

"You must be Frank, it's nice to meet you," George shakes his hand and pets Bella, who has taken an interest in his shoes.

Francesco doesn't correct him.

Mallory repeats this introduction again and again. Francesco wonders what they've heard about him. Has she told them that she's in love? Or that he's clueless but has a nice dog?

"And this is my grandma," Mallory drops his arm to embrace a woman who looks to Francesco to be about his mother's age. How can she be Mal's grandmother? He catches himself before asking this, realizing that it is entirely possible she looks young or is young and that either way, it's not his business.

Her grandmother is a petite woman, he immediately recognizes Mallory's eyes in the older woman's face. Her hair is grey, and wavy curls frame her face, which is plump and only slightly lined with age.

"It's so nice to meet you, Frank." The older woman reaches for his hand and uses both of her warm hands to cover his.

By the time the afternoon has shifted to evening, Francesco feels at home. As the sun sets, someone starts to play music through a speaker.

"I want to stay, but I have to get Bella home," he skirts the truth, which is that his father has had a strict curfew since he was pulled over.

"No worries. I'm glad you made it." She pauses, staring into his eyes. This is it. He knows. This is the moment. He should kiss her now.

But before he can, she's turned her head away, just briefly, to wave at a friend before taking his hand. "I'll walk with you."

He's glad for her company as they make their way toward the park.

"So, I think we made enough for the new wheelchair and then some," she announces.

"What happens to the extra money?"

"It goes to whatever she needs. People wanted to give it to her so it's whatever she wants to do with it."

He tries to keep his face neutral. To hide his skepticism.

"Pretty wild how everyone turned out to help your neighbor. I mean, even if people have their own issues."

"We know how important it is to take care of each other. We're all we have."

Francesco feels a surge of jealousy. He wants to be all she has, not George, not all of those other people. He wants her to say that about him.

She continues, "You probably have family that can bail you out if you have a problem, right?"

He hears Jonathan's words from the night they were pulled over, "My dad can't bail me out..."

"It's not like that. My dad's the reason I was late. I have to work for what I have."

She laughs and turns away from him. "Sorry, not trying to be insulting, but everyone works. Not everyone has what your dad has."

"You know who he is?" Francesco asks.

"Not specifically. But what I mean is, how long would you last if it weren't for your dad, or your mom helping you out? If you really had to try to make it on your own, could you?"

This sounds like a challenge and Francesco answers faster than he should have, "Of course. I never ask them for help as it is."

"If you say so."

They walk together in silence. He needs to salvage the evening. Rushing ahead of her, he turns to face Mallory, blocking her in her tracks.

"Ok, let's make a bet. I bet I can go for a month without even asking my parents for anything. Just doing things on my own. With what I make from my own work. No advantages. No special favors."

She laughs again. "Well, it's not really like that, I mean, yeah, sure, the bet's on. But it's one thing when it's a month. Another thing when it's forever."

His eyes drop. He needs to try to unfuck the situation. Her voice interrupts his panicked thoughts.

"But since we're betting, what are the stakes? If I win… then what?"

He smiles. "If you win, I donate $1,000.00 to any charity you want."

She scoffs and repeats the word charity but nods her head in agreement. "Okay, fine then. What if you win?"

"You go on a date with me," Francesco says too fast. He waits for her to argue something back about hetero-patriarchy or whatever those words are. She just stands, head tilted to the side, and smiles.

"You're on."

When they get to the park he turns to her. "It's getting late for you to be walking alone," he stops short of saying *around here.* "I think Bella and I should take it from here."

She nods, and before he can gather the courage to lean down and kiss her, she's flung both arms around him, squeezing him in a bear hug.

Shit.

Has he been friend-zoned?

He tries to enjoy the moment and not overthink.

"Hey," he calls out to her as she starts to turn away to head home, "here's my number. In case you… want to text me or something." He hands her his phone, and she copies his number into her contacts. She doesn't offer her number, to his dismay.

CHAPTER 14

May 2022

Francesco shoves the remainder of his books into the locker and slams the door shut, no homework this weekend. Only prep for finals.

Have you thought about college?

The voice from his memory asks him again. He sighs, opens the locker door again, and digs a history book out from the back. He considers shutting the door again before grabbing his math book.

But that's it.

A jab in the back and Derek's voice bring his attention back.

"Party at your place tomorrow night?"

"Yeah, uh, sure," Francesco begins to answer but catches himself. Does this go against the bet? He anticipates the conversation that will follow. They'll want his parents' booze, and it is his dad's house, so there's that…

"I've been thinking," Francesco walks beside Derek down the hall, Scott and Finn rush to catch up with them. "I've been thinking since it's been warm out, we should have a barbecue."

That should work.

"Barbecue at your house. Okay then," Derek begins to respond.

"No," Francesco cuts him off, "I mean barbecue at like, someplace else."

"Someplace else?" Derek stops, his face twisted in disbelief.

"Well, like a park or something?"

Scott gives him a playful punch on the shoulder. "What? You afraid to leave your dog home?"

"Shut up about my dog," Francesco begins, "and no, no, it's not my dog. I'm just tired of always doing shit at my house. My dad is being an ass."

"A park? And then where are we gonna go?" Derek asks rhetorically, Francesco can tell. He doesn't need the accompanying gestures to show him Derek wants to know where they plan to get laid in a park. Derek provides the gestures anyway.

"Besides," Scott cuts in, "your place has the pool and the guest cottage. But if you want to do a cookout, I can bring some burgers and hotdogs and…"

"No," Francesco is losing his patience, "Not my place, ok?"

They round a hallway and Francesco descends the stairs, picking up the pace.

"What the fuck? Is it that time of the month?" The guys laugh.

"Fuck you, Derek." Francesco pushes the door open; the afternoon light pierces his eyes and he pulls the shades out of his pocket and puts them on. They cast sepia filters over the trees, the courtyard, and the guys.

"No," Derek walks uncomfortably close and stares down into Francesco's face. "No, fuck you, Francesco. Where the fuck have you been recently, anyway?"

"What?"

The other guys are standing close, but they look away. Francesco thinks Scott looks uncomfortable. Derek continues to raise his voice, "All I know is, I gave you an advance on my meds to sell and the last time we hung out was that party almost a month ago. I know you sold that shit by now. Greedy bastard, you keep avoiding hanging out. What's the matter? You on to bigger and better things?"

"No, what? No, I didn't even sell it all. I haven't been partying. I don't even give a fuck, here," He grabs what's left of Derek's meds out of the bottom of his backpack and throws the amber bottle toward the taller boy. He doesn't move and the bottle bounces off his chest and hits the ground. Scott ducks to grab it before it rolls away.

"Well, what the fuck have you been doing?"
"I've had to work. For my dad." Francesco lies, partially.

"Whatever, fucking pussy. You don't want to party with us? Fine. More booze and bitches for the rest of us, right?" He turns to the other guys who nod in agreement, but none of them will make eye contact with Francesco.

"Fine. But is that all you guys give a shit about? Partying at my parent's cottage, or the Lake House, or wherever else as long as I'm paying? I just don't get why we can't do normal shit like other people."

"Normal shit?" Derek uses a mocking voice, "you're the one who's suddenly on the wagon and just wants to have some stupid cookout. What do you think we stick around for?"

The words hit Francesco. One look at Scott's face, then Finn, and Declan. He can see it now. Eyes darting side to side in awkward glances.

"Fuck you." Francesco mumbles. He walks away before anyone can make excuses. Before anyone has a chance to try to cover for Derek or jab him in the side and stage whisper that he said the quiet part out loud.

It's not true. Francesco thinks it can't be. He's just got a bug up his ass.

Unless it's true.

He opens his car door, not bothering to look back.

Fuck them. *Fuck them.*

He tries to replay the scenes in his mind. Junior High, the last few years. When had they just hung out? Gone fishing together? Played video games?

He can only picture Jonathan, smoking cigarettes and making bad jokes while they sit on his floor.

He thinks of Mallory.

It would only be for a month, for us, it's forever.

Fuck them. He doesn't need them. He doesn't need his dad's money. He has Bella.

And Mallory.

CHAPTER 15

"My school has a dance coming up," Connie announces. She proceeds to describe the dress she saw online, "I need it for the dance, Daddy." Francesco never noticed it before. She tells him she needs the dress. Doesn't ask. Instructs.

Is that what he does too?

He looks down at his plate for answers. It's still empty. Margie hasn't come out of the kitchen yet. He can smell dinner cooking.

"Mmmhmm, talk to your mother about it," his father responds, his tone absent.

His mother strides into the room, shoving her phone into the pocket of her linen pants. She's graceful, and always on the move. Nervous and restless, Francesco thinks.

He no longer remembers a time when she wasn't this way. When she had told him every day about the new baby only to disappear into her bedroom, re-emerging without the round belly. Without a baby. And without her oldest daughter.

"Margie," his mother calls toward the kitchen, "I have a meeting in an hour, I can't be late."

His brows furrow, should he help Margie?

It's never occurred to him before. He stands up and heads toward the kitchen.

"Where are you going? Sit down," his father barks.

Francesco stops in his tracks. "I'm just going to see if Margie needs help."

"Like hell you are. I don't pay her to have you do all the work. Sit." His father points to the vacant seat. Francesco knows by the look in his eyes that it's no use arguing.

His mother fidgets with her silverware.

"Cut it out with all that noise, Joann," his father snaps.

A few minutes of tense silence later, Margie rushes in, serving tray in hand.

He feels Bella settle on his feet, but his mind is elsewhere. He's thinking of the group, Food Not Bombs, loading foil serving dishes and containers of food. Donning plastic gloves. Handing out to-go bags to lines of people.

He thinks of this now, watching Margie struggle to balance several trays as his family sits and watches.

I could do this myself, he thinks, maybe not the cooking, but at least filling his plate.

CHAPTER 16

Bella trots alongside him as he wanders the park trail. He hasn't seen Mallory since last weekend at the cookout. She has yet to text him, but he tries not to think of this.

It's getting warmer, and fewer people bike or rollerblade on the path in the height of the afternoon. A busy mom pushes a stroller past him, fast enough that he wonders if the baby concealed inside is getting seasick. In the distance, a group plays frisbee. He stops, squints, and tries to glimpse their faces. He doesn't recognize anyone.

Trees are fully in bloom and his nose itches from allergies. He tries to ignore it, not wanting to look like he's picking. He's certain today will be the day.

Bella, off-leash, runs toward an area with empty picnic tables. Nose to the ground, she sniffs around, looking for scraps of food. He runs to her side before she can snatch chicken bones from a container left under a table.

"Bella, drop it," he holds her shoulder, gently pulling her away.

"Find anything good down there?"

Mallory's voice startles him and as he stands, his head collides with the side of a picnic table.

His vision blurs. He can't tell where she is for a moment. A hand gently touches his shoulder.

"Are you okay?"

He squints. The truth is it hurts like a motherfucker. He nods his head and opens his eyes. The world settles down, the pain subsides into a steady throbbing.

"Oh, me? Yeah, I'm fine. Just trying to keep Bella from chomping on bones."

He doesn't realize he's rubbing his head until Mallory gives him a concerned look. He doesn't want her to feel sorry for him. Does he?

"You poor thing," he imagines her saying, "you better come to my place so I can take care of you for a few days …"

"Sorry to startle you," is what she actually says.

"No worries, I, uh, I'm fine."

No, he decides, he doesn't want her to feel sorry for him. He wants her to forget she ever saw him, ass in the air, digging for a container of plundered chicken wings under a picnic table so his dog wouldn't eat them.

"So, um," he tries to start over, "I'm doing pretty good. With the bet."

"Oh, well, I didn't know that breaking from your parents' money would mean you'd end up dumpster diving in the park," she gestures toward the food container in his hand.

"No," he begins, but Mallory is laughing. He laughs along with her.

Bella has forgotten the chicken scraps. She licks Mallory's hand and turns her back, encouraging the girl to scratch her.

They begin walking together.

"By the way, my grandmother thinks you're cute," Mallory informs him, batting her eyes in a theatric imitation of flirting.

"Well, she has good taste in men, I guess."

Mallory laughs from her diaphragm. The kind of laugh that makes her lean over. As if he's just said the funniest thing she ever heard.

He loves her laugh. He's decided he doesn't care if she's laughing at him.

"It's true," he plays it up. "Though I hope she's not too jealous."

"Jealous?" Mallory asks, her eyes sparkling as a smile stretches across her face.

"Yeah, jealous. When we become a couple."

"And when will that be?"

"Well, in thirty days, when I prove that I'm not the spoiled rich kid you think I am."

"I thought you said one date?"

He stops suddenly, unable to tell if she's really mad at him or just playing around.

"Oh, relax, and no, my grandmother won't be jealous. But Kara, on the other hand, she might."

"Who's Kara?"

"She was the bass player in the band, remember?"

Francesco searches his memory. It slows down his pace and Bella walks to his side, sniffing at his shoes.

"Wait, Kara, with the piercings? And the blonde and purple hair?"

"That's the one. She wanted your number." Mallory says this in a sing-songy voice, taunting him.

"Did you give it to her?"

"Do you want me to?"

"Well, you're not using it, so..."

That laugh again.

"Okay seriously, if you don't want to text me, how about friending me on Facebook? I couldn't find you."

Close to the pond now, the din from the fountain causes him to raise his voice. Bella sniffs around the edge of the pond, snapping at a frog that narrowly escapes her grasp as it dives into the water. She steps forward with her front paws, then jumps back, nosing at the water.

"Well, that's because I'm not on it."

"Oh, right, because it's all old people, well, how about Insta?"

She slips out of her shoes and pulls off her socks, her toenails are painted red and black. It's weird, he thinks, but sexy.

"I don't do social media. No internet at home, not worth it." She shrugs, pulling up the legs of her jeans and rolling them over her knees.

Before Francesco can memorize the sight of her legs, she's treading into the pond.

"Are we allowed to do that?"

Bella romps into the water, following Mallory, water covering her furry back but only up to the girl's waist.

"What?" she calls back to him, "I can't hear you!"

Yeah, right. He takes his shoes and socks off too, tries to roll up his pants, and then gives up and tosses his phone into the pile of belongings and trudges in after them, pantlegs soaked and weighted down.

"Hey, you're not supposed to be in there!" Someone yells from the grass.

"Fuck off!" Mallory calls back, playful, not angry.

"Hey, I thought you couldn't hear because of the fountain." Francesco splashes her.

She splashes him back. Bella jumps and bites at the waves, her tail spraying water as it waves back and forth.

It's not until he gets back home that he realizes he's in deep shit if his father sees him. He can hear his father's voice yelling. For a moment, his mind flashes back to that day. Peering around the side of the house, listening to his father screaming at Carmen.

He sees the last glimpse of his sister before she disappears forever. Blinking back the image, he notices, with some relief, the cars are gone. No one is home. Crisis averted.

Carmen disappeared without a trace. Not even on social media.

I don't have internet so, not worth it...

Maybe it's not that strange that he can't trace her online.

CHAPTER 17

He looks at the clock again. An hour has gone by, and he hasn't completed the page in front of him. Every time Francesco tries to concentrate on the audits, his mind drifts back to the afternoon before. He can see Mallory splashing him in the pond, water soaking her clothes. He rehearses the scene in his mind, wanting to remember every moment.

Bella sniffs under the door to the tiny office. Someone is carrying lunch down the hall. He smells the familiar scent of sauerkraut and thinks it's Alex who works a few offices down.

"Orders a Rueben every day, all I can smell is vinegar and ass," his father complained to him on more than one occasion about this employee.

Fuck it.

"Lunchtime," he tells Bella. She runs to his side and jumps up at him as he rises from the desk. With Bella prancing at his side, he walks down the hall to the staff lounge. Bill's back is to the door, his eyes fixed on the microwave.

Francesco usually ignores the employees. Today he ventures a greeting, "Hey."

"Hi." Bill doesn't take his eyes off the microwave. It beeps, and the man, his dad's age Francesco realizes, pops open the door. Whatever he's cooking smells like watery vegetables and undistinguished tomato-based sauce.

"Um, hey, so, how do you, um, like it here?" Francesco hates sounding awkward, but he's never been introduced to the workers. He should at least get to know them. Since he'll be in charge of them someday.

Maybe Mallory is wrong. Maybe he can use his money to do good things. Be a nicer boss than his dad is. Maybe he can be independent but still have the business and just earn his own way.

Bill removes the TV dinner from the microwave, stirs it in the shallow dish with a fork, and sits at the table. Steam rises from the dish as Bill frowns, considers the question, and then answers, "Oh, yeah, it's fine. Your dad runs a tight ship. It's good."

Francesco opens the refrigerator and finds the bag he brought from home. Usually, he eats lunch with his dad. Take out. But that would violate the bet.

Last night, long after Margie went home, he crept into the kitchen and put together his own lunch. A peanut butter sandwich. He even packed an extra for Bella. She barely waits for him to set it on the floor before gulping it out of his hand.

Bill eyes him suspiciously, frowning at the sight of the dog lapping peanut butter off the floor.

"Yeah, that's good," Francesco tries to make conversation. He isn't convinced Bill is being honest.

Of course not. Your dad's the boss. He reminds himself.

"Yeah, my dad can be a lot sometimes. Intense, you know?"

Bill stuffs a fork full of the steaming hot mixture into his mouth and begins chewing.

"Well," Francesco tries again, "I'll be in charge one day, and I want to try to be a good boss to work for. So, if there's anything you want me to know, you can just, um, talk to me, right? Doesn't even have to be here, I mean we could grab a beer and talk."

"How old are you?" Bill looks skeptical.

"I mean, not now, um, I mean, when I'm here full time. Like as a manager. Because then we'd be colleagues. Right?"

"Not exactly," Bill wipes his mouth on a napkin.

"Look, maybe you don't realize these things and all, but the managers don't hang out with the employees." He eats the last forkful of food out of the container.

"Well, it doesn't have to be that way, right?" He thinks of the cookout. Of Mallory's neighbors. Food Not Bombs. Community. "I mean, I could fit right in with you guys, once I'm working here, right?" His smile fades as he sees the look on Bill's face.

"Sorry, kid, but it doesn't quite work that way. You'll probably want to save that for the managers, assistant managers, you know, your dad will show you the ropes when the time comes."

Bill heads for the trash, tossing the container and plastic fork away before heading out the door.

CHAPTER 18

His father didn't ask him if he wanted to go to the dinner. Didn't tell him he wanted him to be there. With only a few hours' notice, his father flung open the bedroom door and announced the dinner was that evening and they were both going. He hoped to catch up with Mallory.

You could just tell him you don't want to go...

The thought makes his heart race. He doesn't know why but it would not be a good idea to...

Don't upset your mother...

To make his father upset because that's just the way it is ...

She has a condition.

It's better to go. It's complicated. Just the way it is.

"Sorry, Bella, I can't get away with bringing you to this," he breaks the news. Bella slumps down on her belly, whining a brief protest before setting her head on her front paws and letting her dog eyes lay on the guilt.

Francesco pets her head then stands in front of the closet staring at the suits in the back. The ones saved for special occasions. He picks one and as he takes out the pins and sets them on the dresser, his mind drifts to Mallory. He sees himself following her into the pond, the two of them laughing, splashing each other, ignoring the cries of outrage from passersby.

The suit is stiff and formal. At one point, he would have thought it looked good on him. But now, as he stares at himself in the mirror, all he can think of is what Mallory would say if she saw him in the tailored Italian suit, designed to match his father's.

Just like your life. He hears her voice in his head, taunting.

Mom and Connie aren't accompanying them. As his father drives him to the venue, a restaurant and banquet hall downtown called Fortuna's, he explains the reason for the occasion.

"Got surprise news today."

"Oh, yeah?"

"Finally got Lyra Group to sell that damn residence in the slum."

"Oh, well, that's good. I mean if it's in a slum?"

"Christ," his father begins, lighting up a cigar, a habit he saves for special occasions, "what did I always tell you? Think about it. The one thing they aren't making more of?"

Francesco nods his head, "Land."

"Exactly."

"What's it going to be? Condos? Or apartments?"

"Too much overhead, no one wants to invest in that shit these days."

Francesco is bored already. He tries to listen, but Mallory's laugh, her eyes, her curly hair, haphazard from the wind, that's all he can think about.

"Did you hear me?" his father's voice louder now.

"Huh? Sorry, was thinking about a math test. At school."

"Don't worry about that shit," his father waves the thought away with a hand and repeats himself, "going to make it storage units. That's where the money is. Almost no overhead. A gift that keeps on giving."

"Makes sense." Francesco nods.

Will he really have to think about this shit all day someday?

"Now, you're gonna get some practice tonight. And you're
going to meet some other heavy hitters. Pay attention, don't
fuck up, don't embarrass me, ok?"

"Yes, sir." Francesco agrees.

As his father turns off the ignition, Francesco unbuckles
his seatbelt and starts to open the door. The sooner they get
in there and eat, the sooner this will be over.

"Not so fast." His father reaches out to pull his arm, guid-
ing him back into his seat.

So much for just getting this over with.

Francesco fidgets in the passenger seat, trying not to look
his father in the eye.

"You're going to be full-time soon. Starting tonight,
you're going to be more involved. You've got to learn a few
things."

His father's phone chirps, he checks a notification and
stuffs the phone back in his pocket before continuing. "I'm
springing this on you last minute because it was sprung on
me last minute. That's how it goes sometimes. You don't
let an opportunity pass just because you weren't expecting
it, understood?"

Francesco nods his head.

"You're gonna meet with a guy named Charles Getz. He's
from Bonvenuto Real Estate. Pay attention. You're going
to be seeing a lot of him in the coming months."

"What? Why?"

"Because you're going to spearhead this project and
Charles, he goes by Chuckie, he's going to be your liaison."

Francesco shifts, he doesn't want to have a liaison. Doesn't
know what one is but doesn't want to sound stupid by asking.

"He's going to be your contact person," his father elaborates. "So, you're going to be in charge of certain tasks on this project. It'll be like a test. If you have questions, you come to me. Don't do anything stupid, and don't embarrass me."

Francesco nods, suddenly wishing he could keep doing boring audits.

"Now for the good news," his father pauses. Francesco ventures a glance at his face. He's beaming, eyes lit up. "You're going to have a real role in this, and that means you get real pay. Plus, since you're dealing with Chuckie, you get a referral fee when all is said and done. So, all in all, you're looking at about ten k."

"Ten thousand… dollars?" Francesco blinks, trying to digest the news.

"For this project. And there will be others. As long as you don't fuck up. Got it?"

"Got it."

Francesco doesn't consider how this fits in with his bet with Mallory. It will be his money. The money he made honestly. By being a liaison. A contact person.

Over dinner- calamari alfredo with sparkling water for him, red wine and steak for his father, and eggplant parmigiana for Chuckie, he learns what he'll need to do for the ten grand. He'll be in charge of PR.

"Think of it like being an influencer, like on YouTube, but for the project." Chuckie tells him between bites of a meal his father secretly calls "Italian for lightweights." His dad hates it when people order eggplant parm almost as much as he hates it when they order spaghetti as an entrée.

"What is this, the kids' table?" he likes to joke.

"So, do you want me to make videos?" Francesco asks, hoping he doesn't sound as stupid as he feels.

"Not exactly. But you will talk to the media, and deal with questions from residents about the buyout process. You're going to field calls and deal with the rabble. Not the most glamorous job, gonna be honest. But you do it well and there will be more opportunities next time around."

"Don't worry, he'll have it covered," Francesco's father cuts in, patting Francesco on the back, enacting confidence Francesco doesn't quite believe he really feels.

"There are more details, we'll talk about it during the week, just want to make sure you understand your role in this."

"Of course, he does, he's my son." His father spares him the burden of answering for himself.

"When are the notices going out?" his father changes the topic.

"Tomorrow. Should have the place vacated in a month, razed by July fourth."

"Ah, just in time for a cookout, right?" His father sips his wine, smiling. Chuckie grins too as if they are in on a joke that Francesco hasn't figured out yet.

CHAPTER 19

Francesco walks taller as he leaves his dad's office a few days later. Having spent the day responding to calls- mostly people whining about the terms of the sale from Lyra Group's buyout and asking questions that he had no idea how to answer- he anticipated catching up with Mallory at the park.

"The key to this thing," his father prompted him that morning, "is to be polite, no matter what. Remind them to look at the positives. This is a generous opportunity to start a new life somewhere. They're getting a payout that is more than some of these people make in a week. Any questions beyond the basics, refer them to our lawyer, his number's on this form."

His father had pushed an outline of the sale proposal across the desk. Beneath the explanation of the payout and terms of eviction was a phone number for the company's lawyer as well as the contact information for Chuckie and a few other guys whose names he recalled from discussions at the business dinner.

He felt bad for some of them, confused, crying, and demanding answers. But it was just business. And they were getting a buyout. A really good deal, his father had said.

Bella stayed home today, he needed to concentrate without her distracting him. The first order of business would be to pick her up at his parent's house and then head for the park. If memory serves him, it's Food Not Bombs day.

Bella bounding by his side, Francesco makes his way across the trail to the old side of the park. Broken glass dots the walkways, and the small play area is occupied by adults hovering close together, making drug deals, he assumes, and not by children playing on the swings and slide.

He can see people gathering by the picnic tables. Soon he'll get to tell Mallory the good news. Ten thousand. His own money that he's earning.

As he approaches, he notices something is off. No one looks happy to be there. Raincoat, who isn't wearing a raincoat on this sunny afternoon, looks like someone just died. When he finally sees Mallory amidst the crowd, she's sitting next to the guy with Locks, wiping something off her face.

Tears?

Bella runs ahead, darting right for Mallory. Her bulky body lumbers as close to sitting on the girl's lap as the dog can manage. Francesco picks up speed as well.

"What's wrong?"

She doesn't look up. Only stares into the distance as Bella licks tears from her face. Francesco feels a stabbing pain in his heart followed by anger. He imagines fighting whoever made Mallory cry.

"What is it?" he asks again, his voice higher than he intended.

She slowly reaches into the pocket of her jeans and pulls out a piece of paper. It's been folded several times and the print is streaked in some places; he thinks where her tears have hit the page.

He takes the paper from her outstretched hand and as he unfolds it, his heart stops.

He recognizes the letterhead.

Bernardoni Realty.

It can't be.

His hands move in slow motion, like in a dream.

In his mind, he sees George of the beret and Pringles hairstyle, shaking his hand.

He doesn't have to read the letter to know what it is.

Somewhere between his line of sight and the typed words on paper he sees the couple sitting in lawn chairs, talking with Mallory.

The sea of faces and bodies, dancing to music, carrying plates.

Mrs. Votti, who finally would get her electric wheelchair.

Mallory's grandmother, welcoming him with a two-hand shake.

He forces them all out of his mind.

"This must be a mistake," he says the words out loud, forcing himself to read the words even though he already knows full well what's written on the paper. There were so many of these letters, all stashed neatly into envelopes.

He brought them to the post office, just the other day.

"This must be a mistake."

Mallory still doesn't move, even with Bella licking close to her eyes.

"Can you believe those sons a bitches think they're the good guys?" Raincoat asks him.

"What do you mean?" he stammers.

"They're giving a buyout to anyone who moves out in two weeks. Two weeks, that's all. But they'll pat themselves on the back and try to say a piddly thousand dollars is their idea of generosity." She turns and spits on the ground. "Disgusting! I hope they rot in Hell."

"Well, maybe it's not that simple. I mean, I think I can help, but it's not that simple."

She turns to look at him, but her eyes are vacant, her expression one of stone.

"I can help," this time with confidence.

Raincoat folds her arms over her chest, waiting for him to elaborate.

"That company? The one that's buying, it's my dad. My dad's company."

Raincoat narrows her eyes, and her lips tighten, he's afraid she'll point an accusing finger at him, and before she has the chance he continues.

"I'll talk him into making a better deal. I work for him now. I work on this project; they'll listen to me." Even he doesn't believe that last bit. He can't read her reaction; Mallory's face hasn't changed.

He continues, "I'll, I'll um, I'll get a better buyout. We'll negotiate. How much does everyone want?"

"Nothing." Mallory stands now and walks toward him, her eyes brewing with rage, even as her voice remains level. "We aren't for sale."

"You don't have a choice. Let me help you. Be reasonable. I mean, it's complicated but I …."

She cuts him off, "Don't bother. This is what you don't understand. What you'll never understand. You aren't going to cut a deal for us because you're not one of us. You have your priorities," she looks down at the letter, grabs it from his hand and returns it to her pocket, "and we have ours."

"Mallory, please, it's not that simple…" he's whining now. He doesn't want to sound weak, but his heart is racing. Images flood his mind. His mother's bedroom door closed.

She has a condition.

Doctors coming to the house, and his father yelling at them behind closed doors. His mother walking down the stairs weeks later, rail thin. His father smashing a chair against the wall when little Francesco asked when the baby would come. Long days of silence followed by shouting, breaking furniture, and more doctors.

His father's voice asking a question he couldn't understand, "See what happens when you upset your mother?"

It's not that simple, he hears himself say.

"Just go back to your trust funds and your mansions and leave us alone."

She turns her back and Raincoat puts an arm around her.

"Come on, Bell," Francesco tries to keep his voice from breaking as he calls his dog back to his side. She reluctantly joins him.

CHAPTER 20

Francesco turns on his side again, grabs his phone from the nightstand, and checks his notifications. Another hour has passed, and he still can't sleep. Every time he closes his eyes, he sees Mallory's face, despondent. Then angry. Scenes he barely remembers and doesn't understand play on repeat. He can't tell memory from waking nightmares. Blood on the living room floor. Days and nights filled with silence.

His stomach feels sick, heartbroken. Mallory can't be mad at him. Can't give up on him. He'll fix it.

But you can't upset your mother. Do you see what happens?

This is different. He'll talk to his father. In the empty space between his last text message just before midnight and the rising of the sun, he stares up at the ceiling trying to clear his mind enough to rehearse what he'll say. He pets Bella with one hand while trying to imagine the right approach, the right words, the right way to keep from upsetting his father.

Mother- she's delicate. Has a condition.

When waking thought gives way to memory, Francesco can't tell if he's dreaming or if his mind, too tired for censorship, has simply wandered.

His mother is younger but looks older and spends her time roaming the house in her pajamas. Sometimes she doesn't shower. There are doctor visits, pills, and periods when she's gone. In the hospital. And he can't visit.

And there is no baby.

His father is busier than usual and has no time or patience to hear about the award he won at school or the play he tried out for or that his best friend is moving.

But one day his father comes home smiling. A rare good mood, Francesco runs to see what is in the box his father carries.

"Just what the doctor ordered," he leans down and winks at Francesco, setting the box on the floor.

"It's for your mom. A surprise!"

Francesco thinks it's a baby, to make up for the one that hadn't shown up.

"A puppy!"

His mother was in the room behind him, lingering in the doorway, looking indifferent toward the surprise. The puppy is dark brown and tiny. Francesco can carry her easily.

"Look, Mom, a puppy!"

She stares into space at first, then smiles, regarding the squirming puppy.

"Beautiful. Bella. Beautiful," is all she says.

But in the weeks that follow, his mother retreats to her room again. For a few days, she even forgot to feed the puppy. Francesco had taken Bella in as his responsibility and can't understand why his parents continue to argue.

"I got you the damn dog like the doctor said!"

"I don't want a dog, Pat, I want our fucking daughter!"

Francesco is happy again, with the puppy to play with and talk to.

When Francesco walks down the stairs the following morning, the sound of his father's voice greets him. It's the tone he uses for Christmases or dinners out, when he's hoping to impress someone. Francesco breathes deeply and follows the sound.

"Hey, wheeling and dealing, I heard Chuckie's pleased with you so far."

His father sits on the couch, pouring over ledger books strewn across the coffee table. Usually, he works in the study and at the office. Only on rare occasions, when he's pleased with himself and wants to show off, does his father bring his work into the dining or living rooms.

Francesco's mouth dries up. He forces a hello and then blurts out the remaining words before he can change his mind.

"Dad, there's something we need to talk about."

"What, one of the rabble give you a hard time? Don't pay attention to them."

"No, Dad, I think, I mean, what if," he takes another deep breath and exhales what he's been trying to say, "You can't go through with the deal. The apartments have to stay apartments."

His father's face darkens into a deep maroon. All is silent for a moment, then his father's voice bellows into the room. It shakes the floors. Bella slinks behind Francesco at the sound.

"What the fuck are you talking about?"

Francesco looks down. A litany follows. "You've worked all of one day riding my coattails and now you're qualified to tell me what to do? Who the fuck do you think you are?"

Francesco wants to apologize. Wants to slink away to his bedroom and drop the subject. But something holds him in place.

"You can't do this." He looks his father in the eye, not bothering to shout back. "People live there."

"They're getting a buyout. Fucking thieves! They'll complain and bitch until they rob you blind..."

"Bullshit!" Francesco's voice louder now, arms folded across his chest, "A little bit of money if they move in two weeks? Really? Who the hell can even pack and find a new place in that time?"

"How dare you." His father's voice is soft now, shocked. "How fucking dare you." He starts to pace the room. Francesco thinks he may drop the conversation. Come back later when they're both calm. Maybe then they can negotiate.

The sound of a coffee mug crashing against the wall indicates there will be no calm negotiation.

"I don't want to hear another fucking word about this. The sale is the sale. The terms are the terms. We're holding a press conference tomorrow and you're supposed to be there, so whatever the fuck has gotten into your mind you better get it out."

"No."

His father's eyes widen. Francesco fears the old man may have a stroke. Instead, the older man makes a dash in his direction, leans back, and punches Francesco in the face.

He hears the sound of a scream, and it takes a moment to realize it came from Connie, not him.

How long has she been standing there?

"Go to your room!" his father bellows at his sister, who stands frozen in the doorway watching them. The older man turns to Francesco again.

"You're not going to ruin this! Do you understand? You're not going to ruin me! Do your fucking job!"

"No! I won't do it." Francesco pauses, his face is throbbing from what will likely be a bruise in a few hours. "Fuck you. Fuck your money and fuck your business!"

His father's face turns from red to pale. Francesco no longer understands what he's saying, or why, he just keeps yelling, "You're the reason Carmen left! You selfish, greedy asshole! Take all your money and stick it up your ass! You're the reason Carmen left and never came back and if she can leave, so can I!"

A heavy thud echoes into the room. The ground shakes behind him. His mother, who had also entered the room without being noticed, is on her knees, arms wrapped around her middle as if she's been stabbed, face twisted in anguish.

"Now look what you've done." His father's heavy hands shake him by the shoulders, shoving him toward his mother who is managing to cry silently on the floor.

"Look what you've done to this family! You want to be like your sister? Get out! Get OUT!"

Francesco runs for the door with Bella by his side. His heart pounds in his chest. Is this really forever?

Is this how Carmen felt?

CHAPTER 21

If he planned to leave, he would have packed a bag with a change of clothes. Some food. Layers to help him prepare for the spring breeze that makes him walk faster to stay warm. Food for Bella. He tries not to think about what he just did. Or what he'll do next.

Adrenaline and dread pour over him as he replays the scene. Living without his father's money is no longer just a bet. Mallory will have the answers.

When he and Bella reach her apartment building, there's a mass of people standing out front.

Another cookout?

He realizes as he gets closer. They're holding signs. A few have bullhorns. They're yelling something. The few cars that drive through the streets in the surrounding neighborhoods honk their horns. Some drivers shout in anger out the windows.

Bella finds Mallory in the crowd and the girl smiles to see the dog running toward her. Her expression grows cold as her eyes fix on Francesco's.

"I know you're pissed. You have a reason to be, but I want you to know, I quit. He wouldn't negotiate, you were right. I quit. I walked out. I'm done with them. I want to help you."

She regards him, her own expression not changing.

"What's going on here?" He motions to the signs and bullhorns.

"An eviction defense action. We're not leaving. And the public is going to know that developers want our homes for storage."

"Please, let me help. I want to help."

She pushes a sign toward him. He takes it and stands with the others.

Housing is a human right!
Housing is a human right!
Housing is a human RIGHT!

He joins in the chanting.

He recognizes George and thinks he notices Kara with a few others who have chained themselves to the entrance of the building. As he chants along with the crowd, he recognizes someone else.

Ralph Squires, one of Chuckie's assistants. He's talking to News Five and gesturing toward the crowd. Another news van pulls up. They stand in line to talk to Ralph. No one is interviewing the residents, though their cameras pan the scene.

The sharp smell of menthol passes by Bella's snout. She stops, raises a paw, and turns her head. So many people, their fear smells sour and sharp, like vinegar. Head low, she strays from the boy and follows the familiar scent of the girl from the park.

Yelling rings deep in her ears. They yell in a rhythm and she's padding along the parking lot in time with it now. There was food last time she was here, and if she tries, she can catch a trace of it in the wind.

People were happy then. Some shared their scraps.

No one is happy now.

Cars arrive. In the back of one, she sees the face of Alsatians, judging her. She kicks her back legs sending stones skipping across the pavement. The Alsatian, with brown and black fur; long snout, tall ears, turns to peer out the car window. The Alsatian's eyes squint at the sight of the crowd.

Bella smells something new, and her hair stands on end.

More people arrive then, a crowd dressed from head to toe in what must be sweltering black attire. They give other members of the crowd fist bumps and hugs before standing off to the side, creating a barrier between the protestors and newly arrived police, some patrol cars have German Shepherds enclosed in the back seat, waiting for orders. Francesco recognizes Officer Dimples.

Why would the police be here?

He reaches for Bella but realizes she's left his side. His heart races as he looks from one end of the growing crowd to another. He can't take off looking for her, the gathering has grown too dense. A brown blur catches his sight. Relieved, he watches as Bella weaves around the crowd, sniffing at the ground and nudging an occasional protestor to pet her. He starts to make his way closer to Bella, but doesn't get far before others, homemade signs on cardboard in hand, convene in the space between them. Someone hooks up a speaker and begins playing songs he doesn't recognize.

Cars pull up and people jump out of them, gathering banners and signs and joining in. Some bring their own banners with names like Fair Housing Justice and Eviction Defense Squad.

Still holding his sign, he walks to the perimeter of the protest, wanting to be closer to Bella, and Mallory, who has, as usual, found her. Closer to the road now, he can see a line of police cars descending on the neighborhood. Officers emerge dressed in bulletproof vests and SWAT gear. Some carry shields. He's seen this in video games and on the news, but never in real life.

Why are they dressed like that?

A familiar voice amplified through a bullhorn, shouts.

"I don't see a riot here!"

The crowd answers "Why are you in riot gear?"

Mallory stands in the front line, facing off with officers standing behind shields, batons in their hands.

What the fuck?

Bella has found the girl, and the menthol smell she recognizes fills her snout. And the vinegar smell is getting stronger.

There are others now, Bella sees. They've brought sticks. But they don't smell good. They don't smell like people Bella wants to play with.

She hovers close to the girl as the anger grows louder.

One of the officers pushes forward into the line of protestors, knocking people back. They stumble to the ground.

"Hey!" Francesco drops his sign and runs toward the police. "Hey, what are you doing?"

Someone grabs his arm. Officer Dimples.

"You? Bernardoni?

"Yeah, yes."

"I saw the news, don't worry, these scumbags aren't going to get away with trashing your dad's new place."

"What are you talking about? They're not trashing it. We don't need all of this," he gestures to the cops in riot gear.

"Stand back, kid, this ain't a place for someone like you."

Another voice carries over the commotion, through a scratchy loudspeaker in one of the patrol cars.

"Clear the area. This is now declared a riot. You have until the count of five to clear the area or you will be arrested."

Bella shifts her weight from paw to paw. Bad. Even the cars yell. She smells her boy nearby and walks toward him, then back. She paces, whimpering. The girl can't hear her.

Bella needs to go to her boy. He gets in trouble when she's not there. But she also needs to stay.

She needs to sit.

And stay.

"What are they doing?" Francesco demands.

"You need to go home, kid. Your father will have my badge if you get hurt here."

"One…"

"No! You get these cops out of here, these people aren't doing anything wrong."

"Two…."

"Housing is a human right…"

"Three…"

"Get out of the way kid, you need to clear the area!"

Francesco begins to respond, and the rest happens in a haze of slow motion.

Mallory steps forward, standing on her toes to try to maintain eye contact with a cop who has pulled one of the protestors out of the crowd, knocking him to the ground. A group of officers advances toward Mallory.

Francesco runs in her direction.

"Clear the area… this is an unlawful protest… you will be arrested…"

A brown mass lunges from the crowd, barking at the officers.

Bella feels fear. The anger makes her skin tremble. The vinegar smell chokes her. She whimpers and tries to reach a paw to the girl. Then there is shoving. There is falling. Crying. Yelling.

The vinegar smell so sharp it burns her eyes.

The bad men rush forward.

She must not.

Must not do it.

Must not.

Bella growls a warning. Then louder.

The scent burns now.

Must not do it.

The smell of lead and metal is close.

Her growling becomes snarling. She bares her teeth at the men with sticks and shields. Legs and arms too close, she snaps at the air.

Please take the warning. Don't make me do it. It's bad.

Fur standing on end, tail low sweeping side to side, she barks one last warning before leaping forward, no choice left.

Mallory screams "No!" dropping the bullhorn, she jumps in front of the dog.

Shots are fired.

Screams erupt from the crowd.

A pool of blood spills into the road.

Francesco's blood has turned to ice. His stomach lurches, and his eyes follow the path of red streaming from the body that moments ago had been animated. Chanting.

Some of the people dressed in black rush to the body, first aid kits in hand. The police pull people from the crowd, dragging them into patrol cars and vans. Ignoring the lifeless body on the ground.

"Bastards."

The words are a whisper at first.

"All bastards. You're all bastards."

A hymn only he can hear. He watches Mallory's blood flow. It extends over the ground. Over the sky. He can see only in shades of red.

"Bastards!" he begins yelling. Turning to face the row of cops still assembled with their shields out.

"You're all bastards! All of you! Bastards!"

He hears an officer give a command, and another says, "No… Bernardoni's son." but it doesn't register.

"Bastards! All of you! All of you! All of you!"

Others are screaming now. A bottle grazes the side of an officer's face mask. The remaining officers charge the crowd.

He doesn't see it. Only red. Only blood.

He sees it on the buildings, their boarded windows, in the alleys, and at bus stops. Red flows under the bridge, at the port, amidst groups of pigeons that take flight as he approaches, in a daze, head throbbing.

Smoke from distant factories spills red into the sky. The train tracks give way to trees, their red limbs hiding him, branches blocking out the sun.

He stumbles. Falls. And the redness disappears.

CHAPTER 22

Narrator

You know about Mallory, now. There was no saving her. Especially with no one to respond to the crisis for the first hour except street medics.

But I know what you're really wondering. And I know you won't read on until I tell you. Ruin a good story with your impatience.

But it's the way you are.

So here it is: No.

The dog doesn't die. Not then anyway.

Where she goes and what she does is for later. And while we're on the subject, I'd like to remind you a good many people were just beaten and a good many animals of different species are killed every day.

But you only care about the dog, don't you?

Go on, then. Keep reading.

I wasn't there when it happened, but I heard about it. You could say a little bird told me. I couldn't go to him if I wanted to. Just had to wait until he found me. Eventually, he did. They all do. Some arrive before it's too late.

CHAPTER 23

Francesco

The sounds of his heart racing with every step eclipses the noise of traffic, the echo of music filling the streets behind second and third-story windows, and voices calling to each other from street corners.

The soundtrack is miles behind him, but he doesn't notice. In the dark, apartment buildings give way to warehouses and lots protected by fencing and razor wire, where commercial trucks have been corralled.

It's been an hour since late-night traffic rumbled overhead while he charged past encampments under bridges, not noticing the people huddled near tents. The Passaic continues its journey, littered riverbeds give way to cat tails and trees. A lone shopping cart, abandoned on its side, the last relic of the cityscape. He didn't notice it. Hearing only chanting, then gunshots, screams, his own voice.

You're all bastards.

Seeing only waves of red. Not the squirrels who scatter as he approaches, the raccoons ducking behind trashcans, protecting their loot, not the tree whose roots tangle into the ground. The root that catches his foot trips him and sends him tumbling in the dark.

If he doesn't wake up all the way, the sun won't hurt his eyes. He discovers this as his eyelids part just enough to let in the hot white light and then shut hard, sending him back into darkness. Waking brings the pain in his back to a crescendo, bringing questions better left unanswered.

What happened? Where am I?

CHAPTER 24

Brief waking moments bring the same bright light and a rush of sounds.

I am you. I am you. I am you. The words were spoken by a raven looking down at him in pity.

"Is Bella Dead? Mallory? Where am I?"

A squirrel stuffing seeds into extended cheeks eyes him as voices run together, speaking in unison, interrupting each other.

"You've got to eat these little bugs…"

"You stepped on my tail…"

"While they're nice and fat and juicy…"

"Wait 'til he gets a whiff of this…"

"They'll be back soon, get your babies and run…"

His head spins. He can't lift a hand to cover his ear. Can't move at all.

"Enough," another voice, loud but not demanding, brings the chatter to a halt. "Let him sleep." All is silent again.

CHAPTER 25

The pain is gone. Warmth stretches over his face, across his arms, and down his trunk to the roots beneath the ground. A soft rain tickles his face, and squirrels run along his branches, retreating to their nests. It itches.

The rain heavier now soaks into the forest floor. He didn't know he was so thirsty, drinking the water into his leaves, bark, and dirt. Into the mouths of frogs that he now understands are also him.

Thunder rolls along the Passaic in the distance. It is his voice. With a bolt of lightning, he can see. He sees himself on the ground, arms, and legs at odd angles, eyes closed.

He understands now. The body on the ground is not him. What a relief. Its arms are bent at strange angles. Its eyes closed against the sun. Face scratched and arms bruised. It may not survive. It doesn't matter.

What a relief.

Francesco remembers this feeling. Once, during the winter break of his freshman year, his family had gone on a cruise. He doesn't remember if that trip had been to the Caymans or if that was the Hawaii vacation. He remembers the salt tanks.

"You want to brine yourself?" His father had chided his mother, who was fascinated with the idea. She read the pamphlet for days before they arrived. Connie wasn't interested. Francesco was.

On the second level of the ship, past the lounge, the pool, the saunas, and the massage room, the newly installed saltwater flotation tanks were located.

"I'll never know why you have to waste my money floating in salt water when you're already on a ship that's floating in the ocean," his father begrudgingly booked the appointment for his mother.

"I suppose you want to go, too," his father sneered at him.

He didn't reply, but his mother, saving him the embarrassment, insisted Francesco have an appointment, too.

His mother went into one room, he and into another. Following the instructions laminated and posted on the wall, Francesco had removed his clothing, removed his necklace- a confirmation present- and showered briefly before stepping through a small door into a completely dark room.

A void, separated from all of normal life with its bright colors and loud noises and sunlight and people and drinks and performances and suntans and girls in swimsuits and perpetual ocean on all sides. Once he closed the door behind him and stretched into the saltwater tub, only as deep as a regular bath, all sense of space and weight evaporated.

He was floating.

For an hour and a half, he remained suspended in water, divorced of gravity.

Like now.

In this place, that is very much not a cruise. Far from his parents, from anything luxurious, or even civilized.

Here he remains.

Floating.

I'll be dead soon. Or am I already dead? Is this Heaven?

"It is. And you aren't," a voice, the big voice he's heard before, echoes through the woods. As if a Greek Chorus speaks in unison.

It's ok. I'm ready to die. I'm not afraid.

"You have work to do." The Chorus tells him.

His head hurts as streaks of light escape through the branches of trees leaving trails, the echoes of colors that won't stay still. Work. Audits. Real estate.

"No. That is not your work." The Chorus replies to his thoughts.

Bella. Reality begins to crystalize in his mind. Home. School. Family. Bella, and with it a surge in adrenaline, the anxiety returns.

Where is Bella?

"With friends. Rest. You have work to do."

Who are you?

"We are you."

CHAPTER 26

His body is weak. It shivers. He can't move his limbs.

"You can if you try." The Chorus tells him.

No, no, I can't. But he's already lifted an arm. He tests his fingers, then a leg. His body creaks like dry wood, but he's able to sit up. He pulls himself to his feet.

He can smell savory odors from deep in the dirt. He tastes a rainstorm on the way. On instinct, he reaches for his phone. It's gone. He doesn't know what day it is, how long he's been wandering in the woods if he's truly been unconscious for days.

His stomach groans a hungry challenge. He turns in circles. The scent of a plant calls to him. Part wood, part mint. Before he can question how he knows this, he's already pulling at the plant, stuffing the leaves and spindly twigs into his mouth.

He reaches for another with berries that remind him of candy.

Not this one, the chorus tells him.

Are you sure?

Not this one.

He moves on, staggering on rubbery legs to the edge of the river. Before he can think twice, his body lunges and grabs a frog that had been sunning himself on a rock. He's had frog legs before. He could make a fire somehow and…

Not this one.

Are you fucking kidding me? What am I, a vegetarian now?

The frog eyes him before speaking in a faint voice, "I am you."

Startled, he jumps back, dropping the frog who gives a final glance before leaping to safety.

What the fuck is going on?

CHAPTER 27

Pat Bernardoni

This was not the way Pat Bernardoni imagined his press conference going. Chuckie and Ralph look at him, their faces are pathetic, and concerned. Fuck them. The stunt Francesco was trying to pull could have gone under the radar, only making a mess at home for him to clean up. But no. Some radical terrorists had run at the cops who had to defend themselves and right there in the thick of it, his idiot son, screaming and ranting and running around in the mix. And then the boy had taken off.

If he had one thing to be grateful for it was that none of the news channels managed to get Francesco on audio. God only knows what he was carrying on about.

"What the hell was he doing down there, Pat?" Chuckie had called hours after the melee when he saw Francesco's face on the news. "I didn't even see him, Christ it was crazy."

"Well, he wanted to try to smooth things over, talk sense to the people."

Chuckie sucked in his teeth then, "There's no talking sense to these people."

Now, sitting in the television studio, Chuckie avoids meeting his gaze. Ralph approaches, claps him on the back, "We're going to find him, don't you worry."

Pat grunts but avoids changing his expression. "My wife is a nervous wreck. For all we know one of those terrorists could have knocked him over the head. May even be holding him for ransom."

"Any word from the cops?"

"Not yet, my wife keeps calling every hour."

"Mr. Bernardoni," an anchorwoman summons his attention. She looks good, he thinks, though her outfit isn't flattering her best features. Someone should tell her, he thinks, but not him. Can't risk the trouble if she's one of those feminist types.

He tries to smile, forcing his face into stoic order.

She waves him to follow her into a spot in front of the bright lights and cameras.

Someone reaches over her shoulder to hide a microphone wire. A tech approaches him with a microphone as well. He clips it to his lapel, this a familiar routine.

The interview begins with formalities. Pat Bernardoni is no stranger to cameras. He knows the importance of pausing. The power of looking away at key moments, holding space for emotions that aren't present.

"What do you think happened to your son?" the anchorwoman asks.

She, too, knows the importance of exaggerated expression. Her brows furrowed, lips turned down, caricatures of concern.

"Only what I was told by the police. My son, Francesco, was just assigned to this new project. He went to try to speak to the residents of the building and was met with confrontation. A riot."

Bernardoni shakes his head at the word "riot" as if it's bitter meat.

"He was attacked. By some extreme left-wing types that were part of the riot. I believe he may have been kidnapped."

He stares into one of the brighter camera lights then, a trick he learned that comes in useful when it's time to conjure salt water from his eyes.

"Do you have a message for the kidnappers?"

A beat, silence is good to build tension, and he replies, "Please. Don't hurt my son. My wife and I, we've already lost our oldest daughter. Please don't put my family through another loss."

He feigns a cracking voice before continuing, "If you are looking for a ransom, whatever you want, get in touch with the authorities." His voice is stronger now, he faces the camera square on. "Turn yourself in."

Chapter 28

Squatters Arrested in New Bernardoni Building
  The Passaic Tribune
  June 18, 2022

It's been almost a month since Bernardoni Realty acquired an unsightly building in the southern district of Belton, a once-thriving working-class district. But the deal has been fraught with turbulence and trouble, as Bernardoni has faced some resistance from former tenants.

First, there was a confrontation between tenants, radical activists, and police that left a young woman dead and resulted in the disappearance and possible kidnapping of an heir to the real estate empire, Francesco Bernardoni.

Just this past weekend, police cleared remaining squatters who refused the offer of a rapid relocation stipend, a stipulation that was offered, Bernardoni said, out of his concern for ensuring tenants have a fair deal.

"There's no law that I have to do this," Bernardoni explained, "my colleagues are in a hurry to break ground on a new project. I have to make them happy. I want to do what's right for these people, so I offered a very generous package for them to leave in two weeks. Like a job, two weeks' notice. Very fair."

But Bernardoni said he was surprised when very few residents took him up on his offer. What's worse, for the second time, things turned violent.

"Police have had to go to the location several times. First, with the riot, it was sad because a young lady lost her life. My son, on that same day, my son disappeared and may have been kidnapped by a dangerous element that is using this situation to attack me, my family, and my business. And now the police had to go back in because people were squatting. It's illegal. They could have taken my offer, but they chose to break the law."

What could have been a reason to celebrate has instead been a headache for Bernardoni Realty and more personally, for the Bernardoni family.

"I'm stunned. Every day, when I wake up, I think 'what is going on in this world?' My son is out there somewhere being held against his will because someone is upset with me. We just want him back home."

Authorities say Bernardoni's son was present during the violent riot that resulted in one casualty, yet police have not been able to locate him since the crowd dispersed and they are not ruling out a possible kidnapping. Police are asking for anyone with information on Francesco Bernardoni's whereabouts to please come forward.

Chapter 29

Francesco

In this life, time moves slowly. The sounds of his favorite music, the voices of his friends, and notifications on his phone are like remnants of a dream. The voice he hears now comes from the trees, the rain, mosquitoes, birds, squirrels, and an occasional deer or rabbit.

He might be crazy.

He doesn't know.

He knows only that when he follows the voices, he finds food. The plants, seeds, and fruits he's allowed to eat. The Chorus tells him it's safe. And they tell him where to find water.

The voices speak in unison now, more often than not. When it splinters, the commotion makes his head ring. It makes him nauseous. Eventually, he passes out and when he wakes up, the voices speak as one once again.

Days ago- was it three days? A week? He thought he was headed back toward town. Was certain he'd find the bridge or the warehouse. But he was wrong. The dense trees gave way to a clearing in the woods, and frogs sang in a swamp. He had looked around, his stomach aching from hunger.

But the voices didn't weigh in, so he didn't eat. He kept walking. Late in the day, rain had begun to fall. Soft at first, it sang to him. Each drop another note in a chord vibrating down to the fine hairs of roots deep in the ground. In the absence of food, he ate up the music and felt satisfied. The music changed keys, a soft rain to a downpour, and he took shelter beneath a canopy of tree limbs.

He felt lonely then and wanted to hear The Chorus. He heard only rain at first. Then the voices came, splintered, discordant, competing.

Have you forgotten me already? One sounded like Carmen.

He lifted both hands, covering his ears. They would not subside.

Each raindrop a broken violin string.

"I tried to tell you, but you're just like the others..." another voice chastised.

"No roots," another screamed in his ears.

He cried, leaning his forehead against his knees.

He strained to remember remnants of his old life. The electronic music from the video game he and Jonathan used to play. Even the sound of Jonathan's voice.

My scholarship!

But the rain only used it to taunt him now.

Then he tried to hear Mallory's voice. To hear the sound of her laughing at him, or even yelling at him- *you're not one of us, and you never will be!*

But the rain only grew more insistent.

They're taking us down... Down to the ground... Using dynamite... And the earth will shake...And then where will you build your castles in the sand?

All of it nonsense, competing in his head, his head throbbing with pain. His eyes throbbing with tears. Water and salt. Rain and dirt.

And then he slept.

CHAPTER 30

In his dream, Francesco is warmed by a fire. One of the better fires he's made in his time in the woods. It lights right away before splinters stab at his calloused fingers. It burns hot, the smell heating his nostrils and warming his throat.

The sun is setting, but the colors of bark and leaves and grass and shades of orange on the horizon are more vivid than anything he's seen. This is how he knows he's dreaming.

He feels something pull at his arm and turns to see Bella. *You're here.*

At that moment, he wants to tell Bella all about the Chorus and the voices of the rain and the frogs, but time is limited. He knows this but doesn't know how he knows it.

Like you don't know who the voices are, but you know we are you, Bella tells him.

He wants to ask why. He wants to ask how to make The Chorus speak. To control it.

As if she knows it, Bella puts her paw on his shoulder, he feels himself return to center.

"Bell, are you dead? Am I dead?"

Bella licks his hand and steps two paws onto his lap, her amber eyes level with his. Her eyes sparkle, then become the color of honey. They fade and for a moment, he thinks he's looking into Mallory's eyes.

"Is Mallory dead?"

It's Bella's face, he realizes it now, her eyes.

Wrong question, she answers.

"What's the right question?"

Bella turns her face away from his, looking into the distance. He follows her gaze. He wants her to talk to him again. The Chorus answers.

Are you awake?

Bella turns away from him.

No.

Facing the sunset, she pads a few feet away, then stops to look back at him over her shoulder.

Are you awake? The Chorus is louder now.

Bella, come. Come. Sit...

The fire crackles and Francesco looks down instinctively. When he raises his eyes again, Bella is gone.

He tries to call her name, but his lips fail to part. He hears his voice calling to her but it's only in his mind.

Are you awake?

He rises with a start, and for a moment, his heart stops. Bella is there, it wasn't a dream. He trains his eyes on the fur, the dog's body that had been sitting, watching him as he slept. His eyes adjust to the early dawn light.

The creature comes into focus.

Are you awake?

Not Bella.

The animal approaches slowly, eyes focused on his.

A wolf.

Francesco feels the animal's hunger. Feels the saliva spread in his mouth as the wolf licks his lips.

Not this one, the Chorus echoes. The wolf's eyes shift. He heard the chorus too.

Not this one.

He lowers his muzzle, sniffs at the dirt, and gives Francesco one more longing gaze before leaping into the distance and disappearing into the thick trees.

CHAPTER 31

Francesco's stomach gurgles and growls. Today he's thinking of pizza, hamburgers, and meals prepared by Margie with a heaping pile of seconds or even thirds to eat if he wants it.

His stomach roars.

Perhaps this is why he couldn't take his eyes off the mushrooms. Plump, round, thick. They grow at the base of a tree. His mouth waters. He reaches a hand toward them.

Not this one.

He hesitates. His hand hovers in the air, outstretched in the direction of the mushrooms. Not every kind is edible, but these look hearty. And wouldn't he know if they were poisonous?

Not this one.

Aren't all poisonous foods red? Or striped? Had he heard this once? He feels lightheaded. He's wasting away. Hasn't had enough to eat.

Not this one.

"Shut up!" he yells the words aloud. The voice. The Chorus, his crazy thoughts. "It's your fault!" he rants, a fist raised in the air. "Show me some real fucking food. Show me how to trap a fucking squirrel, I'm *starving*!"

The words repeated, *not this one*, but he doesn't hear it. The sound of mushrooms, ripped from their stems by his hand, is almost enough to make him wince.

I'm fucking *hungry*.

He mashes the thick, chewy top of the mushroom into his mouth. As he chews, his tongue, then his gums, start to tingle.

It can't be worse than starving.

Is the last thing he thinks as the trees begin to sway. The light fragments. He doesn't feel himself stagger and then hit the ground.

CHAPTER 32

A chasm of pain rips through his stomach. He imagines the wolf pulling chunks of flesh from under his ribs. He wants to scream but can't. The wolf ignores his pain and continues to take hot, sharp bites out of him.

This can't be happening. I should be dead. Soon. Please.

Blood drips from the wolf's mouth. He licks his lips and blood- Francesco's blood- splatters. It splashes against his face. Suddenly cool and now Francesco realizes he's burning up. He's on fire.

Of course, it's a sex worker.

This deep voice is not the wolf's. It speaks the words casually. Not the voice of a predator. It doesn't even sound hungry.

Where do you get that from? another voice, incredulous, asks.

The original voice continues, "It's all in the lyrics. *Arty Tart?*"

The wolf disappears before the second voice can offer the rebuttal from somewhere in the darkness, "That's what you're going on? It could be about a pastry chef."

"Gimme a break. You don't even believe that excuse you just made."

The voices laugh.

"It's true!"

The debate heats up as Francesco feels something wet, cool, and comforting on his face. His stomach rolls.

"And besides, so what if Lalena is about a sex worker? Sex work is real work."

"I'm not saying it's not real work, I'm just saying there's no way your man Donovan would have written a song about a sex worker."

"Sounds to me," water drips on Francesco's nose as the explanation dances somewhere in the distance, "like that's exactly what he did."

"You're wrong. Wrong. Wrong. Wrong."

The other voice begins to hum.

"Make yourself less annoying and hand me the eyedropper, would ya, bae?"

Francesco can't see the two men. His head is throbbing, relieved only temporarily by the sensation of cool and wetness. These voices aren't trees. He knows it now in comparison. Of course. How did he miss it before? Humans have a distinct voice. Different from trees. And frogs. And plants. And wolves.

And dogs.

These are the piercing voices of humans.

For the first time, he's aware the presence of humans feels different. He feels it in his fingers, his legs, his feet. His…

Where are his roots? He can't feel the ground.

Francesco tries to ask, and with great effort, he manages a groan.

"Take it easy, buddy," The hand on his wrist gives him a gentle shake along with this command.

Do I have a choice?

"I don't know if you can hear me," the other voice begins. This voice speaks faster, and sounds younger. Still older than him, maybe. Francesco realizes the human voice is talking to him, "but if you can, I'm going to give you some medicine, ok? Don't bite down on this. And one… two…"

Something passes over Francesco's lips. It bumps his front tooth, and he feels something wet spray over his tongue. He thinks of a dentist's tools. But this isn't water. It tastes like pine and grass. He starts to choke and swallows the mixture instead.

Then there is more.

Warmth spreads over his stomach. Relief. The pain subsides.

"All I'm saying," the voice begins again, and the hand on his wrist gives another gentle shake, "is it's in the lyrics."

Francesco drifts into a deep sleep.

CHAPTER 33

Joann Bernardoni

Joann replays the Medical Examiner's words as if looking for clues to prepare her. Her palms and fingers tingle in the early stages of numbness she recognizes from her knitting days. She loosens her grip on the steering wheel. Cars glide in and out of her lane on the New Jersey Turnpike as she drives north, but she hardly notices them until one careens too close in front of her.

She almost slammed the brakes too late.

Almost, she thinks, heart racing. She recites a Hail Mary silently, then loosens her grip on the wheel, breaths, and without realizing it, continues to squeeze the wheel tight at ten and two like her father taught her, as traffic picks up around her.

The Examiner said he tried to call last week, but her husband, Pat Bernardoni, hadn't gotten back to him.

"I assume he's traveling for business. I understand your husband is a busy man and this can't be an easy time for you. I saw the notice in the paper..."

His voice trailed off into a distant echo as Joann processed what he said.

Frank had been found in the Hudson River.

"It appears he may have been pushed but more likely," the man hesitated on the phone, "he likely jumped, Ma'am. I'm sorry to be the one to tell you, and we can't confirm it's him …."

"It's not," she replied, cutting him off. "My son has no business in that area, plus, he was a happy child. He would not," she stopped, the words caught in her throat before speaking the words, blasphemy, impossible, unthinkable, that he insinuated. "He would not commit suicide," tears ran down her face as she spoke the words though they came out a high, urgent squeal.

Tears well in her eyes now recalling the conversation.

"Remember Ma'am, we still don't know," and "no identification," and "need you or Mr. Bernardoni to come identify the body."

A horn in the distance returns her focus to the traffic ahead of her. She screams and her body tightens in anticipation of a crash. But the truck is in the next lane, horn blasting again in self-righteous warning. The offending vehicle, a white SUV whose driver speaks on his cell phone, one hand gesturing wildly to accentuate his point to the absent listener, speeds up, appeasing the larger vehicle.

"Would you concentrate on the *road*? God damn, Joann, you need to stop worrying about the boy," her husband's voice condemns her from the back of her mind.

She grips the wheel tight again, this time in anger. He knew. And he ignored the message. Joann clenches her teeth. This is the last straw.

"It's your fault!" she yells to the empty car, sobbing.

"Look at you," her husband's voice taunts in reply, "falling apart. Weak. You can blame me all you want, Joann, but it was you who spoiled him. Make him weak. Like you."

She almost misses her exit as she thinks of her rebuttal in the imaginary duel. As she pulls off the highway, Joann tries to steady her breathing. Her husband doesn't know about her conversation with the Medical Examiner. He's at work, as usual. She didn't bother to tell him, not wanting another fight.

As she parks outside the morgue, her chest tightens. First, it was Carmen. And now Francesco. Her only son.

She feels the familiar signs as her breathing becomes shallow, her hands cold and sweaty. The world sways and her head becomes light and foggy. She reaches into her bag for the amber bottle, digging past an emergency pack of cigarettes she hides from her husband, who thinks she quit completely three years ago. She digs deeper through the junk.

"Why do you carry around so much shit?" her husband asks, demanding an explanation even now from miles away.

She ignores his voice in her head, collapsing onto the steering wheel and crying.

It takes Joann twenty minutes to calm herself enough to walk through the door. The Medical Examiner appears moments later and guides her down a hall. White, sterile, clinical, she walks through Limbo. A place of not knowing, where the dead wait to be claimed.

He speaks to her in a voice she thinks he cultivated over the years. She imagines he calls it the "crazy mom voice" and puts it on like surgical gloves whenever he has to deal with someone like her.

Patient. Patronizing. Not quite natural.

The moment arrives. In a small room, surrounded by stark white walls, under the glare of a painfully bright light, Joann waits as a technician wheels a gurney in. An electric buzz distracts Joann. Was it this loud the whole time?

She thinks it may be coming from the light. Or she may faint.

Her heart pounds.

This is it.

But it can't be.

My son wouldn't do this.

He was happy.

This is it.

The last straw.

"I'm leaving you for good this time," she imagines herself saying to Pat after breaking the news in the daydream she's now engrossed in.

"I had to identify our son! You threw him out, and then you didn't even tell me when the Examiner called!"

"Mrs. Bernardoni?" The placating voice interrupts her.

She blinks. Back in the room with the buzzing light and a corpse. A body…

Don't talk about him that way!

Lies beneath a blanket in front of her.

Not my son.

"Mrs. Bernardoni, you can take your time. Whenever you're ready."

He says this, but Joann thinks he doesn't mean it. The way a server drops your check at the table and says "Take your time," when they really mean, "I have other things to do and you've been here long enough."

She takes a breath, closes her eyes, and nods her head.

She hears the soft rustle as the sheet is removed from over the body.

Joann opens her eyes.

She hovers for a moment, somewhere near her body, the way she's learned to do during the worst of Pat's episodes. She sees brown hair, longer than she remembers ever seeing on her son, but he's been gone long enough for his hair to grow shaggy.

Her muscles tense. She holds her breath as her eyes scan the body.

But there's no need.

She exhales with relief, then remorse.

"He's not my son." Right hand over her chest, she breathes heavily now, not in panic but release. "Not my son."

Francesco is alive.

As she drives home, praying her thanks to the BVM, recalling the name her mother gave to the Virgin Mary, mother of all mothers, tears return. It wasn't Francesco. But the body, the boy in cold, dark, Limbo in the basement of the Morgue remains unclaimed. Some mother's son jumped- or was pushed- from the George Washington Bridge.

This thought, and the ongoing worry about her own son's disappearance, plague her for weeks to come, pushing aside any thought of leaving her husband.

CHAPTER 34

Francesco

Francesco smells the rain outside before he can hear it. He hears its persistence, clamoring, before he can see it descend like a wet mob demanding entry only to surrender, sliding down the windows. He doesn't remember drinking too much, but if the howling and burning in his stomach, nausea he can practically taste, is any indicator, he's going to spend today regretting last night's choices.

Thank God Bella hasn't been begging to go for a walk yet. It's Sunday. Must be Sunday. They have time. He's ready to drift back to sleep when another smell slips in, it overpowers the smell of rain, dirt, and spring. It's skunky, thick, and heavy.

Jesus Christ, Jonathan.

He wants to tell his friend to put that shit away. Christ, he better have made sure his parents aren't home if he's going to do that shit in the main house and not the pool house.

He tries to open his mouth and saliva rolls over his tongue. He clamps his mouth shut hard, willing himself not to vomit.

"Let me get some of that," a stranger asks.

Who the fuck said Jonathan could invite someone else over?

The voice sounds familiar. Not Jonathan. Not Derek. Not one of the other guys. But familiar.

Who the fuck is choking him out when he's hung over? Smoking in his fucking room?

A deep voice, soft, young, tells someone that he's going outside to take care of the goats. Francesco forces his eyelids apart. The room is hazy, lights dim. Two men he doesn't recognize are in his room. He tries to bolster himself up in bed, but a sharp pain in his gut leads him to reconsider.

One of the strangers, a guy in his late forties- maybe fifties- notices. He's got bushy hair and a rebellious beard. He reminds Francesco of the character from the old Harry Potter movies. The big guy with the Scottish accent. Whatever his name had been, Francesco can't remember. Jonathan was more into that shit than he was.

And where was Jonathan?

Francesco's eyes adjust. His heart races, breath catches as he sits in stunned silence.

Someone has trashed his room. His computer, all of his good shit is gone.

He's about to scream, to call out the intruders, demand they explain themselves, when a new realization dawns on him. Indignation turns to panic as he realizes that he's not home.

Across the room, standing near the door, another man gives him a tentative glance. He's lean, and his hair falls from the top of his head in small box braids.

"Looks like our guest is awake, Brent," this man says. Not Brent, Francesco hears it now. Bread.

"I don't know who you are," Francesco begins, "but leave me alone. My family has money. They'll give you anything you want."

As he blurts out the words, Francesco realizes this is no longer true. He no longer has a family. He didn't need their money. He feels his cheeks burn with shame.

"It's okay, kid, luckily we don't need your family's money. We have everything we need right here. But thanks for the offer," the younger of the two men says. His voice is calm, but his smile makes Francesco question if he's joking. His companion, the man with the beard, approaches the bed. Francesco braces himself for an attack, but the man only puts a hand on his companion's shoulder, as if calming him before he can say something regrettable.

"Hello, welcome back to reality, bud," the man named Bread smiles at him, pushing the bushy whiskers out in both directions. Francesco stares as this man lifts a joint to his lips, takes a hit, and exhales slowly, tipping his head away from Francesco. He's wearing a Pink Floyd shirt and camo pants, an image Francesco finds both confusing and jarring.

The hairy man speaks again.

"My name's Bread. Ya know, like the band, or the stuff you put your PB and J on. This handsome fella here, he's my partner, Kevin."

Francesco's eyes drift from one man to the other. Kevin pushes his glasses up closer to his face, waves the other hand, and smiles.

"How are you feeling?" Kevin asks. He sounds concerned, Francesco thinks, but doesn't wait for a reply before continuing, "You really shouldn't eat random mushrooms, not judging, just, ya know, good thing Chili was in town for the season. They knew how to neutralize that nasty shit you ate."

Kevin paces as he talks, he's restless and wiry. Francesco's mind is filled with questions. He should ask how he got here. Where is here? How long has he been out? But all that he manages to say is, "a lot of people here are named after food."

Kevin finds this funny. Bread doesn't seem offended.

"Well, I gotta go check the engine on the van and take care of the goats, I'll see you a little later, wandering stranger from the woods," Kevin waves, before turning toward the door.

"Frank," he croaks the name out, remembering the way it sounded when Mallory would say it. Suddenly remembering Mallory's face, scenes flash through his mind, reminding him of all that he's given up, walked away from, and lost. "Frank. From Jersey."

"Okay, Frank from Jersey." Kevin makes a gesture of tipping an invisible hat, blows a kiss to Bread, and backs out the door.

The room isn't bad, Frank realizes. It's small, cluttered, and dusty. It's certainly not his room. But it's comfortable in the manner of a rustic vacation camp cabin.

"Welcome to the farm," Bread spreads his hands as if showing off the space. He plops his broad body down into an upholstered chair that looks like it would have been considered old when Frank's parents were young. The chair groans its disapproval, but Bread doesn't seem to mind. He crosses one leg over the other on top of a footstool and takes another hit of his joint.

"Um. Thank you?" Frank replies. The pain in his stomach has subsided to a dull ache. His thoughts clearing now. "What happened? How did I get here?"

"Weirdest shit, actually," Bread now looks like he's gearing up to tell a story that he's enjoyed sharing a few times already. "Kevin, my partner, he saw this wolf, thought it was a wolf at least. Was about to shoot it. Wolf was harassing our goats, or so we thought. So being the peaceful kind of guy I am- I don't really like shooting, only targets and if I had to, Nazis- I tried to scare him off with just my sexy baritone voice. Your wolf-dog wasn't having it. Kept coming around and actually," Bread's eyes are wide open now, he leans forward, his feet returning to the floor, and says each word slowly for emphasis, "your wolf came scratching at the door."

He laughs and takes another hit.

Wolf? Frank remembers something about a wolf. But maybe it was Bella?

"So, Kevin puts his gun aside and decides to be a smart ass, saying "let's see if Lassie has a message from Timmy," and we walked toward your wolf dog and he led us to you. That's one smart beast you got there. Couldn't let him in, though, Kevin's allergic to dogs. So, he's had to stay outside. Been good about it, and hasn't gone after the goats. You've got him well trained." A long toke and moment of silence later, Bread continues, "Now, kid, if only you paid as much time learning your mushrooms as you did learning to train your dog. Kevin wasn't kidding. You nearly died. Chili, they'll be back later. They'll be happy as fuck that you're lucid."

"Chili?"

"Yeah, another food name, as you said. They're our mushroom connoisseur you could say. Word of warning, when Chili comes over. Motherfucker is always hot and is rude as hell about opening windows without asking first, but we let them get away with it because they make the best pizza you ever had."

Frank is more confused now than before he asked. "I had a dog, Bella, but I think the cops killed her. I just took off, lost it, I was in the woods walking around for a while. All this weird shit was happening."

"Your dog grey and white? Look like a wolf?"

"No," he tries to hide the disappointment in his voice, the man had said "wolf-dog" after all, "no she's a chocolate lab mix."

"No, dude, definitely not the same dog. But seems to like you, that's for sure. And sorry about the pigs."

"Pigs?"

"The pigs who shot your dog."

It takes Frank a moment to realize he means police, not other farm animals.

"That's what they do, though," Bread opens his mouth to say something else, but then closes it, appearing to reconsider before taking another drag of his joint.

Frank's head hurts. He isn't sure what Bread is talking about but thinks it may be best not to ask further questions. Not now at least.

"Listen, Kevin and I talked about it, we've agreed to abstain from earth-shattering sex for as long as you need to recover so you can stay here as long as you want."

Frank's host grins ear to ear, then uses both hands to push the air, as if dismissing his previous statement. "Dude, I'm just messing with you. My bad, I'm like the best cigarettes, no filter. Just joking with you but for real, you can stay here to get better and even after if you need to. People come in and out a lot, that's what we do here at the farm, no sweat, no worries my farm is your farm as they say.

Frank nods. "Thanks," he says, but what he really wants to say is that he feels like puking.

Part 2 Frank from Jersey and the Seven Anarchists

CHAPTER 35

Bread and Kevin made good on their promise. After one full day of Frank proving he could keep his medicine, an earthy-tasting potion, and his food, a lot of stuff his father would call "hippie shit" down, it was time for a tour beyond the confines of the fold-out couch in the living room.

"Behind this door," Bread turns to wink at Frank, "is where Kevin and I have our love nest. And where we keep our stash of ammo in case of emergencies."

"Um, boundaries, babe?" Kevin jabs the older man in the ribs, more than playfully.

Frank has never heard of infosec. He wonders if it is an herb or a drug. Maybe they have it hidden in that room too, he doesn't want to pry.

"He was wandering around in the woods half-starved, the kid's probably not COINTELPRO, I'm not worried about it." Bread puts an arm around his partner trying to calm the other man's nerves. Frank wonders if Kevin is ever really calm. He thinks the answer is no.

Kevin rolls his eyes and opens the door, beckoning Frank to follow him outside.

Days of rest indoors have made him sensitive to the sun. Frank winces and shields his eyes with one hand. Following Kevin out of the house is like stepping into a different world. Not the solitude of the woods that recently became so familiar, nor the comforts of his parent's rural lake house. As he steps onto the ground, he feels his roots sinking deep into the earth once again, realizing only then how much he missed the smell of dirt and the hum of the voices.

The cabin, comfortable and homey on the inside, is little more than a shack from the outside. Plants and vegetables grow on wiry frames and in tires painted in color combinations that hurt his eyes. There are large barrels with spouts and something in the distance labeled "compost."

There are also big round tents that remind him of the circus as if people come here to camp. A black van, rust crawling up from the floor, is parked haphazardly on the dirt clearing. Frank looks around but can find no sign of any highway or main road. No other indication of people living nearby. Several feet in the distance, a hand-painted sign with the words "On this farm, we believe all cops are bastards," hangs from the limb of a tree.

To his left and further secluded behind branches, a row of shrubs almost hides a tarp-covered enclosure where goats- actual goats- roam around. One pulls at scraps from a bucket. Another noshes on the side of a bush.

A low rumble like a distant storm draws Frank's eyes to the horizon. No sign of clouds in the sky. The rumble repeats, it's louder. And it's coming from the goats.

Frank can almost understand when a voice, in the distinct human range, cuts in.

"I heard this isn't your dog," Kevin begins. Frank follows him away from the goats and in the direction of a makeshift doghouse constructed from scrap wood and crates, "but this wolf hasn't wanted to leave since you've been here, so maybe you should thank him for saving your ass."

Something in the doghouse stirs, and in one swift motion, the grey creature emerged, slinking toward Frank. He kneels, puts out a hand, and waits for the beast to sniff him. The wolf eyes Frank but remains at a distance.

"Hello?" He feels stupid speaking the words aloud. But Bread told him the wolf came here to get help. And hadn't the wolf waited here for him?

Speak. He wills with his mind. *Say something. Jesus Christ, isn't that why you're here?*

The wolf sits facing him. Silent.

"Well, that's my cue to go take care of the goats. Happy reunion, you two," Kevin clasps his hands together and smiles, walking backward toward the shrubs.

Say something. Dammit, why can I hear the fucking goats but not you?

The wolf turns to the side, facing away from Frank.

What? Are you offended? Then say something.

Silence.

Frank is about to turn away when he hears his father's voice. *You're a real class act. You know what this is doing to my reputation? You, my son, heir to my business, out playing Dr. Doolittle in the woods? And you can't even get that right.*

He squints his eyes, willing the voice to disappear like the scenery.

And look what you've done to your mother.

He doesn't want to think about his mom. Tries not to see her bedroom door closed. Her eyes sunken behind puffy lids.

A dog? What about my daughter?

He doesn't want to think about home. The people he ran away from, or the people he failed.

You'll never be one of us. Mallory's voice, cracking he tries not to see her eyes, the tears, or the image of that last day. She, standing on her toes, pointing a finger at police in riot gear. Bella, growling in defiance. The sound of gunshots.

And how do you think your mother felt? Seeing it on the news? And where the hell are you?

Frank opens his eyes again. The wolf hasn't moved.

"Can you at least tell me," Frank begins, walking cautiously toward the wolf, his tone soft, appeasing, the voice he's heard his father use to make deals? "Can you at least tell me if Bella is alive? Where she is?"

The wolf looks at him and blinks.

"Beellllaaa," Frank says the name again, slowly, the way people do when trying to appeal to someone across a language barrier.

Nothing.

Frank sighs, puts his hands on his hips, and looks up at the sky. In the distance, birds call to each other. Tree branches stretch across, their leaves shading him from the sun, covering the forest in a canopy.

They look like the pictures of nerves like Mr. Sellers has in his biology class. Frank stares at the space between the sky, the branches reaching for each other, but not quite touching. Spreading in all directions. And the blue sky. The space between.

Not between. The Chorus returns. Frank's head lowers to see the wolf. He waits to see if the animal will speak again.

Not between. Not in front of. Not behind.

"God Dammit! Can't you just tell me where Bella is!" Frank is yelling now. Pacing, flinging his arms. The wolf doesn't stir.

Wrong question.

"What about Mallory? Is Mallory dead?"

Wrong question.

"Well, then fucking say something useful!"

I am you.

Frank smacks both hands over his eyes and grunts in despair. What the hell was the point of the voices if they weren't going to help him?

"Trouble in paradise?" Kevin's voice this time.

Frank turns to face him, his cheeks burning. "I don't usually do this, it's just, I don't understand… I mean you said yourself… the wolf… I don't get it."

"Shit is weird. Maybe it's best not to overthink it. You've had a rough couple of days. Come on inside for a bit and rest. Chili's on their way over. They also saved your ass. Chili talks slow, but is better at conversation than your friend there," Kevin nods toward the wolf who now lies in the sun oblivious to them both.

CHAPTER 36

Chili

GhostPepperf12: Heads up, I think I found him.
RedBarren1312: ?
GhostPepperf12: That person you said you were looking for...

Chili reads through the Signal text one more time before hitting send.

They didn't want to say anything at first, but it weighs on them late into the night. Chili's trip to the farm this time was for restoration and healing after a brutal series of actions involving arrests. One even involved casualties. And rest will come, Chili knows it.

They've made a camp in the middle of the first yurt. Big Red, they call it. This was supposed to be a completely off-grid respite, but Chili can never really leave their phone turned off. Too much activity on the Fash-Watch thread. Too many emergencies.

And I came here to unwind.

But the boy needed attention first. It was hard to see the resemblance initially. The kid had puke all over himself, was feverish, and looked like shit warmed over twice.

They roll a sleeping bag across the ground and slip out of their sandals, taking a moment to feel the earth, cool but thawing, before crossing their legs and sitting tall, planted, on the sleeping bag. Stretching their head toward the apex of the yurt. Imagining the stars in the sky on the other side.

They close their eyes and breathe deeply into their diaphragm.

God damn if it didn't look like I was staring right into your face.

They don't want to think about the kid. Duty done. He'll be fine. And now RedBarren is on notice. All the drama is not their problem.

It was a long time ago. Chili had a different name then. They both did.

And I fucked up a lot.

Chili lights an incense stick and blinks back tears, recalling that late January day in 2017. So much clamoring underground, not since the Battle in Seattle had they anticipated so much outcry. Chili had rehearsed the plans that morning, seated in the recliner in the corner of some comrade's living room. RedBarren was Wormwood on Signal then, but her true name, the one she shared only with Chili, was too painful to say, even in memory.

"What's the plan regarding arrest?" Chili asked for the third time.

"No plan. Just a march."

"Are you sure? Because I can get bail money together if there's a solid plan in place, babe."

She pulled at the hair on both sides of her head, closing her eyes dramatically, and repeated, "No plan. Just. A. March."

Maybe she meant it. There were plenty of people marching during Trump's inauguration. But then neo-Nazis showed up and things got out of control fast.

Chili wasn't dressed in black bloc, and knowing they make for a memorable figure, hadn't stuck around when glass shattered in the street.

Maybe that was a mistake.

"You didn't stick with me!" she yelled later, after being bailed out.

"You said no arrests!"

The arguments that ensued in the months after that freezing winter day haunted Chili for years. Their relationship was over long before she was sentenced and by the time she got out of prison last year, they were barely pen pals.

I fucked up a lot of things. But maybe I can do this one thing right.

Lying back on the sleeping bag, folding their arms under their head, Chili let the smokey smell of Nag Chiampa fill their lungs.

Chili thinks about what they said. About the wolf showing up. Leading them to that kid. Kevin wasn't impressed with the stranger.

"You should have seen him yelling at the wolf. Like yelling. Because the animal wouldn't talk to him. Talk about entwhitled." Kevin told them over dinner when the stranger was asleep.

"True, but the wolf didn't attack or run away, right? I mean that is unusual," Bread had pointed out.

Chili listened. What they didn't say was that it made perfect sense. Or it would have if Bread and Kevin had known her. They check the phone again. No new alerts from Signal.

Maybe it was a mistake. Maybe this will be the time Chili texts and she never answers again. Time will tell.

CHAPTER 37

Jonathan

His eyes water as he recalls that night. Jonathan was sure he was going to lose his scholarship. He thought being blamed for Francesco's drugs was the lowest his friend would ever stoop.

Sitting in the auditorium, the smell of grandma perfume in the air, occasional cell notifications going off despite the announcement to *please silence all phones during graduation proceedings,* Jonathan remembers that night a few months ago. He never wanted to speak to Francesco again. Of all his unanswered prayers, why was it this wish had been granted?

"And now," Principal Whitaker drones, "This year's valedictorian, Amee Hobbes."

The audience breaks into applause. Jonathan, leaning back against his seat, uncomfortably hot under the maroon and gold robes, doesn't even try to fake the effort of clapping.

Amee walks across the stage, smiling and waving before arriving at the podium where she adjusts the microphone. Her teeth are perfect. Jonathan remembers Amee back in middle school, relentlessly tormented for wearing braces. The seventh-grade bullies became the ninth-grade jocks.

Many of them chased Amee like dogs searching for a bone when the braces came off. That's how it goes around here. He imagines public school is no better.

And for what?

He leans both elbows on his knees and holds his face in his hands.

And where the fuck are you, Francesco?

Jonathan barely made it through finals. He hadn't been able to sleep without taking extra of his cousin's pills.

He surveys the rest of his classmates in disgust. Derek, Scott, and the rest of the guys Francesco thought were all hot shit. What have they been doing? Partying. Fucking around. Same shit as always.

None of them give a shit that you're gone, you know. Only me. Hell, your own father isn't out putting posters up with your face on them. I am.

"And we'll all face challenges on the road ahead," Amee continues, layering one cliché onto another.

Jonathan tries not to groan out loud. *This needs to be over.*

When the ceremony is finished- big fucking deal- and everyone heads to the party at Derek's or to dinner out with their family before planning their gap year, Jonathan will knock on doors along the other side of the street downtown where everyone swore they hadn't heard of Francesco.

"No, I haven't seen him. Only on the news, that's the kid, right?"

"Shame what happened, do you think he was kidnapped?"

Later that evening, as the June sun's relentless heat subsides, Jonathan will post the Missing Person memes on all his social media accounts. He'll even go old-school and post flyers downtown.

He'll take the bus home and head upstairs before his mother has a chance to make a display of feeling guilty and sorry- for having to work through graduation and for the loss of what they both know is his only friend.

He slips into his bedroom and opens the window, which creaks loud enough to startle him. Too early in the year for air conditioning, he peels his sweaty clothes off down to his boxers, grabs a bottle of Jack Daniels off his closet shelf, and collapses onto his bed.

What the fuck happened to you, man?

He replays the news story in his mind. The yelling and rioting and chaos. And right in the middle of it was Francesco. Jonathan saw the interviews with Francesco's father.

"I believe he's been kidnapped. We need him to come home. Now."

He never liked Francesco's dad. Even now, why isn't he out in the streets every day looking for his son?

You better have been fucking kidnapped, douchebag, Jonathan thinks, taking a swig from the bottle. *Because if you weren't? If you just ran off and left everyone here worried about you? You're a bigger asshole than I thought.*

CHAPTER 38

Jonathan

Jonathan pours a bowl of generic cereal, the kind with more salt and sugar than anything worth writing home about, he catches himself begging God to bring Francesco home. Alive.

Please, God, let today be the day we find him. Alive. Please.

"No!" he replies to himself, banging the milk down harder than he intended to, splashing it onto the countertop. "No. You don't just go and do fucked up shit and then beg God to fix it, like some kind of little bitch. No."

He shovels a spoonful of cereal into his mouth. It's getting stale and the sound of crunching echoes in his mind. Loud. Shouldn't be that loud. He pauses.

And that's when he hears the sound of nails grating against wood getting louder.

"Who's there?" he calls out through a mouth full of partially chewed cereal before gulping it down.

He sets the bowl aside and grabs a steak knife. The scratching at the door continues.

I swear to God if this is kids playing some kind of joke, your asses will be dead.

Facing the closed door, the scratching quickens, followed by a thud. He takes a deep breath and swings the door open.

Before he can process what is happening, he's on the floor, on his back, knife knocked from his hand.

And the dog is on top of him.

"Jesus fucking Christ," he tries to curse between mouthfuls of dog tongue.

He manages to push her eager face aside and sit up, face to face with a thin but energetic Bella.

Tears come to his eyes. He looks to the doorway, expecting to see Francesco standing there in his overpriced pants and designer shirt.

The doorway is empty.

"Bella, where's Francesco?"

The dog sits back and whimpers.

Shit, now I'm thinking she's Lassie.

His heart sinks. He jumps to his feet and walks outside, circling around the building in case he missed something. No sign of Francesco. Bella follows alongside him.

"He's really not with you? You found me on your own?"

He shakes his head, feeling stupid for asking a dog questions.

"Don't bother answering. If you're here, that means he's dead."

CHAPTER 39

Frank

Frank heads back to the cabin after his first real walk around the farm. Stronger now, he can feel his roots growing deeper into the ground again. Sweat drips down his back and he's thankful for the shirt Kevin let him borrow, though he realizes now he should wash it before returning it.

Where is their washing machine?

A bee dashes in front of his eyes, striking him in the nose but not stinging him before hesitating in front of his eyes and flying off.

He thinks a few more days of recovery will be enough to head back to the city. He'll go home and then....

Then what?

A sinking feeling in the pit of his stomach reminds him he has no home. He has no family.

The familiar low groaning he's come to associate with the chatter of goats interrupts his thoughts. He follows the murmuring tenors to the edge of the makeshift pasture.

The goats are locking horns, fighting over the last apple. The bigger of the two, with brown fur and large yellow eyes, bucks back and hollers before snatching the fruit in big teeth. The smaller goat, black with an incomplete white stripe, looks down, despondent.

Frank doesn't hear it in words. He just understands. He understands tyranny and acceptance. The futility of an occasional head butting. He understands hunger. And something else.

He feels it himself. Doesn't need The Chorus to speak to him in riddles. He feels the tumor growing in the goat's stomach.

The smaller goat trots to a water trough and drinks up a few sips before slinking to the ground.

It will be over soon. Frank sits by the animal, placing a hand over her left side. The goat's eyes blink.

It will be over soon. I'll return to the Earth. The trees. The plants.

The wind picks up, shaking the branches of a nearby shrub. Frank remembers seeing the goats snacking on this bush the other day. They cleared as much as they could reach, but leaves remain within his grasp. He reaches for a taller branch and hears the voice again.

Yes, this one.

He pulls a fistful down and offers it to the goat, long abandoned by her mates now. The smaller goat ducks her head and then sniffs at Frank's offering before snatching it away.

He wonders if Bread and Kevin know about the tumor. They'll know soon.

When Frank returns from his walk, the van parked outside of the cabin is joined by an old VW Jetta, in about as fair condition.

He didn't know they were expecting company. Approaching the entrance, he hears laughter and animated voices, and another trying to find entry into the conversation.

"That's excellent praxis, my friend, I can get behind that," Bread's recognizable voice booms through the cabin as Kevin laughs at a joke Frank just missed.

"Okay, but based on what? You can't just be haphazard about these things." This is spoken in a lecturing voice belonging to a young man Frank guesses is in his thirties. His smooth black hair is shaved on the sides and long on top, held fastened with an elastic, but short enough to still stand in spikes shooting in several directions. "Because if you look carefully at Kropotkin's writing, you'll find that…"

He's interrupted by a girl whose long dyed blue hair falls to one side, shaved on the other. The letters E, J, and H are tattooed on her neck and collarbone. "I'm saying not everyone goes about it by reading stuff by old white men, even old white comrades. It's a new day, keep up."

Kevin and Bread laugh, the rebuked visitor pulls his legs up close to his chest and lets his breath out in a huff.

"Well, I need to know what your framework is."

"It's Discordian, okay? Does that work for you? It doesn't matter," the girl replies.

"Technically," Kevin breaks in, pointing a spoon of something that looks like peanut butter, at the girl. "That would be Nihilistic."

Frank can't understand what they're talking about, or why Bread finds this hysterical. As he roars with laughter, both hands on his belly, he notices Frank standing in the doorway.

"Hey, everyone, this is our newest find." He rises to his feet and walks over to Frank, patting him on the shoulder as he continues introductions.

"Frank, this is Miles. Their pronouns are he and they, and what they lack in humor they make up for in just about every other superpower. Also, they liked roller skating after it stopped being cool and before it made a resurgence."

"What is that supposed to mean?" Miles looks annoyed. Frank thinks of Jonathan. Their rituals of deprecation. Had he ever gotten on Jonathan's nerves?

And what has Jonathan been told about his disappearance? Does he even care?

"It means we love you, and you're cool as fuck and people need to know interesting things about you, so they'll remember you," Bread answers before turning his attention to the girl. "And this is Teri Jacks."

"That's not my name!" She grabs a pretzel from a bowl on the table nearby and launches it playfully at Bread. It bounces off his face, but he manages to catch it.

"Thanks for the pretzel," he begins to chew.

"Teri. Just Teri. Bread likes to make everything about Boomer music."

"Yeah, but Don't let Teri fool you, she's the youngest in the group and the only cis woman but that doesn't stop her from making dad jokes." Bread continues, still chewing the pretzel ammo.

"But that's just one of the reasons we love you," Kevin adds.

"So, who is this?" Miles asks motioning to Frank.

"This is Frank from Jersey. He has a pet wolf who isn't currently talking to him and aside from having shitty foraging skills he seems pretty cool."

Bread gives Frank a side hug as he makes the introduction, then leads him to the couch to sit down with them.

"A pet wolf? I'm afraid to even ask. But are we still going to consent to meet here with a stranger around?" Miles shifts in their seat.

"I can go back out, or something, if you want?" Frank offers.

"Nah, he's not a stranger, he's Frank. From Jersey. And besides, we're not planning anything in Minecraft today." Bread cuts in.

Frank scans the room looking for a game console, but doesn't even see a television or computer. He suspects they aren't really talking about gaming.

"The action against Bernardoni is above ground," Kevin adds.

"Bernardoni?" Frank sits bolt upright. He regrets speaking up. The group looks at him with curiosity and mistrust.

"Yeah, Bernardoni Realty and Development. Do you know about them?" Miles asks.

"They mean do you know what a fucking chud the guy is?" Teri asks, popping a pretzel into her mouth.

"Uh, he's he was my uh, well," Frank clears his throat and tries again, "He was my dad. But not anymore."

Silence.

Frank realizes there's a clock ticking somewhere in the background. This was a mistake.

"I see it now," Miles studies Frank's face. "Okay, okay, assuming you had a major bath, haircut, and put on a few pounds, I can see the connection. You're the kid from the news."

"The what?" Frank is taken aback.

"But that kid's name is," Teri scrolls through her phone, "oh, right, Francesco, Frank, clever handle dude. Surprised they haven't figured it out."

"Wait, wait, wait, I need a smoke to make sense of this," Bread lights up a joint and inhales, "you're heir to the Bernardoni company, and you just happen to be wandering in the woods and your dad is going all over the news saying you've been kidnapped..."

"Kidnapped?" Frank interrupts.

"Yeah, kidnapped or whatever, but your dad is also the same chud tearing up housing and telling Elon Musk to hold his beer while he competes for biggest asshat boss of the year?"

"I… uh, I guess?"

"This is what happens when you bring home strays," Miles shrugs and rolls his eyes.

"Okay, but who would think some dude roaming around the woods sick as fuck from eating a bad shroom would be fucking heir to the Bernardoni Empire," Kevin cuts in.

For the first time, Frank hears something like anger in Kevin's voice. His heart sinks. Whoever they are, whatever they're doing, Kevin and Bread have been good to him. Frank's stomach churns with anxiety and remorse. He didn't mean to cause all this commotion. And underneath it all, something else. Frank knows better than anyone the kind of man his father is. But hearing strangers badmouth his dad makes him uncomfortable, even if they aren't wrong.

"And here we are ready to talk about the Bernardoni action in front of the chud's son. Like that's a coincidence?" Miles sounds pissed now, but Frank doesn't care about Miles' opinion of him. In fact, he realizes, he doesn't like Miles. But he doesn't want to cause trouble for Kevin and Bread..

"Um, I can just go for another walk, really it's ok," Frank begins again.

"No!" They bark in unified response.

"So, first thing's first, what were you doing eating mushrooms in the woods if your dad is fucking Chud, Bernardoni?" Teri looks both confused and disgusted.

"We fought and, uh, I left home."

"Oh, this is priceless, let me guess, were you written out of the will for crashing the car?" Miles taunts, up on their feet pacing.

"What? No. It wasn't like that. My dad's deal was going to wreck Mallory's apartment building, and I was trying to get him to reconsider. But there's just no talking to him. About anything. He doesn't care."

"Yeah, you don't say," Miles interrupts, this time Teri pulled at their sleeve, motioning for them to sit beside her and be quiet.

"I get it. I know. I get it now. I didn't want to be part of that anymore. So, I left. I went to help Mallory."

"Who's Mallory?" Kevin interrupts this time.

"Mallory, I don't know her last name, a girl, I guess, a girl I was trying to help." Frank feels his cheeks burn. This isn't happening. His eyes tear up. "I went to the building to help her, and all these people were there for a protest."

"You were there as part of the protest?" Bread asks, leaning forward.

"That's not what they're saying on the news," Miles points an accusing finger.

"Well, it's the news," Teri responds.

"Yeah, I was there with Bella, my dog. And there were suddenly all these people there and then the cops were all in riot gear like in the movies and they started shooting. I think they shot my dog. Last thing I saw was one of them face-to-face with Mallory. They shot her. I think she's dead. I think they're both dead."

Silence, Frank studies the faces in the room as they digest his version of events. Kevin, Teri, and Bread exchange glances. Frank thinks he sees dawning recognition on Teri's face.

"Mallory, that was the girl from North Jersey Street Defense." Teri begins.

Kevin lowers his eyes. Bread nods his head.

"You knew her?" Frank asks.

"Not well. Through affinity groups. Met her once at an event. She was dedicated," Teri's voice is softer now.

"She was a saint. She used to feed strangers, without even asking them if they had money. I saw it happen. I lost it. I went nuts. I saw everything turn red. Like literally, not just how people say it, but everything turned red."

He recounted running and stumbling in the woods, then losing his way.

"I don't know what happened, but weird shit started happening when I woke up." He considers leaving it off there, but continues, "like all of a sudden, I can hear the trees and shit. And I was hearing the animals and the plants, and I guess that's how the wolf showed up. I don't remember a lot. It all kind of runs together. The voice was telling me what was safe to eat. But that one day, I was so fucking hungry. It told me not to eat it, but I didn't listen. Then I woke up here."

No one responds at first. Teri begins crunching on another pretzel, the sound filling the room in the otherwise awkward silence.

"It's pretty fucked up. But I think we can agree that if he was sent here to infiltrate, he would have at least had some decent food. He could have died from the shit he ate, pretty sure his old man wouldn't set him, or a decoy, up for that." Bread interjects.

"I'm just saying it's fucked up, and maybe we need to be careful. Did you check his phone?" Miles asks.

"He didn't have a phone on him," Kevin adds.

"How did you know?" Frank asks.

"Dude, you puked and shit all over yourself. We had to take your clothes off and clean you up before bringing you in the house. No wires, no recording devices no nothing. Just a lot of puke. And shit."

"Um, thanks. I guess?"

"Also, impressive that you walked all the way from Brighton. That must have taken weeks, at best," Teri crunches another pretzel.

"Where am I now, exactly?"

Before Bread can answer, Miles cuts him off, "Better to be discreet for now, right? For now?" they turn to Frank. "All you need to know is you're on stolen land, like the rest of us."

Frank nods, heat prickling his face. Has the farm been bought by his father, too? Or is Miles talking about stolen land the way those weird kids in Civics Club used to talk during debates in school? Before he can ask, Bread cuts in.

"Fair enough," Bread holds both hands up sitting back on his seat.

"Besides," Kevin chimes in, "you've got some time to recover still, according to Chili."

CHAPTER 40

Chili

Miles kicks their sneakers off outside the entrance to the yurt. The ground is no longer cold beneath their feet, even though the sun set hours ago. He reaches to knock on the door out of habit, but before his hand touches the heavy canvas, a low, soft voice calls out from inside the dome in a slow, measured cadence.

"You don't have to knock, come on in."

Chili sits with legs crossed, head high, back straight, both gentle and regal, planted on the maroon sleeping bag. As usual, there is no fire going. Chili seldom needs one.

"Am I bothering you? Do you have time to talk?"

"There is always time. Until there isn't. Now, there is. Sit."

Miles squats low and then kneels on both knees, using their hands to shift some weight off the ground. Even with the sleeping bag underneath, they still feel the sharp, hard edges of the earth. It irritates them, like a sweater that should be warm but is instead itchy.

Sensing this, Chili stretches to the left and grabs two pillows.

"Try these," they offer.

"Thanks," Miles adjusts their weight on the pillows, relieved and aware once again of Chili's uncanny perception of body language.

"Have you met the new guy?" Miles begins, testing the waters.

"You could say that. If you count making medicine for someone in and out of delirium as meeting," Chili pauses, "I did see him once since he's been lucid. Seems to be doing better," Chili looks up at the ceiling, then leans their neck side to side, loosening tension through a series of cracks. "But you mean something else. You don't trust him, do you?"

"Do you?" Miles asks with more intensity than intended.

Chili considers this, then meets Miles's gaze, their eyes soft. "I don't see him as an instrument of disruption. At least, not to us. I've been talking to Jori and Chira. Did you hear about Jori's dream?"

Mile's stomach clenches. Jori never dreams about good things like curing cancer or winning the lottery. Or if they do, they don't share those dreams with the group.

"No, what was it this time?"

"They had a dream of a grey wolf that found a bomb. There was still time to cut the right wire. To keep it from going off. But we couldn't agree on whether to dismantle the bomb or to leave it for someone else to find."

Chili has explained to Miles often enough the way dreams work.

"So, he's a walking time bomb. I don't like this." What Miles really wants to say is that they don't trust using dreams as a compass any more than they like the idea of a stranger being privy to their plans. Especially when the stranger is the son of Pat Bernardoni.

"What about his father?"

Chili lights an incense stick and looks into the distance, "He's not here to do his father's bidding."

"He's a Bernardoni," Miles pushes their hands, fingers outstretched, onto their legs.

"That was a matter he had no choice in," Chili pauses before adding, "you understand." It's a statement, not a question.

Miles's face grows solemn. He puts his face on his hands and nods his head.

"I'm not saying that to be an asshole, Miles."

"Okay. But my adoptive parents were racist, bougie drunks. They weren't Pat Bernardoni."

CHAPTER 41

Frank

Frank wipes sweat from the back of his neck. His hair, now growing shaggy, retains moisture. His father would never allow his hair to cover his ears, to sag into his eye line, or to reach toward his collar.

As he and Kevin carry hay and vegetables to the goats, Frank can imagine his father's voice, "You're going to the barber to get rid of that duck's ass."

He pulls at the tufts of hair with his free hand, a sack of carrots and lettuce slung over his shoulder.

"Not into the long hair I see? No barbers out here," Kevin offers in an apologetic tone. "I can get the clippers out myself if you want, or it'll have to wait."

"It's okay. I'm just not used to it. Everything out here feels different."

A forceful push sends Frank sprawling to the ground. The bigger goat digs his face deep into the sack of vegetables.

"Allister, take it easy, will ya?" Without dropping the hay tucked under his arm, Kevin shoos the goat away and helps Frank to his feet again.

"See? That's when the voice should talk to me. The goat knows I can hear him, why not just ask for some damn carrots?" Frank wipes dirt from his legs.

"Maybe you're thinking about it the wrong way," Kevin offers.

"How do you mean?" Frank rubs at his aching knees.

"Well, maybe it's like any other relationship. Take Bread. Of course, I love him. But if you haven't noticed that man loves to hear himself talk," Kevin is already several steps ahead of Frank who rushes to catch up, closing in on a miniature barn in the distance. "Do you know how many times I have something on my mind, and it's just not worth cutting him off?"

"Ha, I can see that. I mean Bread's cool, but yeah."

"So, I have a choice. I can raise my voice or wave my arms around trying to get his attention, or I can just say 'fuck it,' time for me to knock him out of the way and grab the carrots for myself."

The image makes them both laugh.

"Okay, but what about when I ask? What about the wolf, the other day? I was asking him to tell me shit, but he just sat there."

They've arrived at the entrance to the barn. Kevin drops the hay long enough to unlatch the door. The bigger goat, Allister, trots beside them, bleating and threatening to rear up again.

"Relax, Al," Kevin reaches into the bag Frank is holding and tosses a carrot several feet away. Allister charges in the direction away from the barn to chase his treasure. Kevin turns to Frank, "See what I just did?"

"You threw a carrot at the goat?"

"I manipulated Allister into running away. I tricked him with food. Does he know? Who knows? But I manipulated him because I don't hear what he says and from the looks of things, he doesn't care what I say."

"So?"

"So, you asked the wolf a question. You told him what you wanted from him. That doesn't mean he wants to have a conversation. If he understands you and you're hearing birds and trees and wolves and whatever, then maybe you need to respect that they have their own," Kevin pauses, inhaling and looking for the right word somewhere in the distance, "process. Their own boundaries. Maybe you're overthinking this whole thing." Kevin opens the door to the barn and ushers Frank to follow him inside, closing the door quickly behind them.

"Maybe it isn't for you to go around telling them what you want from them. Maybe this thing you suddenly have is about you listening. Until they're ready to talk."

"None of it makes sense," Frank shakes his head.

"Yeah, tell me about it. Craziest shit I ever heard, but whatever, no judgment, now let's take a look at Clementine."

Heading toward the far corner of the barn, Kevin calls out, "Oh my daaarling, oh my daaaarling." No sound returns to him.

Francesco hasn't seen Clementine since the day in the pasture. He remembers now. The pain. The tumor.

"Um, about that, Kevin," he begins. Light streams in from a small window, illuminating a silky black body, lying on a bed of hay.

"Jesus, what the fuck?" Kevin drops to his knees beside the goat.

"I forgot to tell you. The other day, a few days ago, the same day the wolf wouldn't talk to me, this goat did."

Kevin kneels by Clementine feeling her back, her sides, and abdomen. He leans his face close to hers, listening for breath.

"I didn't think it was actually *talking* because it was different? It wasn't the voice. It was, um, it was pain?" Frank's voice trails off.

On the word 'pain,' Kevin sits upright and stares at Frank. "And?"

"And it was like I was feeling her pain. And I just knew. It wasn't a voice or words or anything, I just knew."

Kevin looks expectant, Frank continues, "Somehow, I knew she has cancer. Or a tumor. And she's dying."

Kevin lets out his breath in a slow sigh. His eyes closed, he nods his head, taking this in better than Frank expected.

"Okay. Well, maybe we should tell Bread soon. He's gonna be torn up. He loves these goats."

Clementine's head moves. She stretches her muzzle toward Frank and opens one small black eye to watch him. Frank doesn't know if dying goats get hungry. But he's hungry suddenly. He tastes carrot in his mouth. Without thinking, he reaches for a carrot and presents it to the goat. She nibbles the edges and then rests her head back down in the hay.

"If he loves them so much, why are you the one who's always feeding them and stuff?" Frank asks.

"Oh, don't let him fool you. Bread loves these little beasts. I do too. But he's a Taurus. He ain't getting his hands dirty." Kevin forces out a laugh.

Frank smiles.

Soon.

The sound of The Chorus startles him. It has been days.

"What's wrong?" Kevin's face is instantly serious, and concerned.

"I heard it again. I just wasn't expecting it. It's been days. And usually, it only happens outside. Which I guess we are, outside, I mean," Frank shakes his head, "I heard it again."

"The voice? Was it Clementine?"

Frank nods.

"She's going to die soon."

"I'll tell Bread," Kevin lifts himself and turns for the door, "if you don't mind, maybe stay with her? Until we get back?"

Frank turns to face Clementine. Her breathing is shallow. He thinks he hears something rattle in her body, a low groan. Her eyes open and fix on his. He's never noticed it before, but her eyes are beautiful. He sees the rich, dark pupil. It draws him in. He tastes grass in his mouth. And carrot. And then searing pain causes his body to convulse.

When Kevin returns, Bread by his side, they're met at the barn door by Allister, rearing, and stomping, and ramming his horns against the outside wall of the barn.

Bread bursts into a fresh round of tears. Kevin puts an arm around his waist.

"I know, babe, I know. But Clem needs you now, okay?"

Bread nods, hands over his eyes, wiping tears. He pulls away from Kevin long enough to pet Allister, trying to calm him.

"I'll stay here with him, you go on and say goodbye to Clem," Kevin offers.

Bread reaches for the door to the barn and hesitates.

"Ok, I'll go with you."

Kevin holds Allister back, giving Bread enough time to duck into the barn before following closely behind him.

"You know," Kevin begins, his back still turned, "maybe I should text Chili in case they know some med-"

Kevin stops midsentence. Bread sees it too.

In the beam of sunlight, Clementine rests peacefully on her bed of hay. She looks light and serene. Kevin thinks he hears her snoring.

But beside her, on the ground, Frank lies contorted.

"Shit, did that crazy white boy fall off something and break his back?"

As if in response, Frank's body convulses. He moans. Blood begins to pour from his nose and mouth.

"Jesus, fuck!" Bread screams, covering his eyes and leaning on Kevin.

"I'll watch him, you go get Chili," Kevin leads Bread toward the door, knowing the older man is prone to panic in situations like this.

Bread gone, Kevin kneels between Frank and Clementine, careful to give enough space in case the boy should convulse again or worse, become violently animated before gaining full consciousness.

He reaches a hand for Clementine. Still asleep. Deep breaths, no sign of stress. Maybe she'll live, he wonders. Maybe Frank also has a gift for taking her illness. He's heard of such things before but never knew of it happening.

The door bursts open again, and Chili enters.

"Thanks and that was fast."

"Yeah, don't mention it. What happened? Did he fall?"

"Don't know. He was sitting with Clem one minute, now we just came in and he was on the floor. A seizure maybe? He was convulsing and blood coming out his nose and now Clem seems fine. She was dying. He knew it. That's why I went to get Bread."

Chili moves swiftly around Frank, their ample body like a dancer. Kevin admires their grace in one of the rare moments when Chili does anything fast.

Chili takes Frank's pulse on his wrist. Then feels for a heartbeat. They lean down low, and Kevin thinks they're sniffing Frank's breath. They reach a finger wrapped in a baggy section of a t-shirt under Frank's nose to collect some blood, performing some kind of improvised test.

Frank begins to moan again. Chili leans down, whispering something Kevin can't understand. Chili removes something from their pocket, a tiny vial. They dab something onto Frank's mouth. A moment later, the boy's eyes flutter, then open. He coughs and tries to sit up.

"Soon. It's coming soon." Frank begins to call out.

"Relax," Kevin tries to reassure him, but Chili motions for him to wait.

"What's coming?" Chili asks.

"It's spreading. Consuming everything. Soon it will be too late."

Frank falls silent again. Kevin watches as the boy's body seems to relax. It reminds him of a horror movie.

"Like one of those movies about demonic possession," Kevin begins, not realizing at first that he's saying the words out loud.

"Eh, similar ballpark, but not exactly demonic." Chili answers as if the conversation is as natural as talking about the weather.

The barn door opens then, and Bread walks in, clearing his throat, "What's happening? Is everyone okay?"

Chili answers, "I can't be sure of the details. But if what Frank is telling us is true, and if it is, I've seen it only a few times before, he may be having a vicarious reaction."

"A what?" Bread asks, lowering himself to the ground near Clementine and gently petting her back.

"He's taking on Clem's pain. Possibly her illness? But I don't think it's gone that far. In this case, that's a good thing."

"He started bleeding," Bread sounds close to tears again, he raises a hand to his mouth. Kevin leans close to him, rubbing his shoulder.

"Yeah, people can have different reactions. A lowkey version of it is crying when you see someone else hurt. But in more extreme versions, the transfer isn't just emotional. Looks like Frank is somewhere beyond the emotional empathy but not quite at the point of full physical transference."

"Sounds woo-woo," Kevin interjects. Then adds, "Not to sound rude."

"It does sound woo-woo," Chili's tone shows no offense was taken, "But that's because woo-woo capitalists take a shred of an idea and run with it."

Frank moans again. This time, his body moves slowly. He begins to raise himself from the ground, his eyes opening but face twisted in confusion.

"What's going on?" Frank asks.

Chili puts their hand behind Frank's back, helping him to sit up slowly. "You may have been connecting with Clementine. Like you did with the trees. And with the wolf. But Clem is sick. And your sensitivity to that was starting to make your body react. You're gonna need some rest, and fluids. Maybe solid foods are not a good idea the rest of today. But not too long. You're already fighting to come back from being malnourished and then poisoning yourself."

"What about Clem?" Frank asks.

Bread is the first to notice. By the time Kevin and Chili turn their attention to the small white goat, Bread is already leaning his full body, face down, over the animal. His shoulders heave as he sobs.

Outside the barn, Allister kicks at the walls and butts his horns, demanding entry. Another cry rises from the distance.

The howling of a wolf.

CHAPTER 42

She lugs another case of bottled water up the stairs to the attic rented from an elderly couple who believed her when she told them she was in town to work as a summer camp counselor. They didn't even bother to ask the name of the camp.

I should warn them not to be so trusting. Maybe that's a conversation for October when the lease is up.

The door to the one-room attic apartment creaks open. She walks into a wall of heat.

Emma.

Her heart races, the cat has tolerated the heat in the cramped apartment, but today was particularly brutal.

Fuck.

She tries not to think about the irony, leaving Emma Goldman to roast alive while she spent the day gathering supplies for the communal cooling station.

A distant meow tells her Emma has not roasted. The fan in the corner of the room, barely sufficient, managed to keep a small section of the room habitable. Bedsheets and blankets rustle and the black cat emerges from her hiding place under the bed.

She drops the case of water on a chair, lifts the cat, and snuggles the animal's face. Emma Goldman purrs.

She's ready to sink onto the bed and relax, the cat still wrapped in her arms, when Emma Goldman reaches up with her front paw and swats her across the face.

"You have to find a better way to get my attention," She replies, eyes closed, rubbing her stinging cheek.

Message for you.

The cat now sits on her lap, tail flicking.

She glances toward a bedside table. Her old cell is still plugged into the charger. She has a notification.

One glance tells her it's from Felix.

Not Felix, that was a long time ago, she corrects herself, Chili.

She doesn't want to read the message.

Emma Goldman jumps up, both paws on her shoulders, staring into her eyes. She hears the cat's voice now from inside her head, reverberating in her ears, pushing against the front of her skull.

Message.

For.

YOU.

She tries to console Emma, stroking the cat's ears. Emma cocks a paw back, ready to strike again.

"Okay, I'll read it." She raises her hands in surrender.

She reluctantly grabs the phone from the table, opens Signal, and scrolls through the message.

Emma looks satisfied. But she looks like she's just seen a ghost.

CHAPTER 43

Frank

Frank stares into the refrigerator, an older model, he's seen the kind in movies. It's got opaque bins for the fruit and vegetables. No digital settings, not even for the temperature. He pushes aside containers filled with leftovers from the last three nights, not trusting anything that isn't fresh.

"Has Bread come out of the bedroom at all today?" Kevin asks startling Frank who didn't hear him come in the door.

"No, not that I've seen," Frank responds, hardly looking up. He doesn't want to be rude, but their options are sparse. Quinoa salad, leftover stir fry, and another leftover dish Bread called curried vegetables. Frank liked the taste, but that was at least two days ago.

"This isn't good. I'll check on him. But hey, I'm supposed to help Chili with the garden today and I'm running late, can you help them?"

"Sure," Frank finds a stray apple and grabs it, crunching as juices erupt in his mouth. It's no meal but better than foraging for berries and seeds.

"Thanks, he's torn up about Clementine."

Frank nods. He wants to tell Kevin that he's sad too, that he cried himself to sleep last night. And that Clementine appeared in his dream happy and playing with a family of goats. But something about it doesn't feel right. How can he be sad? He hardly even knew her.

"Yeah, I'll head out now," Frank gives the apple another bite, devouring half of it as he heads out the door.

The apple is gone long before he makes his way around the side of the cabin to the first section of the garden. Wire racks that look like silos stick up from the ground. Vines and plants dangle from their edges. Painted tires make a path with vegetation filling their centers.

Chili wears an apron with pockets that house clippers and tools and a water bottle. Frank thinks it's for the plants but remembers that Chili is prone to overheating and thinks it may be for them as well.

Chili steps back from a wire rack filled with hanging vegetables Frank doesn't recognize. They wipe their hands on their apron and glance up as Frank approaches.

"Kevin's trying to talk to Bread, I guess, about Clementine. He asked me to come out and help you since he's running late."

"Sure. How's your gardening experience?"

Frank lowers his eyes. He's never actually grown anything, maybe a plant for his mom when he was in school, once. "I haven't done gardening before," he admits.

"No worries. First time for everything."

To his relief Chili doesn't sound perturbed. They point to a row of tools and explain what each is called. Frank strains to commit the information to memory. It's a lot.

"So, take that seed spreader over there," Chili points to something that looks like a sidewalk salter, "and walks slowly over this way to this section," Chili gestures to the far end of the clearing. "We alternate what parts of the land are planted to keep from depleting the soil."

"Oh, that's a good idea," Frank nods.

"It's one of the many things corporate agriculture gets wrong. You can't just replant all in one spot again and again. Gotta keep it moving. Give different areas a break."

"But wouldn't it be impossible to feed everyone? I mean if you just did it that way?"

Chili smiles, "Corporations clear entire forests to over-produce. Most of it gets wasted. There's plenty to go around, but maybe not plenty to give some people every-thing and others nothing." Chili pauses, wipes sweat from their brow, and mists their face with water from the spray bottle. "But I'm rambling. Anyway, start at that far corner and work this way. Remember, walk slowly, and let them fall where they need to. Any questions or need anything give me a holler."

Chili puts gloves over their hands now and leans down, pulling carrots out of the ground in a row in front of the tires.

"Got it," Frank is relieved. The seed spreader is light. Like pushing a shopping cart. Easier, even. He starts with a section of land under direct sunlight, clear of trees. He's sweating and should have brought water with him, not wanting to make the trip back just for a drink now.

The seed spreader makes a quiet hum as he walks- slowly, Chili said. He feels the humming on the ground soon. It vibrates. He feels it in his roots. Yes, his roots, they've been missing lately, with all the time spent indoors and the sad-ness over Clementine's death.

Not death. Release. The Chorus reminds him.

A blackbird with red stripes on their wing watches him from a nearby tree.

Is it you? Are you the one talking? Frank starts to ask. Kevin's voice echoes in his mind.

You're overthinking.

He continues past the bird, letting the hum of the seed spreader take him from himself again. He feels the vibration in his hands now. Feels static from his palms to the instrument to the ground and beneath. An instrument. A tool. A means to a larger end. One seed to a garden to a goat's mouth to a bird's beak, to a wolf's muzzle to a baby to a woman to a tree to a bolt of lightning.

And why not be an instrument?

With no family. No home. No Mallory.

An instrument. A seed spreader.

Propagator, protagonist, propagandist. The Chorus whispers.

Frank stops walking. Releases his hands from the machine. Closes his eyes.

"I'm here. Make me an instrument." He speaks the words aloud and hears his own voice in the rustling of leaves. Feels it in the sun, smells it in the decay deep beneath the dirt.

Make me an instrument of your message. He hears the words echo in his mind this time.

To his left, a bee whirs by, narrowly avoiding his ear. Beside his foot, ants march in formation, fulfilling their duty far from his sight. Behind him, the wolf pads out from the forest, silent panting barely audible but Frank feels it.

Make me an instrument.

He feels his palms tingle, the static spreads up his arms. It grows warm and courses down his body to his legs and then his feet and into his roots.

I am here. He declares softly.

No, the Chorus responds. *I am you.*

He repeats the words. Eyes still closed. Oblivious to Chili's shadow cast as they approach, watching.

I am you.

He knows when the wolf has come to his side, sitting close to his right foot. Frank resists the urge to open his eyes.

Make me an instrument.

He feels his roots grow. Feels them brush against the roots of carrots and lettuce and peppers, radishes and eggplant, and then shrubs. Feels them roll along the ancient roots of trees.

I am you.

He smells the harvest that hasn't grown yet. Sees it picked from the ground, adorning a table. Through his roots he feels the ground torn apart, feels the blood of hands cracked and calloused, the pain of backs bent and burned under the sun, of elbows and wrists enflamed.

Feels the heavy burden of exhaustion as the bodies retire to crowded shacks and drift to a brief respite of sleep where the day's torment will only repeat in illusion before the dawn comes.

Hears the whimper, cry, then scream of pigs sent to slaughter. Tastes the blood in his own mouth.

I am you.

Sees rows of bandaged hands chopping at the assembly line. Then feels the stiffness in his joints, feels the blood splash onto the slaughterhouse floor.

Sees the young woman take the bus to the grocery store before the sun has risen. Feels her hip and knee throb as she paces the hard floor stocking shelves.

He sees Margie, standing in his parents' kitchen, pulling pork chops and Brussels sprouts and leeks from the refrigerator, lining them along the counter. Sees her bend to get the cutting board, feels the pinched nerve shoot up her side. Hears her child crying alone as the daycare empties out, all but the teacher's aide gone for the day.

"We've talked about this before," the young aide scolds Margie when she finally rushes in to retrieve the child.

"I know, I'm sorry, I couldn't get out of work any sooner," comes the reply.

And another cracked and bleeding hand pulls at the ground to give up another carrot, spills blood as raspberries are pulled into the bucket, wipes sweat from the brow of a wrinkled face, tired eyes trying not to think of home and whether it was a mistake to come here after all. And if it will ever get better.

Frank falls to his knees, buries his face in his hands, and sobs.

CHAPTER 44

Chili

Chili checks their phone. No reply yet. They sent the message. Did their part. That's all.

I'm just a Messenger.

The kid has been showing signs Chili recognizes. They've seen it before, though not frequently.

Need to keep an eye on him, Chili thinks as they slip on their sandals and leave the yurt to wander the grounds. Sun is setting. It's Chili's favorite time. The cool evening is almost comfortable for him. Thanks to an oily mix of cloves and peppermint, the bugs leave them alone.

And there's Frank. Up ahead. Walking the tree line in the distance, a grey mass Chili now recognizes as the wolf wanders by the boy.

That's something Chili's never seen.

It's one thing for a person to open up, connect, begin to set down roots, and feel all of nature, something Chili's had more than a taste of since adolescence. But having an apex predator take an interest in your development?

That's unique.

Chili walks the dirt path toward the trees, keeping enough distance to not interrupt Frank or scare the wolf. They know this is an important time for Frank too. He's begun walking after dinner. Then sitting, staring up at the sky in a sort of meditation, the wolf at his side.

Chili thinks they understand the reason.

Their foot crunches hard on a twig and it snaps beneath their weight. The wolf looks over his shoulder, stoic. Frank turns slowly, showing no sign of shock or irritation, his face shows a rare serenity.

"Sorry to disturb you. I enjoy a good evening walk as well." Chili comes closer now. Something else has changed. The boy's eyes have aged. The others can't see it, but Chili can.

"No worries. I was just thinking," Frank begins, his brows dip, furrowed. His hair is growing long, and shaggy bangs hang in his eyes, but Chili thinks he's trying to find more words. "I was just thinking, but not really. It sounds crazy, but I feel like I have to come out to… to… feel things?"

Chili doesn't respond. These moments are golden. Frank needs to feel what he's saying as much as he needs to feel what he comes to the woods to feel. Chili knows this. They hold space for Frank to find his words. The boy shifts his weight, looks away, and then says, "It's new. I think it's new. Sometimes I have dreams that I've done this before. As a kid? But I don't remember. But I have to come out here and it's like… like filling up a car with gas? But I'm the car. And I don't know what the gas is, exactly? But it's out here."

Frank looks to Chili, his eyes looking for understanding or judgment.

A mosquito buzzes past Chili's ear. They remain still and for a moment they can see her. They remember the first time she began talking about the trees. She used the same analogy. Chili can't smile. Can't laugh. The boy will think he's being mocked.

I wish you were here. I wish you could see for yourself…

Frank leans against a tree and raises his eyes, staring beyond Chili as if they were not there. The wolf circles and sits at his feet.

When the moment feels right, Chili responds, "You make a good analogy. Another way to think of it is eating. What you get from being out here," Chili motions to the trees as they say this, "is like taking in a meal. But it's energy. Not food."

Chili watches to see a look of recognition, to see that Frank is following along. The boy's eyes drop to the ground. He looks nervous, Chili thinks. They continue, "And you have always done it. You just haven't always known it."

"Why is it happening now? I mean, why am I noticing it again now?" Frank asks. His voice is low as if he's trying to stifle emotion.

"It is a birthright of all beings. One that we are robbed of by the societies created for us. One that some of us learn to reclaim. Some teach others to reclaim it. Others stumble upon it through," Chili pauses, waving their hand as if to summon the words to describe it, "an awakening."

"Was it the mushrooms?"

Chili can't stifle a chuckle then, "not the ones you were eating. No. This began, I would guess, with your eyes being opened some other way."

Some other way...

The words hang in the air and Frank hears horns honking. Chanting. Yelling. A chaotic mob surrounds him.

Housing is a human right...

Housing is a human right...

Housing is a human right...

He feels his eyes burn. Sees police in riot gear pulling protestors from the crowd.

Hears the gunshot.

Some other way…

He feels his eyes open. Blood runs into the street.

In the distance, he hears himself screaming, "Bastards! You're all bastards!"

He's lost track of where he is. Oblivious to Chili waiting for his response. He's forgotten the wolf at his feet.

He feels his eyes open wide, taking in the boarded-up windows, the camps under the bridge, the warehouse, the train tracks, the trees, and the birds.

His eyes no longer see red, he feels his skin tingle as if thousands of eyes are opening, wide, all through his body.

I am you, the voice reminds him.

The older person before him comes into view. The soft eyes, round face, oversized shirt, and long hair partially shaved. Chili blinks slowly, looking Frank in the eyes.

I am you, he hears the words again.

CHAPTER 45

Frank

The pull-out couch is nothing compared to the luxurious full-sized bed Frank used to share with Bella back home. But in his early weeks in the cabin, his body needed sleep. After each evening walk, he'd part ways with the wolf, take a warmish shower, the cabin's water isn't ever really hot, brush his teeth with an extra toothbrush Kevin gave him, and pull the couch out into a narrow, springy bed. Within minutes, he'd be fast asleep.

His body has been healing. No longer waking at nine or even eight in the morning, he now wakes throughout the night. The first hints of light in the sky signal it may be close to four in the morning. Didn't someone say it was summer now?

He squints and tries to ignore the light shining into the cabin windows.

He missed graduation. It hadn't occurred to him before. Did Jonathan make it? Did his friends at school know or care that he was gone? Did he even have true friends at school?

And Bella? Where was she?

Dead? Like Mallory?

He dreams of that final scene, a blast, and everything turning red. And other times he dreams of Bella walking through strange neighborhoods. In his dreams, she cries for him, howls, and whimpers. He tries to call to her, but before he can reach her, the wolf appears. Somehow, he knows that if she sees him if she tries to run for him, her tail wagging, eyes filled with excitement, the wolf will devour her. He has to stay back, stay silent. Let her go. He doesn't want to.

But it's just a dream.

His head buzzes. He wants to go back to sleep, but a deep hunger forces his mind awake. He tries to ignore the gnawing in his stomach.

Out. Come. Out. The voice beckons him.

Yes. It's what he needs. More than a sofa bed. More than a King-sized bed with pillows stuffed in satin pillowcases. More than comfort. He needs to walk among the trees.

Rising carefully but still unable to avoid a hearty creak erupting from the couch, he finds his shoes and slips out from the cabin, avoiding further noise so as not to wake the couple he assumes is asleep in the room nearby.

The dawn air feels cool and refreshes his skin. He can smell growth beneath the ground. Smells the grass and dirt and earthworms. Smells fish for the first time and understands there is water nearby. A cardinal calls in a tree nearby. Leaves rustle in the morning breeze.

In the distance, a grey mass slinks along the tree line and he recognizes the wolf walking toward him in no hurry. Something new pulls at the edges of his mind. Something from his dream the night before. He feels its familiarity but can't put words together to narrate the story.

The wolf had been there. And Bella. He wanted to follow them both. But something had happened. Something surprising. He had been so close, only turned his back for a moment. Long enough to light a match. Throw a bottle. Watch the explosion.

A chill spreads over his back.

I've been reading too many of Bread's crazy manifestos.

The dream, barely a glimpse of remembrance, has fallen back into the caverns of his mind. His eyes remain on the Wolf, scenting the air and settling, paws stretched forward, outside one of the yurts.

Frank approaches and is surprised to hear voices from inside. He recognizes Chili's slow cadence. Kevin mutters something. Laughter follows. He hears a voice he's come to associate with contrarian arguments and criticism and realizes that Miles is there as well. Probably, Teri too, he thinks before hearing her voice break in.

"I think he could be an asset. I mean we all start somewhere," she says.

"It's too risky. It's risky even having him here this long." Miles's voice.

"He may have more to offer than any of us can appreciate." Chili's deep voice. Slow words. Then silence.

Frank shouldn't be eavesdropping. They are way too into privacy. Like they're hiding from the FBI or something. Maybe they are. But the wolf stopped here. Led him here. He's supposed to hear something.

"Or this could all be a big mistake," Miles finally responds.

Frank listens for a few moments more. Long enough to hear them planning something called a banner drop. He hears his father's name and understands it's about him. His business. The damage he's doing. Again.

He'll help. He'll talk to Chili later, Frank decides. And he'll help. The wolf must be satisfied now because he rises to his paws and trots into the distance. Frank understands his cue to leave. He walks the grounds, taking in the fresh air before the heat becomes oppressive. By mid-morning, it's already shaping up to be a brutally hot day. Returning to the cabin, he finds Bread inside preparing a meal.

"You're just in time to play prep-chef, wash your hands, and help me out with this meal, okay?"

Frank runs his hands under the sink faucet, using something that looks like a stone but is lemon-scented soap. He doesn't know how to cook but doesn't want to admit this.

"Bread?" Frank begins, wondering if he should keep his interest in the action to himself. He's not supposed to know about it. He was technically eavesdropping.

"Yep, that's me, fluffy and full of carbs, what's up?" Bread jokes.

"I wasn't trying to listen, but I was up early this morning. I heard people talking. In the tent? About my dad's business. I want to help. I can help. I need to."

"Need?" Bread asks, his tone neutral.

"Yeah, yes. I need to. I need to…" he struggles to find the words, "I need to make things right. That my dad has done? Like, my dad's work paid for me to have things. But I see where his money came from. And I need to… to um … to like give back? So I need to help."

Bread puts a cutting board and knife on the counter and begins lining up zucchini, onions, and vegetables Frank doesn't recognize.

"Well, you can help for now by chopping these up into small pieces for dinner." Bread winks. He's smiling. Frank's glad to see it. After his beloved goat died, Bread cried for days and was brooding and silent for just as many days. It hadn't been the same, Frank realized, without his jokes and laughter. Without the wide beard lining a grin.

"But you may also be able to help with the protest. I think Chili is set on it happening at some point anyway, so may as well radicalize you sooner rather than later."

Frank doesn't understand what "radicalize" means. He's heard the word on talk radio shows his dad used to listen to, but what they were describing was nothing like what he and Bread now discuss.

Bread explains what a banner drop is, his animated gestures make Frank glad he put the knife down first. Frank learns they're planning to drop banners on several overpasses along the highway. He recognizes some of the locations. The banners will be taken down after a few hours at most. As soon as the police are called and can respond. But for those few hours, everyone on the north and southbound lanes of I 95 will know that Pat Bernardoni Destroys Affordable Housing.

Dad will shit.

But that's only the first action. For all of Miles's worry, Bread seems to have no problem spilling the details of his group's discussion.

As he chops zucchini and something he learns is a rutabaga, Frank also hears of a campaign of actions that will target several big developers, including his dad.

"So, what are you guys? A rogue team of Social Justice Warriors? Are you, like, Antifa?" Frank finally asks.

Bread laughs as he washes a serving tray that looks like something made in an intermediate pottery class. "We are antifascist, which is what 'Antifa' means, by the way. I kinda like your description, actually," Bread pulls at his beard and considers how to answer. "Rogue team of Social Justice Warriors," he repeats, chuckling.

Frank has given up on expecting an answer and returned his attention to the rutabaga, it's hard to cut and smells bitter. But it feels good on his hands. He can feel his roots growing into it, drinking up something.

Energy, Chili had said.

"As for your real question," Bread interrupts his thoughts, "we each belong to various groups and coalitions of," he pauses, "concerned residents of Earth. Activists. Anarchists, and socialists, we try not to beat each other up over theory. What counts is what we do."

Frank is still confused. It occurs to him that every time he talks to Bread he ends up more confused than before he asked his questions. Nevertheless, he continues, "So, what do you do?"

"A big part of what we do," Bread pauses to chew a baby carrot before arranging a handful of these and other vegetables on the newly cleaned tray, "is called 'mutual aid.' Basically, when we know people need something, we try to get people what they need."

"That sounds good." Frank ponders aloud.

"Yeah, it pretty much is. But some people don't like it."

"Why not?"

Bread reaches deep into the fridge and removes a head of lettuce and some bean sprouts.

"Well, think about it like this. If you found out that you could get everything you need from your comrades, that you didn't need to ever go to a store, would you still go out and spend money to get things you didn't need to pay for?"

Frank considers this. He wants to ask about the word comrade- but he doesn't want to lose focus. "I guess, I mean maybe I might go to the store to get something that was new, that other people wouldn't have? Like a new phone," he wants to say a new phone when it occurs to him he's been in the woods for how long? At least a month? Maybe more? With no phone. He hasn't even missed it. "I mean I guess maybe not even a phone. Unless I was back home. Like before, when I was just having a normal life before the thing happened, I might have wanted certain sneakers, a car, or a new phone. But I haven't had those things. I've been out in the woods, then here with you guys, and I guess it's been ok to not have those things."

"Betcha weren't hanging out with wolves back when you were busy texting your friends, am I right?" He gives Frank an exaggerated wink.

Frank nods and can't help smiling. "Right. So, it's like friends who just get together and trade stuff? Like how do you get gas for your car and stuff?"

"Not a perfect system. We're not completely self-sufficient. Hell, Kevin and I aren't even completely off the grid. But mutual aid helps free people from having to be dependent on shopping. So back to the point and why people would get mad," Bread stops to eat another baby carrot, "If you stop going to the store because you don't need to, what happens to the store?"

Frank's mind flashes to a memory. Three years ago? Maybe five? His parents had taken him to a fundraiser in southern Jersey. On the way there, they passed row upon row of vacant strip malls.

"I could put all of this to good use," his father had commented. He could tell by the outline that several had been Dom's Diners, a chain with a telltale status of an Italian-looking man holding up a pizza as if he was preparing to throw it in someone's face.

"What happened to them?"

"Went out of business. Couldn't keep up. Survival of the fittest in business, Frank," his dad had told him.

He pushes the rutabaga cubes onto an oiled pan, "I guess, they go out of business right? So that would hurt the businesses."

"Not as much as the businesses are hurting the community. You've seen that for yourself, sounds like? But yeah.

They'll lose money. Lose profit. Lose the opportunity to exploit people." Bread is busy chopping something too now, on a counter on the other side of the small kitchen. Frank is careful not to accidentally bump into him. "But corporations, and the heads of corporations, and the landlords and bosses, they're threatened by the idea of mutual aid. It's why it's illegal to give away perfectly good food past expiration dates. So that food gets wasted. And people who try to give it to the community, like Food Not Bombs? Get targeted and criminalized."

Frank's head perks at a reference he finally recognizes. "So you do that stuff, and you do protests and drop banners and… how do you get money to pay for the stuff you need to pay for?"

"Some of us work. And some of us are supported in other ways. As I said, we're still stuck with the capitalist framework. But we're helping each other to not be dependent on it. So yeah, we respond to issues like housing, healthcare, police brutality."

"What does police brutality have to do with anything?"

"Who do you think is hired to protect the stuff rich people have?"

Frank flashes back to the crowd outside Mallory's apartment. One patrol car after another pulling up. Cops in riot gear. German Shepherds. He nods.

"I want to help. I have to."

"Good. Put the onions in the pan with the rutabaga, in the oven at four twenty-five, and I'll talk to the others about it."

CHAPTER 46

Jonathan

It was always more fun riding in Francesco's car, Jonathan thinks.

Francesco's dad's car, he corrects himself.

If Francesco was here, they'd be someplace fun. At a party. Someplace cool, on a Saturday night in the summer. And Francesco would probably bust his balls the entire time, talking shit about his retail store shoes or his single mom's TV dinners she pops in the microwave on her one night off each week. And Jonathan would want to punch Frank in his prim little nose about five minutes into the night.

But it would still be better than parking his mom's beat-up Camry in the parking lot of Frederickson's Plaza, in front of the bowling alley that everyone's avoided since sixth grade. The one next door to the liquor store. It would be better than suddenly becoming invisible in Francesco's absence. Invisible, that is, to everyone except Bella, who has become his shadow.

"And I 'preciate it, you know, no offense?" Jonathan slurs this with a heavy tongue, one hand splayed out in a gesture of surrender, the other gripping a bottle inside a paper bag.

"I 'preciate everything you do for me, Beeella."

She licks her lips and whimpers, stretching a paw toward him in double motion. Like the gesture a parent uses to tell a child it's time to quiet down.

"Oh, don't look at me that way. You know what I mean." Jonathan continues. Bella hunkers down and rests her muzzle on her front paws, resigned that it will be another long night.

He can tell he's upset her. He didn't mean to. This must be hard on her, too, he reminds himself. Looking out the windshield, Jonathan can see across the road, the city lights beneath him. He remembers coming here with Francesco, and sometimes with Bella, in Middle School. Not for the bowling. Not even for the booze, but because across the road, the sparse woods then not yet cleared for the road and retail stores below the cliff had fascinated Francesco.

"An' he would always want to just go there? You know? It was dumb? But he loved that shit," Jonathan tells Bella as if she's been following a story that began in his mind. She doesn't talk back. Jonathan continues, "Not even to smoke weed, well, that came later. And then we used ta bring the girls here. Sorry, you didn't get to go along for that."

Jonathan thinks of the times back when stealing away to forbidden places was a source of excitement. Not a sign of emptiness.

The woods are cleared now. Against the black of night, a scattering of lights remind him life has gone on. For some people.

"But not for me!" His voice is louder now. Bella grunts. He ignores her. "What about me? Francesco? What about me?" Hot tears form in his eyes. Bella rises to her paws, leaning up against his right shoulder, and she begins to lick at the corner of his eyes. He doesn't stop her.

"What am I supposed to do? Why did you leave me? And why the fuck should I even care? Because YOU," he points an accusing finger at the sky, "you were an asshole. You were always an asshole! But I still need you! You sonofabitch! I need you!"

The scene before him is washed out with tears like a ruined painting. The bottle falls from his grip, he covers his eyes with both hands, leaving Bella to lick at his fingers as Jonathan's shoulders heave. Nothing left to shout, he cries into the empty night.

CHAPTER 47

Frank

In a few hours, it will be warm. The sun will be up, and Frank will begin to sweat. The first pink hues haven't graced the sky. The overnight chill hasn't fully given way to humidity. Frank welcomes it all as much as he welcomes the third trip, by van, into a nearby city.

These protests, Frank has learned, aren't like the one at Mallory's. Noisy crowds are traded for covert, clandestine actions in these protests.

Direct Action, Chili explained, before the first one several weeks ago.

"Direct Action gets satisfaction!" Bread had joked.

It was true. Frank thinks this now as he slips through the pre-dawn streets, spray paint can in hand. He heads around the north side of the building, flinching awkwardly as he notices his father's name, a name he no longer claims, on a sign.

Bernardoni Realty, LLC

Another one of his father's buildings. Seeing the name brings a surreal surge of familiarity.

He shakes the can of spray paint hard, a nervous tic. Chili keeps watch several feet behind him. Kevin and Bread have the southern corner of the building, and Miles and the others are keeping watch by the surrounding streets.

Frank finds his canvas. His arm is stronger now. He's gotten used to the strained hand-eye coordination as the black spray paint flies from the can and begins to fill in the message.

"Make it chunky. We want it to be readable", Kevin explained to him back when they practiced in his yard.

Frank slows himself, covering the same area again, thickening the lines on each letter as he spells it out.

P-E-O

He rings the O a third time.

P-L-E

He reinforces the lines on each letter, trying not to think about the name on the sign. Trying not to see his father's face.

Imagines the building is just brick and concrete.

He underlines the word in lines of heavy black spray paint. Somewhere on another side of the building, Miles paints "A" with a circle around it. Bread is leaving words of antagonism. A quote from one of his many books. The others are much better. They can do bubble letters and scripts.

Beneath the darkened horizontal line, Frank writes another word. The spray paint can rattles and he throws it aside, grabbing another from his backpack to continue the job.

He steps back to admire his handiwork.

PEOPLE

———

PROFIT

It's not bad. He's getting the hang of it.

"Ok, let's go!" he hears Chili's voice through the silence. It brings him back to awareness.

He runs in the direction of Chili's voice. Moments later, they pile into the van. On the way back to the cabin, the group is mostly silent. It's become a ritual. The surge of adrenaline has cured Frank of any early morning drowsiness. His eyes are open wide. He can barely remember a time when he and his friends sneaked Adderall from the family medicine stash and traded, or sold them at school so they could feel like this for a few hours.

His heart pounds in his chest. Another target finished. His first time, he was so nervous he almost fainted. By now, his anxiety is excitement.

He hears his own voice in a distant memory, "But that's someone's property. They worked for it."

"Did they?" Chili had asked.

Frank had thought of his father's words, "When you're successful, people get jealous. They try to steal what they're too lazy to work for."

"Did they work for it?" Chili had repeated.

"You're not one of us and you never will be," Frank heard Mallory's voice in response. He remembers a scene at his dad's office. Had he tried to be buddies with one of his dad's staff, in the breakroom?

He had, and he had been snubbed. Because everyone- Mallory, his dad's employees, even his dad, he realized- everyone understood but him. He understands now.

"No," he told Chili, "No they didn't."

"Companies like this commit violence," Chili had gone on to explain, "and us? We're creating disruption. We're creating discomfort. We're creating art. We are combating their violence."

Frank understands. His eyes have been opened. Pink streaks across the sky precede the sunrise. Soon, the rest of New Jersey will awaken. Soon, someone will show up for work. Their art will be discovered.

And Pat Bernardoni will have plenty of discomfort, Frank smiles, imagining the look on his father's face when he hears the news.

CHAPTER 48

A week later, Frank is again huddled in the back of the van with Kevin, Chili, Miles, Bread, and the others. This trip takes longer, it's harder to stay awake. This morning he's more tired than excited. He knows the adrenaline will kick in. His stomach roars in protest. He tries to ignore it. They ride in silence as if conversation this early in the morning will carry through the stillness and give them away.

Frank wishes he could watch out the window, but it's still dark and he's crushed between the bodies of his older comrades, in the middle of the seat. He closes his eyes, listening to the spinning of the van's tires keeping rhythm on the road. Not quite asleep, his mind drifts into trance.

He imagines Jonathan, a pang of guilt stabbing his chest. He'd all but forgotten his longtime friend. Out of sight, out of mind. But he can see Jonathan. He's slumped over the steering wheel in his mom's beat-up car. Frank's heart hurts for his old friend then.

Jonathan stares out the windshield at the sky, yelling something. Frank settles deeper into the trance and hears Jonathan calling his name.

"I'm here, dude, I'm fine," Frank answers in his mind.

But he's not on the scene. He can't get through to his friend. He tries to reach out a hand to shake Jonathan's arm. His hand grabs Jonathan's wrist. His friend drops a bottle of cheap booze onto the floor of the car.

He's crying.

Frank tries to speak but no words come out.

He squeezes Jonathan's wrist, shaking him, trying to make him snap out of it.

"I'm here, bruh, I'm here. Knock it off you sound like a
…."

Frank looks down at his hand and sees a familiar paw. He sees now. He's not in the car. Not with Jonathan. He's watching from a distance. In the passenger seat, Bella reaches out to Jonathan, pawing his arm and wrist, trying to distract him from his misery. Trying to get his attention.

The young man, still slumped over the steering wheel, ignores her.

Frank doesn't know if it's a daydream, fantasy, or prophecy. He feels sad for his friend, excited to see Bella, and also, something like jealousy. He should be there. That was his life. What is he doing here?

Bella should be with him. His dog. Should have come for him if she's still alive. Why hadn't she? And why was Jonathan crying so much? What was he missing?

I am you, The Chorus louder than it has been in days, startles Frank. His body bolts upright, rigid, eyes open.

To his left, Bread is silent. His hands are peacefully folded over his belly as he looks out the window. To his right, Miles bites the nails on one finger while their other hand picks at a loose thread on a black balaclava. Kevin drives in silence. Everyone in the van focused on the work at hand.

No one noticed The Chorus or his startle response. The van slows. Frank can barely make out the scene unfolding outside. Narrowing streets and older homes, some of them boarded up, through an early morning filter of black, grey, and blue.

What are we doing here?

It takes a moment for his eyes to adjust and for his subconscious to remind him. He's been here before.

Everything looks different now. Whatever light illuminated the colors and details of the 20th-century architecture by day has been stripped away and distorted in the twilight hour. But he recognizes enough to know they're driving through the place his friends- and he- once called The Stones.

He hears Mallory's laugh clear enough to make him turn his head, peering into the empty streets as the van comes to a stop. He's blocks away from where she used to live. Nausea creeps over him. He's glad he hasn't eaten in hours. His stomach flips. In memory, he hears the chanting, confused screaming, and gunshots. The soundtrack of his last visit.

"We're here, everyone out, we got work to do," Kevin announces in an unusually soft tone. Of course. They're in a residential area this time. Mostly residential, except for the construction zone up ahead. Behind the orange temporary fencing and sign: Bernardoni Realty: Coming Soon! Luxury Storage Units!

He pulls a black balaclava over his head and packs spray paint into his backpack. Chili, Miles, Bread, Kevin, and the rest of the crew have filed out of the van, covered from head to toe in black as well. Even with experience, he can barely recognize Kevin and Chili once they're dressed in black for anonymity. He hears the rattle of a spray paint can.

"Keep an eye out for surveillance," he hears someone- Miles, he thinks- whisper a warning.

They split up in pairs as planned. Miles remains a few feet behind him. He steps over a piece of construction barricade and ducks under a break in the fencing.

In the darkness, the new construction is a warehouse. Mallory's home had been constructed for efficiency. A concrete box with windows and little balconies. But he remembers the signs of life. The Puerto Rican flag in one window, Black Lives Matter flag hanging from another balcony. The plants dangling from open windows. He remembers the barbecue, music, and laughter.

All gone now.

The storage building is cold, grey, empty. As he approaches, his heart races. His hands sweat inside black gloves and he steadies his grip on one of the spray paint cans. This place looks like an abandoned prison, all signs of life, gone.

He follows the plan to his spot, aware from the sound of footsteps that Miles is keeping watch behind him. Time is running out.

He pulls the cap off the spray paint can and takes a breath.

Just one line, he prompts himself, *just one line like you talked about* and that's it.

Shame on Bernardoni Realty. Four simple words. He aims at the wall, this ugly building, his canvas.

Shame.

A thick S completed.

Shame on Bernardoni.

He sees his father's face in his mind. No. Not one line. Not good enough.

"What they do is violence," he hears Chili's explanation.

He hears the gunshots.

Sees Officer Dimples, "Your father will have my badge, get out of here!"

Sees Mallory on the ground. Red flowing from her lifeless body.

Blood.

He raises his hand. As if in a trance, another message emerges.

"Frank," Miles hisses behind him, "what are you doing? That's too much! That's not what we planned!"

The spray paint can hisses. Frank can't stop. He can't follow the plan. He can't hear Miles.

"Frank! Come ON! We've gotta go! What are you doing?"

The hissing closer now.

Frank ignores it. He methodically replaces the empty can with another. He's not done.

"NO! What are you doing? Cover that up!"

Miles demands now, his voice louder.

"What the fuck is going on?" Kevin's stage whisper is joined by arguing.

"Grab him!"

"Someone stop him!"

"What the fuck!"

Frank smiles as he signs his work. Because this message is personal.

He turns to see his friends gathered around him. He can't read the expressions on their faces under the black masks.

"C'mon, we'll talk about this later," Chili's voice carries over the escalating argument.

CHAPTER 49

Police Investigating Property Attack Related to Kidnapping of Bernardoni Heir
Passaic Tribune
August 25, 2022

It's been months since a group of violent radicals descended on the new Bernardoni building in a riot that turned deadly and which authorities also believe resulted in the kidnapping of Francesco Bernardoni. Son of the well-respected NJ developer, Pat Bernardoni, the disappearance of his only son coincided with plans for the younger man to follow in his father's footsteps.

"He was weeks from graduating from the Academy and was already training to take a prominent role in the business," Bernardoni said. Though the tragedy hasn't slowed the development of a new storage unit and work on several other new acquisitions, Bernardoni said he and his wife are beside themselves and only want their son to be returned home safe.

In recent weeks, several buildings in the Passaic area have been attacked and vandalized. Just last night, the newest building on 3rd Street in downtown Brighton or the first time, a message was left that appears to be directed at the Bernardoni family.

The message, spray-painted in black and red, reads as follows:

Pat Bernardoni,

Mallory's blood is on your hands. Stop your greed. Give your money back to the people. Your karma is coming- are you ready?

People will learn the truth about you.

Frank

When asked about the cryptic message, Mr. Bernardoni insists he believes the vandals are holding his son hostage or have coerced him to participate in the destructive actions.

"I have no idea who Mallory is. As for blood on my hands, this is obviously the work of some kind of very disturbed person."

Authorities explained various symbols and slogans on this and other buildings in the area as related to anarchist ideology, a dangerous anti-government movement. For now, Bernardoni is increasing his security presence at all of his buildings.

When asked if he is afraid for his safety or the rest of his family, he said "I've dealt with these kooks before, environmental nuts and fanatics. They can be dangerous, but we have lots of very good, very capable law enforcement officers and I put my trust in them."

CHAPTER 50

The woman pushes the door to the attic apartment open, the now familiar smell stings her nose. Dust, but something else. She's come to think of it as the smell of the early 80s. Like orange shag carpeting and Atari consoles, the smell is preserved in her mind.

Her parents' house didn't smell that way in the 80s. The cleaners and cooking staff wouldn't allow dust to settle long enough. As a girl, her feet slid across polished hardwood floors, shag carpets in olive green or baby-shit orange were things she only knew about from movies. And memes.

She blinks, her eyes adjusting to the darkness. In the dim light, Emma Goldman meows a greeting. The cat weaves between her feet.

"Strange, thinking of them after all this time." She speaks aloud as if the cat was following her memory.

Emma G. didn't disagree.

The woman closes the door behind her and heads for the nightstand, her extra phone charging.

That's when she hears it.

Emma Goldman's voice, like chimes, reverberates from the floor beneath her feet to the steep arch above her head.

Time to go home.

Emphasis on the word home, the cat's voice urgent. Piercing.

"This is home for now," she kneels down, extending a hand to pet Emma G. The cat refuses her affection, in a rare act of aloof defiance.

Your home.

For the first time in years, she can see it. The long dining room table, an altar adorned with plates of plenty on holidays and during parties. A desolate island most other times.

Except for the occasions when her father would sit, sometimes puffing a cigar, leafing through the paperwork.

The room open, spotless, empty.

Barren.

Red Barren. She thinks, of the old account she used years after she left home.

Go home. Now.

Emma Goldman leans her front paws against the woman's legs, stretching into her. The cat driving the point home with the kneading of her soft paws.

"Over my dead body," she answers.

Emma flicks her tail in response. She can see the disappointment in her furry roommate's eyes.

I don't have to explain myself to you.

She collapses on the bed, staring up at the pitched ceiling above her. Studying the cobwebs. The kind that finds their way into rooms that are cleaned seasonally.

Chili's words flash in her mind.

I found the person…

Good for you, she thinks.

Emma bats at her toes with sharp nails. She pulls her feet up, bolting upright and sitting on her feet before the cat can attack again.

Emma leaps onto the bed, poised to strike in a hunter's pose. Tail twitching still.

"I'm not speaking to you right now," she says aloud, ignoring the irony.

She pulls her laptop from a corner of the bed, intending to check her email. A notification catches her eye.

A new headline.

A campaign on the east coast. Trolling a developer by tagging his buildings.

Good praxis.

She thinks this as Emma Goldman begins purring louder.

Clicking the link, she recognizes a name.

Her mouth goes dry.

CHAPTER 51

Frank

The drive back to the cabin was bad enough. The silence carried a different heaviness. It wasn't the typical stillness of shared adrenaline and anticipation. Rather it was the kind of silence Frank recognized from his childhood. The silence his father used to send a message: you've fucked up.

It was only a matter of time before a full-on storm would erupt. Waiting for it to happen was always worse than enduring it.

But for Bread and Kevin, Chili, Miles, and the rest of the anarchists, there was no yelling. No name-calling. No throwing furniture or threats. There was an extended silence. Minimal recognition that he was even in their presence.

Two days later, Frank wanders the grounds outside the cabin. The crisp morning air is refreshing. The sound of birds was the closest he's had to communication in days.

Had he fucked up that bad?

It hadn't felt wrong at the moment. He watches as light spreads across the goat pen, illuminating the edges of leaves on the trees that surround him. It felt right.

The Chorus hadn't told him to do it, but then, does he have to wait for the permission of- whatever it is- to talk to him before every move he makes?

He rounds the edge of the lawn. In the distance, he can see Allistor, the widower goat, noshing hay. Frank's heart hurts. Tears form in his eyes.

I've got all the food now. But I miss her. Allistor tells him. He walks toward the animal. Since he lost his mate, Frank noticed he hasn't been as belligerent. Less aggressive.

He should tell Kevin to get another goat, a friend for Allistor.

Forest is bigger than it used to be. The goat tells him this as he approaches. Allistor's eyes are lethargic. Frank wonders if he, too, has some illness. He stops a few feet in front of the animal and closes his eyes.

He feels the hay in his mouth. Senses the flies buzzing around his back. Feels the heaviness of hoofs on the ground. Stomach gurgling as the hay is digested. Feels the sun on his muzzle. Emptiness in his heart.

The body is well, he hears The Chorus respond.

Reassured, Frank opens his eyes. Allistor regards him, turning his head so one yellow eye looks directly at him. The goat begins to chew another mouthful of hay. Frank thinks the animal seems droopy, and sad, or is it just him?

He thinks of the construction site again.

Was he wrong to go off-script?

The wind picks up and he hears voices on the breeze.

Was it right? Was it wrong? Who was it for?

"It was for Mallory," Frank speaks the word as if explaining himself to Allistor.

"Was it really?" Allistor replies.

Frank blinks. He wasn't expecting this.

"It was for Mallory," and then, taking a chance, he adds, "you understand, don't you?"

Allistor continues to chew. Lips pulling back over prominent teeth, as if ruminating on the question, before answering, "It was not what she needed. It was what you needed. Be clear, the difference."

He shakes his head, flicking a long ear to deter a fly from getting too close. Allistor suddenly turns his head and Frank follows the animal's gaze. Chili is walking toward them, no shoes on their feet, an oversized tunic-style shirt hanging over jeans.

Chili waves, a relief to Frank who hasn't been feeling welcome since the action. He waves back.

"Mind if I join you? Or is this a private party?" Their voice is calm and gentle as usual. They aren't angry. Frank releases tension he didn't realize he's been holding. He smiles.

"Fine with me, Allistor was just giving me life advice." He remembers how the conversation began and adds, "I think he's lonely. But I don't think anyone's going to listen to me after...."

"After the other day at the construction site?"

"Yeah. I mean, I kind of get it, but I don't get it. What's the big deal?"

Allistor wanders a few steps away as if to give them privacy.

"It may or may not be a big deal," Chili begins.

Sometimes Chili can be helpful. And other times, they just make things more confusing. Frank wonders if they're just trying not to take sides. He shifts his eyes toward Allistor who has moved on to grazing on a nearby shrub.

Chili continues, "If it is not a big deal," they look off to the sunset, speculating as they speak, "then it will be chalked up to someone making a cryptic but nonsensical post. It will be brushed under the rug. Maybe will intimidate your father a little." They take a deep breath, rubbing the palms of their hands together, then return Frank's gaze, "but if it is a big deal, it could implicate the crew in your disappearance."

"But how?"

"Your father either believes you've been kidnapped, or he's using that narrative to deflect from your involvement in the protest the day Mallory was killed."

"But that's not true," Frank laughs, "I wasn't kidnapped."

"What is and is not true is often irrelevant. The story suits your father."

"But how?"

"The truth is, you disobeyed him, left home, he disowned you, and you joined in a protest." Chili crosses both arms across their chest, then adds, "a protest that ended in a fatality. Truth is relative to the narrator. They say it was a bunch of violent radicals."

"But it wasn't!" Frank raises his voice.

"I know that. Everyone who was there knows that. But more people weren't there. And they get the story from those who control the narrative. They're being told what to believe."

Frank's stomach turns as the implications of what happened start to sink in.

"So," Chili continues, "the story of a millionaire's son is abducted, carried off by dangerous radicals, that makes your father the victim. The story where he throws you out of the house for challenging his business decisions? That story makes him the villain."

Frank nods slowly. "So, you think the message will lead him to you guys? That he'll find me here? And they'll assume Kevin and Bread kidnapped me?"

Chili pauses for a moment, closes their eyes, and lets the breeze pass. Frank wonders if they're having a seizure. He's not used to people answering so slowly. Allistor bleats, as if he, too, has grown impatient. Chili finally answers, "It is possible, though not easy, for our work to be traced. It depends on how much effort," Chili tilts their head side to side, looking for the right words, "how much resources are put into it."

"What does that mean?" Frank tries not to sound frustrated.

"When your father thought he was dealing with a group of kids spray painting his buildings, his response was likely to be minimal. How much would anyone invest in finding out who did a few hundred dollars worth of damage to a building?"

Frank's chest tightens, he knows where this is going.

"But now that your father has cause to believe that he's being targeted by the kidnappers," on the word 'kidnappers,' Chili raises their hands and makes air quotes, "now it's a different matter. Now he can justify putting more money into an investigation. Maybe getting the FBI involved. Now the narrative emerges. His son is now the Patty Hearst of…"

"Patty Hearst? Who's that?"

Chili pauses for a moment before answering, choosing their words carefully. "Patty Hearst was the heiress to Hearst Media, at one time they made all the newspapers. Then one day she shows up with a radical group- clowns really, but they started robbing banks."

The idea makes Frank smile. For a moment he imagines himself robbing banks, imagines the look on his father's face. Hears his voice shouting in a rage, *my reputation!*

"They killed people, and not their oppressors. They were … misguided. And it shocked the country. Here's young Patty, armed to the teeth, broadcasting messages shaming her father into giving away his money to the poor."

"Well, that's not a bad idea, right?"

"The idea? No. Their execution is a different story. Eventually, she gets caught. Then the story changed. She was brainwashed, tortured, all these stories that play on the deepest fears of rich, white Americans."

"So, was it true? Was she brainwashed into doing it? Or did she just want to avoid getting in trouble?"

Chili's mouth turns down in a look of ambivalence. They shrug their shoulders. "Only she and the Symbionese Liberation Army, that's what they called themselves, only they know for sure. And she had the most power. Her narrative prevailed."

"So, that's why everyone is mad? They think that I'll Patty Hearst you?"

Chili smiles. "Yeah, pretty much."

"Well, I won't. I want to stay. But if you think there's a real chance that they could find me here, I mean, I don't want to bring attention…"

"Gonna be a house meeting about it this evening. You're invited of course. We're gonna talk about it there."

The morning sun has begun to take effect. A light sweat breaks out on Chili's face.

"I just felt like it was the right thing to do."

"You felt that?" Chili asks.

Frank nods.

Chili considers this, staring off into the distance, "sometimes there is no right thing. There's just the thing you do. And then there are consequences. And you deal with the consequences when they come. Are you prepared to deal with the consequences?" Chili looks somber now, their eyes heavy with grief Frank hasn't seen before.

"I am," he answers.

They walk back to the cabin together.

In the distance behind them, Allistor bleats.

"I'll mention your idea to Kevin. About getting another goat." Chili says.

CHAPTER 52

Frank stayed out as long as he could. He watched from a distance, nervous, as a rusted blue van, then a clunky VW Rabbit pull into the dirt path in front of the cabin. Aside from a brief lunch with Chili, Frank avoided the cabin today.

He doesn't want to be paranoid. Tells himself he's better off in the field keeping Allistor company. The goat, who has been following Frank from the safe distance of a few paces all afternoon, continues to act aloof. One eye on Frank, hay dangling again from his mouth, he hasn't been the best company.

The daylight fades, and Frank guesses it's going for eight o'clock. He recognizes the figure emerging from the Rabbit, Teri. Frank likes Teri. She wears her hair shaved on both sides and long on the top and back. He remembers the first real conversation they had.

"What do those initials mean?" he asked about the English letters tattooed on her neck.

"Nothing." She smiled back.

"Why would you get letters on your neck that don't mean anything?"

"Absurdism."

He admired Teri but was also afraid of her.

He wonders what she's thinking now. Knowing what he did. What would be her fuck-you to him?

Another figure walks toward the cabin. Miles. Frank's stomach tenses. He remembers how Miles hadn't trusted him in the first place. Maybe he had been right not to want Frank involved.

He recognizes Jori, black and blue hair shimmering in the evening light. He thinks Jori and Miles are partners but can't remember if anyone ever confirmed that. They usually travel as a pair. Jori's always been quiet toward him. He doesn't know if it's suspicion or just being shy. She's the best artist in the group. When others are leaving symbols or three-word slogans, Jori makes art.

Chili, Bread, and Kevin are already inside.

Frank wraps his arms around himself, noticing the cool evening air for the first time. He sees movement behind the van and as his eyes adjust, the grey blur comes into focus.

The wolf.

"Have I let you down, too?" Frank asks.

The wolf sits, scents the air, and stares at Frank.

It's time to go. The wolf tells him.

Frank walks closer. The wolf remains still.

"Go where? Leave? Leave here? Go in the house? What?"

The wolf looks over his shoulder, into the distance. The woods. It occurs to Frank, and not for the first time, that he still doesn't know where the hell he is.

"Go where?" he asks again. But when he turns back to face the wolf, the animal is gone.

"Frank," Chili's voice calls to him from the doorway to the cabin, "the meeting's starting."

Frank nods. His heart races as he walks inside. It's much warmer in the cabin, a combination of the remnants of trapped daylight and the bodies of his comrades. Kevin and Bread sit on the couch together, not arms around each other like usual, but upright and serious. At some point, Chira had gotten here, but Frank didn't notice. She sits in a folding chair in the corner. Chira has a knack for unfiltered honesty. Something Frank usually doesn't mind, but dreads now, knowing he'll be the target of her unflinching assessment.

Miles and Jori huddle together on an oversized chair. Teri sits on a footstool to his right. Chili pulls a folding chair up for Frank and sits beside him on a cushion on the floor. Even though the group assembled forms an imperfect circle, Frank can't help feeling like he's facing a firing squad. He hears his heart pounding and wonders if the others can hear it as well. His throat dries up, eyes dart from Jori to Chira to Bread. He tries not to look at anyone for too long.

Bread starts to light up a joint, but Kevin pulls on his arm, and Bread puts the joint in a small pocket of his shirt.

"Thanks, everyone for being here," Bread begins, rubbing his hands together. Frank thinks he looks nervous too. "We've all had a lot of feelings about what happened, but we've also had a few days to sit and process and hopefully let some of those initial feelings settle."

Frank wonders if they'd been talking about him already. Of course, they were. They have cell phones. Why wouldn't they have been texting each other?

Bread continues to talk. Frank tries to force himself to pay attention but there are so many words, "we're here to try to agree on the best thing to do next," he says a lot of things. "This is not about punishment. We need to make sure everyone feels safe. And that everyone feels heard. And we may not like everything everyone has to say, but," Frank thinks he's trying too hard. Like he's trying to avert an argument that hasn't happened yet.

He wishes he would just stop. Let the fireworks explode so he can deal with whatever happens next. Instead of all these words.

"So, everyone is going to get a chance to say what they need to say. And we'll talk together about what happens next. But it has to be all of our ideas. So even if you don't usually like conflict, this is a time to say your piece."

Just fucking say it already, Frank thinks, just get the yelling over. But now Chira is talking. Frank tenses.

"I had my reservations, to begin with," Chira looks right at him, Frank's eyes burn, and he tries to look away without seeming rude. "Not because of who his father is, but because he's not well vetted." She motions with her hands as she speaks, flipping them, palm up again and again, like a magician twirling invisible scarves to keep the attention of the audience. "Even then, I admit, Frank went from being a rando to reading some solid lit, he didn't have to do that. He's been helping out around here, he didn't have to do that. And, yeah, he fucked up. In a serious way. But that's also our responsibility as a community because he had a crash course in radicalism. That's our bad as well as his. So, what next? He's part of the community now. He's got some work to do, but if he's willing to do it, why not work together as a community to improve? And that's my piece."

Frank's shoulders relax. Maybe it won't be so bad.

Bread nods, "Thanks, why don't we just go around the room and end with Frank's reaction, after you get to hear from everyone?"

No one contests this. Chili rubs a hand over their mouth before speaking, "There are some real safety concerns. And that needs to be taken seriously. This isn't all-or-nothing. It's not a question of whether Frank stays or goes. It's a reminder of training. And self-care. And the importance of working together. Working like a team, not as individuals. And that's a big lesson. It doesn't get internalized all in one shot. That's my piece."

Teri speaks next, "I think there's a ton of unchecked privilege here. And it put us all at risk." Her voice is loud, but she's not looking at him. She yells into the room as if he's not even there. "I mean, it's one thing for Frank to have this vendetta with his dad, but if that's all it is to him, then he's not about the work we're doing. So, I mean, Frank," she turns to him now, her eyes piercing into his. "If this is a family vendetta, that's fine. Take it outside of the collective space. Because if you're doing an action with us, you're doing it with us. It's not about you. But if it's just about you? Well, that's fine, but you don't need to put us in danger to do that. That's my piece." She wraps her arms around her waist. Mouth pointed down in a scowl.

Frank can feel his cheeks flush. His face is hot with shame. He wishes he could leave the room. Tell them all to fuck off and storm out.

Listen, The Chorus echoes in his mind, a rare occasion when he hears it indoors. *Be silent; listen.*

Now it's Jori's turn. Frank tries to listen, but he's already thinking of what Miles will say next.

Listen, The Chorus repeats.

"So, I don't really know you, so none of this is personal. I think the decision to do what you did was reckless. I don't think you should be part of future actions. And I think your staying here puts Bread and Kevin in danger. And that's all I have." She shrugs as she says this, looking over her shoulder to Miles.

"Well," Miles begins, "I'm not gonna say I told you so, but I never really felt comfortable about us just letting someone in so soon, especially under such dubious circumstances. I don't think it was a good idea, and it's a reminder of why we usually do things the way we do them,"

On "usually," Miles opens their eyes wide, emphasizing the word in a way that twists the knife further. Frank feels his face turn hot again.

He thinks of the wolf. Of Allistor. Tries not to panic. He wants to run. Or to shout. To tell them all to fuck off.

Miles continues, "This is what some of us were afraid would happen, not that we knew this exact thing, but we knew it wasn't a good idea. And so now I think the only remedy is that Frank leaves. I think we have some responsibility for where he ends up since we've taken him in, or since Bread and Kevin have, but I don't think it's a good idea for him to stay here. I never thought that was a good idea. And we can talk about how to arrange to help Frank move on somewhere else, but I think that is what needs to happen. And that's all I have to say for now."

Kevin uncrosses his legs and leans forward. He's the only one who speaks directly at Frank from the start, "Listen, what you didn't wasn't okay. I think you get that. You're a young guy, I mean literally, a few months ago you were a kid finishing high school, and then all this stuff happens, and then you're in the woods and then you're here, so I can say mistakes are mistakes and it's a learning curve. I'm ok with that. And I like you staying here, but," Kevin breaks eye contact, looking to the ceiling and trying to choose his words, "but I think even for a little while it would be a good idea for you to be living somewhere else. Even if it's just until this blows over. For all of our safety. That's all."

Frank doesn't disagree but hearing Kevin's words hurt the most so far. He closes his eyes, trying to push away tears. Not wanting to look weak. He hears Bread's voice next.

"I agree, Frank, I agree with what Kev said. And I just want you to know it's not personal. It's just a safety thing.

And it doesn't have to be permanent, but for now, it's not safe for you to be here. I'm sorry."

Frank nods. He can't look up. Instead, he studies the wood on the floor. Looks for hidden faces in the Rorschach test of its grain.

The room is silent. Then Chili speaks up, "Frank, you can respond, or say anything you want to say now."

But he can't. Because if he starts talking, his voice will crack. He'll start crying. And he can't do that. He takes a deep breath, still mesmerized by the wood on the floor.

"I didn't realize," he begins to speak slowly, careful not to let his voice tremble, "what could happen? I thought that spraying one thing or spraying another, what's the difference."

"There's a big difference, though!" Miles cuts in.

In unison, Bread, Kevin, and Chili respond, "You had your turn," and "It's Frank's turn."

Miles sits back, folding their arms over their chest.

"I know that now. And I don't know. It felt like the right thing to do. But I didn't realize what could happen. But, I think no matter what," he inhales, not planning the words until they come out of his mouth, "I think no matter what I should leave. I feel like I need to go back. Somewhere out in the world. I don't know where. So maybe it's not an issue."

"We have some funds, to get you started. And some comrades you can stay with." Bread offers.

"I don't know. I think I need to maybe try to be on my own." Frank can't meet his eyes.

"It's going to be near impossible. It's your choice, but this isn't punishment. We want to make sure you're okay. Being on your own makes that less likely. Maybe sleep on it?" Kevin adds.

There's more discussion. Formalities. Security measures mostly. Frank doesn't understand most of the conversation. His mind is already distracted by the words he hadn't planned to say.

That night, Frank dreams he's walking through the woods, trailing behind the wolf whose grey lumbering presence is illuminated by a full moon. He stops to watch the moon. When his eyes return to the path ahead, the scene has changed. No longer in the woods, he's now in the park. He instinctively looks for Bella, before remembering she's not here. And now, neither is the wolf.

"Pick up the gun," a voice tells him. He turns to see a stranger. A man with an AR-15 strapped over his shoulder. "You don't have time to wait. They're coming."

"Who's coming?" Frank asks.

"They're coming for you. No running away this time. Get a gun," the man's tone is sharp now, he points to a pile of weapons on the ground.

I don't know how to shoot, Frank thinks, but he walks toward the pile anyway.

"You don't have to do that, you know."

This voice he recognizes.

Mallory.

He turns, looking for her, but the park is empty.

"They're coming." Mallory's voice tells him, "Time to make a choice."

He wakes drenched in sweat.

CHAPTER 53

Chili

Chili's mind is clearest in the hours before dawn, a habit. The cool air the last three mornings was a welcomed break from the sweltering late summer heat. Their apartment has been neglected in recent weeks, so much time spent at The Farm with Bread, Kevin, and their new recruit.

Frank is on their mind now. Chili stumbles through the kitchen in need of caffeine. Something scampers out of the sink and behind a row of spices before they can turn on the light.

Another of the anonymous crew of drain-dwelling bugs that used to make their roommates scream.

"She's just trying to stay alive, like us," Chili used to tease. They're all used to the intruders now. And the mice that take shelter in the old walls every season when it rains, or the weather turns cold.

Chili turns on a small light over the stove. They twist the dial; click, click, a blue light surges from the burner. With a kettle over the flame, Chili stands and watches, eyes growing dull, their mind wandering elsewhere.

All in all, the meeting hadn't gone bad. Frank agreed it was best to vacate the cabin for now. Wise choice. Chili doesn't like the idea of the young man trying to make it on his own. He's come a long way, but not far enough.

"But it's his choice, nothing we can do about it," Kevin had confided to them after the meeting that he, too felt responsible to make sure the kid was taken care of.

"Maybe we can introduce him to some trusted friends," Chili suggested.

The kettle whistles soft at first, escalating to a shrill, urgent alarm. Chili turns the stove off. They open one cabinet, then another. Had they really run out of tea? Reaching a hand toward the back of an overhead cabinet, Chili finds a crumpled box. Two teabags remain. They drop one into a chipped mug, stained yellow inside despite being freshly washed.

"I feel responsible for him too, but it's his choice," Chili had tried to reassure Kevin. And himself. What he hadn't mentioned was why he felt responsible for Frank.

Steam rises from the mug as Chili carries it into the main room in the cramped studio apartment. Heat from the tea pricks his face and opens their sinuses.

Chili feels responsible because they know who Frank is. *Who he is to you.*

Chili sits on the futon and pulls their phone down from an end table. They check Signal for any news. On a thread called PunchNazis, a user called Armageddon29 posts an update of a neo-Nazi cell they've infiltrated.

"They're planning a 'Save the Whites' protest to coincide with Indigenous Peoples' Day. Buses coming from NY and PA…"

Several emoji reactions, followed by photos of three men with requests for information for doxing purposes.

On another thread called ClimateCrisisReact, a lively discussion is taking place as members of the group plan an action for Labor Day weekend, still a few weeks in the future.

"We need volunteer medics and donations of cases of water bottles. Also, need legal observers…"

Chili scans a dozen different chats before scrolling down far enough to see what they can already deduce. No reply from RedBarren1312.

Damn.

But you knew this would happen, a voice in their head reminds Chili.

They knew she wouldn't respond, at least a part of them knew it. But they hoped to be wrong.

Let sleeping dogs lie.

Chili sips the tea. It's dark, rich, and almost tastes like chocolate. Spicey. Cardamom, cinnamon, and orange peel, they can taste so many nuances in one sip. Cracks of sunlight begin to peer through the clouds, and the shadows in the room adjust.

Time to make a decision.

Chili starts to replace the phone on the table, before reconsidering. They pause for a beat. Then another. Finally, Chili types another message. It's a one-way conversation now. Something Chili typically avoids. It feels creepy. Like stalking. But they have to do it.

If you've seen the news, you can guess the rest. Soon he'll be out of range. I won't be able to protect him.

They put the phone face down now, not expecting a reply.

CHAPTER 54

The notification, louder than a text, longer than an email, indicates a new Signal message. She jolts upright, throwing off the covers, eyes now open and alert. Only a moment ago she had been lost in a nightmare. In a jail. Working. Fingering dozens of keys on a ring, trying to find the right one.

"You've got to get me out of here, fast," someone in a cell had called to her. But the harder she tried to flip through the keys the more time slowed. She dropped them several times. Just before waking, she could hear the heavy footsteps of a guard coming down the hall somewhere behind her.

"Hurry, we're running out of time," the voice pleaded.

She tries to catch her breath. The late summer morning is cool but her body is drenched in sweat.

She draws a symbol on her phone with an index finger to unlock the security code, then types in a number as backup security. She has a message on Signal from the last person she wants to hear from.

If you've seen the news…

She hasn't seen the news. Not in well over a week. At least, not any news outside of the information coming through encrypted threads online.

She pushes the power button on her laptop and types in the local news channel. She meant to reply to the first message. Hadn't she? Part of her didn't believe it could be true. Just another ploy to get her to respond, and a low blow, if that was the case.

But was that their style?

They were both older, maybe wiser. Why still hold a grudge?

Federal prison, for starters, a voice inside her head reminds her.

She doesn't see anything noteworthy at first as she scrolls the headlines.

They probably meant their news, realizing now they've been separated by not only years but miles. She types in the names of several news stations in the NY and NJ area. Rows of headlines fill the screen. A bank robbery still under investigation in Patterson, a three-car pileup on a highway in Butler, and drama at a school board meeting in the Pompton Lakes area.

And then she sees it.

For the first time in decades, she sees the name she denounced. She expected it to be traumatic, seeing the familiar face in photos and videos. Reading the name of the business that mattered more to him than his family and their future.

Instead, she feels nothing. As if watching glitter fall inside a snow globe. Far on the outside, watching a scene she's not a part of.

Bernardoni Realty Target of String of Vandal Attacks
    Bernardoni Developments Subject of Street Vandals
    Extremists Descend on Bernardoni Buildings
Big deal. Was she supposed to feel sorry for him? Pat Bernardoni hasn't changed much, to look at the photos.

He's aged. His money couldn't keep time from wearing lines into his face. He looks weak, far from the figure who used to loom large.

She's about to close her laptop, wondering why the peace of time and distance had been disrupted over something so insignificant when another headline catches her eye.

Bernardoni Heir Feared Kidnapped

And another.

Pat Bernardoni Pleads for Son's Safe Return

And another.

Bernardoni Building Vandalism Spree Linked to Missing Bernardoni Heir

"What the fuck is going on?" she asks the empty room.

CHAPTER 55

Frank

September 2022

Frank feels at ease since the decision was made.

"It doesn't have to be permanent either," Kevin's told him repeatedly this morning, as the slender man buzzed around the kitchen making breakfast. It had been a full spread of tofu scramble with stir-fried vegetables, oranges, fruit smoothies, and toast. Usually, Bread was the house chef. Frank wondered if Kevin was feeling guilty and trying to make it up to him.

It doesn't matter.

Frank understands.

Even Miles seems to have chilled out. Acted almost friendly toward him yesterday.

As he finishes washing the breakfast dishes, an awareness sets into his bones against the backdrop of the running water. He was only ever meant to stay for a little while.

"Got a minute?" Bread's voice breaks Frank's concentration.

"Sure."

"Want to show you something," Bread beckons him to follow out the door. His band t-shirt is covered in dirt and dust. Frank doesn't recognize the logo or the name of the band. He follows Bread out toward the goat field. "New member of the family, Kevin told me what you said about Allistor."

Tears form in the corners of Frank's eyes. He doesn't know why. As he and Bread walk toward the barn, he sees it. No longer one silhouette, head slumped, a despondent eye fixed on him as he chews hay. Now there are two.

He feels a magnetic pull as he approaches them.

"I'm really still virile for my age. Don't let my, um, condition, fool you," Allistor tells his new mate, motioning with his snout to point toward the spot where his testicles should be.

The petite white goat bleats in response, but Frank hears her reply.

"I'm not really into having kids. Do you have any carrots? I love carrots."

He shouldn't be eavesdropping and slows down, giving them space.

"Are they happy?" Bread asks and Frank can tell he's nervous.

"Well, Allistor definitely is. The other one likes carrots."

"Duly noted." Bread laughs. "I thought maybe before you go, you can name her if you want?"

Frank looks at the two goats playfully trotting side by side before stopping to nosh on a shrub. He could call her Mallory, but was that insulting to do? Or maybe Carmen, or name her after his mother or…

The white goat stops and looks at him then. She trots toward him and stops, answering for him.

Frank walks the grounds for the last time as the sun sets. Tomorrow, he'll leave. Everyone has reassured him it's only temporary, but Frank knows he'll never be back. As he walks along the shrubs at the edge of the clearing, the sound of rustling stops him in his tracks.

The hair on his neck stands on end. Chills prick at his spine.

I've done it now.

The memory of Miles's reaction flashes through his mind. "He's put us in danger."

He stands still, heart racing. He can hear his pulse pounding in his ears. Whoever is in the shrubs can hear it too, he's sure of it.

The police. The FBI. They've found him.

He's too far from the cabin to make a dash for the door without drawing attention to himself. As his mind races, replaying all the scenarios; the police in riot gear, someone undercover, a SWAT team, a grey creature pads from the shrubs out into the open, facing him.

The wolf's fur is illuminated with the glow of the evening light.

Frank breathes a sigh of relief.

All this shit's going to my head.

The wolf approaches him then stops in his path and sits, scenting the air.

Time to move on, the wolf tells him.

"I know," he replies aloud.

Your work begins.

"Work? What work? Why do you keep saying that? I don't know what my work is."

We show you, The Chorus answers.

He closes his eyes, breathing in the warm breeze, feeling the branches and leaves rustle. When he opens his eyes, the wolf is gone.

CHAPTER 56

I Am Frank: Rash of Threatening Messages Lead Authorities to Copycat Theory
Passaic Tribune
September 2, 2022

In the past week, more than a dozen acts of vandalism spanning a 200-mile radius in the Pompton Lakes area led authorities to question: is this the work of extremists responsible for the abduction of the heir to the

Bernardoni Development empire? Or is this the work of several copycat vandals?

Pompton Lakes Police Sargent Dennis O'Toole is leaning toward the copycat theory. They look for any excuse to emulate people close to celebrities. Unfortunately, in cases like this, it means that whatever the kidnappers or people associated with the Bernardoni disappearance do, you'll have dozens of others trying to follow suit."

He also fears that the actions of the original vandal or vandals give legitimacy to others who may be looking for a way to channel their destructive tendencies.

"It emboldens them, and that's what we have to look out for."

In recent days, the acts of vandalism targeted an Amazon warehouse, a parking garage, and even a prestigious private college. The messages seem to be escalating in hostility and violence.

As Sargent O'Toole reports, "You start with an anarchy symbol here and there, and now we've got spray paintings of guillotines and outright threats. 'We're coming for you,' and 'heads will roll.' The common denominator is they're all signed 'Frank.'"

Some compare these messages to the works of those like the mysterious artist known as Banksy, but O'Toole thinks this comparison is dangerous. "We don't want to glamorize and glorify this kind of destruction. These are not harmless, victimless acts. They cost thousands of dollars and are now making real credible threats. It's nothing to take lightly."

Authorities still have no leads on the suspected kidnapping of Francesco Bernardoni. While some speculate that the mysterious "Frank" may actually be Francesco, those closest to Francesco, such as his father, Pat Bernardoni, adamantly denounce this narrative.

"My son is not a political extremist. He is the victim of extremists. And we want him home safe." Pat Bernardoni said.

Anyone with information on the identity or identities of the vandals calling themselves "Frank" is asked to call the Pompton Police tip line.

CHAPTER 57

Pat Bernardoni

Pat Bernardoni is in his home office when he hears his daughter Connie's voice calling to him from downstairs.

I told her not to yell through the house.

Her voice carries but he can't hear what she's saying. It sounds like "Policeman here to see you."

Pat Bernardoni pushes his chair back from the desk, rubs his eyes, and exhales. It's a wonder he can get any work done with constant interruptions.

"Daaaaad," Connie yells again. Footsteps thump up the stairs. Before she can burst into his office, something he's also told her a million times not to do, he's up and walking for the doors.

He meets her in the hallway. She's wearing her riding outfit, no longer brand new, and not on a riding day.

"Change into play clothes. Those are expensive and you're not going riding until Saturday," he barks.

"Daddy, why is there a policeman here to see you?"

"That's my business, not yours. Now go change into play clothes." He points toward her room. She sulks, arms folded across her chest, but doesn't talk back.

Descending the stairs, Pat Bernardoni sees the visitor whom his daughter has let into the house without his permission.

I'll deal with that later, he thinks.

"Can I help you?" Pat asks, his tone intentionally aggressive.

"Mr. Bernardoni, sorry to bother you. I'm Hector Malone, private investigator with the North Brighton police."

The investigator is in plain clothes but flashes a badge as he introduces himself. A man in his thirties dressed sharp, hair clean cut.

"Any leads on the punks who vandalized my properties?" Bernardoni remains curt. The first attack cost him, but there have been more than a dozen since then.

"No, sir. That's what I was hoping to talk to you about. We think the vandal or vandals may also be responsible for your son's kidnapping."

"Well then I would hope you're putting adequate resources behind this case," Bernardoni keeps his voice level.

"In cases like this, we've found it beneficial in the past when there is a, um, when the family," Malone stumbles on his words. He regroups and tries again. "In cases of missing persons, we find it tends to expedite things, expedite leads, that is when we can offer some kind of reward for any information useful to apprehending the missing person."

Bernardoni doesn't respond. Silence is power. He watches as Malone becomes more visibly uncomfortable. The younger man attempts to keep eye contact but is the first to avert his gaze, searching the room for something to focus on. His hands, originally casually by his side, now fidget with his pockets. Malone bites his lip and rubs one thumb over his ear. Bernardoni recognizes these nervous tics.

Finally, the younger man speaks again, "Usually, in cases like this, it's typical for the community, or in many cases, the family, to contribute to the award money, for when the missing person is found."

Bernardoni scowls.

"My buildings are vandalized, my son is missing, and the police want to extort money from me to solve the case?" He jabs an index finger into his chest as he says this.

Malone's eyes widen, he contorts his mouth beginning to form words but then pauses, as if reconsidering what he originally intended to say.

"I mean, it would be customary and would help move things along if we go this route, but we don't have to."

"You know what I suggest?" Bernardoni paces in front of his guest, one hand in the air, pointing with his index finger as he speaks.

"What's that, Mr. Bernardoni?" Malone asks.

"I suggest your department takes the money that hard-working Americans like myself are already paying you through our generous contributions, and I suggest you use that money to find whatever thugs are trashing my buildings and disrupting my business, and I suggest you offer a reward or do whatever it is you do, to find my son."

He stops pacing. Close enough to Malone to see the remnants of a few acne scars on his cleanshaven face. Malone takes a step back, looks to the floor, smiles, and then answers, his voice steady for the first time.

"I would be careful, Mr. Bernardoni," he begins.

"Excuse me?"

"I would be careful," Malone raises his head and looks Bernardoni in the eyes, "because so far this is a missing person case suspected to be a kidnapping. And as such, the public is watching closely." Malone maintains eye contact; he pauses for effect. "And so far, there is no theory connecting any personal connections to Francesco's disappearance." He emphasizes the words 'personal connections.'

Bernardoni feels his blood pressure rising at the insinuation. He starts to object, but the younger man cuts him off.

"We don't want the media, or some nosy philanthropists in the community, or even your business competition to start to openly question why the Bernardoni family isn't putting their resources into finding their kidnapped son."

Bernardoni feels heat rise in his face. He tries to maintain a blank expression but feels the pulse in his neck beginning to throb.

"And you better watch whom you threaten. I'll have your badge. I'll sue you, Mr. Malone."

Malone smiles. "No one is threatening anyone. And a man like you isn't really interested in whatever I have. I'm just suggesting that we both have an interest in making sure your reputation doesn't get dragged through the mud. Doing all we can- all we both can- to make sure Francesco is home safe as soon as possible is the best way to ensure that. Right?"

Bernardoni walks toward the younger man, his voice low and seething with anger, "If anyone has information about my son, they have a moral obligation to come forward. I don't pay people to fulfill their moral obligations. I won't be extorted by criminals."

Malone raises both arms in a shrug. "Point taken. We'll continue to keep the investigation open and will keep you posted on any leads that come in."

Bernardoni smiles, "I appreciate you doing that," his voice saccharine and sarcastic.

"Thank you for your time. I'll see myself out," Malone turns his back on the older man, calling over his shoulder, "have a good rest of your day, Mr. Bernardoni."

Pat Bernardoni watches the investigator through the window. Sees him get into his car, check his phone, glance once more at the house and pull away from the curb.

"Son of a bitch," Bernardoni yells, slamming his fist on the back of the couch as he walks past it. Whatever stunt his son was up to, whatever this latest bullshit is, it's starting to take a toll.

He's doing this to ruin me.

Well, the little bastard won't succeed.

Bernardoni heads for the stairs. His wife stands silent regarding him with a look of disgust on her face.

"How long have you been standing there, snooping into my business?"

"Long enough to know it wasn't just your business when it's our son you're discussing," she answers.

"You're not well, dear. Go back to bed. You're misinterpreting things like you always do when you have one of your little episodes."

"Fuck you!"

Bernardoni stops short. Never has his wife ever spoken to him this way. He's too shocked to respond at first, and she takes the silence as an opportunity to continue.

"You have more money than God and you won't offer an award for our son? Our only son? For Christ's sake, what is wrong with you?"

A slap interrupts her. Losing her balance, she stumbles to the floor.

Bernardoni speaks in a firm, slow cadence, "I said," he begins, "your mind is befuddled. You're having another of your episodes. Now go to your room."

All I do for this family, he thinks, *and this is the thanks I get.*

Part 3 Back to Brighton

Chapter 58

April 2023

Frank

Frank walks through the alleys, winding his way through the section of the city his friends at the Academy used to call The Stones. Strangers walking by in the dim light would think the fur around his neck is the trimming of his jacket collar. If they come closer, they'll see the truth.

A possum dangles over his shoulder, little paws clutching his collar, tail twitching in annoyance when he walks too fast.

"I don't want a bumpy ride," the creature hisses in his ear.

Frank has almost forgotten the possum is there, lost in thought as he recalls life at the Academy seems distant. As if he watched it in a movie once and remembers some themes but not the details of the plot or the characters. That was Francesco Bernardoni's life, not his.

In that life, he didn't know The Stones even had such labyrinthine alleys. He didn't know about the vibrant art community that ran along 112th Street and included a recording studio where indie musicians in the area often got their start. He didn't know that Bart's Place, the bar on the corner of Broadway and Columbine, had been one of the first meeting places to exist downtown, before the rest of the city sprawled in all directions. Didn't know that the owner, Bartolomeo Mangino, was the direct descendent of the original owner who was driven out of town for aiding immigrant labor organizers and anarchists in the 19th century.

He didn't know that the homes had been built by Italian, Polish, and later Irish and Russian immigrants, some of whom died in the tenement-like conditions, while a few others broke through and became the same kind of slumlords that used to terrorize their own families.

In his old life, he had no idea that later waves of residents, mostly African American, some Dominican, and Haitian, had been drained of their wealth and kept captive by a generations-long cycle of redlining and price gauging. His father's father had made a fortune through his role in the cycle. But no one ever told Frank this story.

He speeds up his pace, stretching his legs to step over puddles and trash left on the ground.

Whiskers scratch at his neck as the possum leans his snout closer to Frank's ear.

"Are you trying to kill me?"

Frank smiles at his melodramatic companion, "I've wanted to see you play dead."

"Not funny."

"The sooner we get back, the sooner we can eat," Frank whispers in the dark, no one around to question whom he is talking to. A memory occurs to him. His family is seated around the table for a dinner party. His parents' guests, Mr. and Mrs. Doherty, owned a construction business that often worked with his dad.

Mrs. Doherty had been as quiet as her husband was gregarious. At one point in the conversation, Mr. Doherty, having made his way through the better part of the white wine the adults were sharing, had set down his cloth napkin, raised his index finger in the air, and began to rant.

"We have a new aide helping Mother. I can't even begin to tell you." He rested his forearms on the table and leaned closer for emphasis. "You just can't find good help anymore."

"Oh, George, really, we don't need to talk about this now," his wife tried to interject. He ignored her.

"She's got a name I can't pronounce, for starters. Showed up late twice in the first two weeks she was caring for Mother."

"To be fair, dear, she takes the bus, all the way from the old neighborhoods, and the bus was late."

He speaks over his wife again, "But then, I stopped in to visit Mother, and as I am leaving, this woman asked me if I could take her home because one of her kids- God only knows how many she probably has- was sent home from school. Probably fighting."

"No, dear, he had a fever," Mrs. Doherty tried again, but her husband was on a roll.

"Anyway, of course, since I was standing right there, what can I do? So I drove her home- used the old car of course- and Pat, I'm telling you, it's not the old neighborhood you and I knew growing up. Your father, rest his soul, would be turning in his grave! These people leave their trash everywhere."

What Mr. Doherty hadn't known, or at least hadn't said if he did know it, was something Frank has learned in the weeks he's been squatting in the old neighborhood- The Stones. Where his parents' neighborhood had weekly trash pickup guaranteed by the city, the neighborhoods on the northwestern corner of the city had only had trash pickup twice in the weeks since he's been here.

Frank walks past overflowing trash cans and dumpsters. To the joy of the rats, raccoons, and fishers he's seen roaming about, but to the dismay of everyone else, the area has been neglected by the city.

"Stop, there, that's a good one," the possum points with a snout toward one of the dumpsters. Frank reaches into his pocket and removes a bag. When they're close enough, the creature stretches from Frank's shoulder and balances on the edge of the dumpster. He sniffs the air for a moment before part-crawling, part-diving into the refuse. Frank hears the sounds of the animal scurrying about in the dark.

"Do you need me to come in there to help?" he asks.

In response, the possum scurries back to the ledge, an unopened bag of bread dangling from his mouth. Frank opens the bag, and the possum drops the food in, then returns to the trash.

When the bag is filled with treasures; uneaten donuts, a sack of potatoes, a box of pasta, a bag of bread, a box of crackers, and some sugar packets. Frank slings the bag over his shoulder and waits while his furry comrade scurries up his arm, attaching himself to the man's collar with all four paws.

He remembers the first time he walked this way with Mallory. How he had noticed the darkness and staggered streetlamps. It wasn't just light the community had been deprived of. A few nights ago, Mrs. Jenkins, who lived next door to one of Frank's favorite encampments, had a stroke. Her nephew, Lyle, had begun desperately banging on doors, calling for help. The noise had awakened him from a deep sleep.

Frank had run come outside of the abandoned house where he'd been staying to find out what was wrong. Lyle, who must be only about twelve, was waving his hands in the air in a panic.

"Aunt Jeanie, she fell, and she's not talking. I called 9-1-1 an hour ago and they haven't come yet. I need help!"

No nurse or doctor came to the door in a two-block radius, but a neighbor had been able to give the older woman a ride to the hospital, another half hour away.

As he walks the streets now, Frank feels closer to Mallory. But even she is becoming a distant memory. In his past life, Frank didn't steal. Well, only on occasion, but not like now. Not for survival.

"Steal from the big box stores, not from locals." He learned this from a fellow traveler, Bea. She'd shared an empty house with a group of three friends who had offered Frank shelter in the weeks after Chili dropped him off- at his insistence- to live on the street near Mallory's old building.

"Hey, you got anything for us?" A high-pitched voice breaks his concentration. He feels the Possum rearrange himself on his shoulder to look down at the ground as Frank turns his head in the direction of the voice.

A bushy skunk emerges from between two overflowing trashcans, babies in tow.

"These bins are trash. No good food. Can you help?"

Frank lowers the bag from his shoulders, eyeing the box of donuts. He first thinks of leaving the jelly-filled powder donuts with the Skunk, what the hell, he never liked that flavor. But something stops him. He smiles, grabs the box, and lowers it to the ground.

"Here you go, the good stuff. Enjoy!"

The little ones scamper around the box, "Dessert for dinner!" one squeaks.

The Mother Skunk turns to Frank, a smile of gratitude on her face, and bows to him, "thank you, you're a saint."

He shakes his head. "No saints. No Gods. No masters. Eat up."

He slings the sack over his shoulder again, gives the Possum a chance to settle in, and continues to weave through the alleys, picking food from a few more dumpsters, distributing bread, crackers, and cookies to people huddled around burning fires inside rusted garbage cans as he made his way to the place he now calls home

CHAPTER 59

Narrator

You may find it hard to imagine life before the internet. Unless that is, you happen to find yourself wandering in a daze in the woods. Head in the clouds, hearing voices as you wander through the wilderness.

And if you ever have the chance to bask in the relief a week unplugged can bring, imagine that disconnect lasting longer. Weeks become months.

No emails to check. No social media notifications. The legend of Frank from Jersey became an internet sensation. But Frank, the man, went through one day and the next, oblivious.

No idea he'd become a meme. Photoshopped images of himself standing with Bella scraped from his socials, a wolf superimposed over the dog's body. Then a raccoon. And a possum.

CHAPTER 60

Frank

Frank climbs the dark stairs, his dumpster treasures in hand, possum on his shoulder. When he reaches the landing, he sweeps aside the curtain taking the place of a door. Before he can call to the others, a raspy voice carries from just behind his right ear.

"Honey, I'm hooome! Did you make me some cupcakes?" The possum pronounces it 'chupcakes,' but only Frank can hear him.

Roxie looks up from the beanbag chair in the corner, "You're home, Frank! And I see you have Popcorn with you." She tolerates the possum, and Frank thinks she would like him even less if she could hear some of the rude jokes he makes.

"We're home and we have presents." He holds up the bag bulging with food.

Roxie walks toward him, helping to unburden the load, and sets the sack on a small table in what was once a living room. Lia emerges from one of the vacant bedrooms, she's claimed it as an art space and sanctuary in the abandoned house.

Lia is as brooding as Roxie is assertive. A petite woman with dyed white and purple hair, Lia lingers in the shadows as Roxie relights chunky candles. What little electricity they have is rigged off grid and they use it sparingly.

Popcorn, the possum fond of hitchhiking with Frank, leaps with grace from the man's shoulder to a bookshelf. He walks along the spines of books with names like Kropotkin, Marx, and Goldman displayed, oblivious to the library's contents.

When Frank and the others are preoccupied sorting through their food, Popcorn climbs down the shelf and squats in a corner, where he found some old pamphlets, relieving himself in peace.

He remembers the first time he found Frank. Alone, overheated, and confused. The man wandered the streets and was the butt of some of the possum's cruder jokes at first. But the animal pitied him after a few hours and led him to this reclaimed house. A place he knew often had good food, and good people who shared it with him. They would take care of the man, Popcorn thought.

He was right.

Popcorn scurries along a wall toward the small sofa and climbs onto one of the cushions, circling before settling down. He sniffs at his tail and licks at his front paw, watching the silhouettes. Frank and Roxie would make good mates, he thinks. But he knows by their scent they haven't consummated their relationship yet.

He credits himself for introducing them. In time, he thinks, they may settle down and have some of their own young in this nest. One big happy family.

"And when you do," Popcorn says aloud, "you better bring me some chupcakes."

Frank is the only one awake in what he assumes is early morning. Two, maybe three A.M. Roxie is curled on a hammock, snoring softly. The light of the moon outlines her face. Lia has wandered off again. Frank knows not to ask questions. Lia comes and goes on her own timing.

He's gotten used to having livelier conversations with Popcorn than with the mysterious woman who after all these months is still a stranger and likes it that way.

"She's not a fed, she's just shy. We love her as she is," Roxie told him back when they first met.

Each floor of the old house has been reclaimed by the Possum Crew. They called themselves that before he met them, adopting Popcorn as their mascot and giving him the name based on what they thought was his favorite food.

It's a good thing they can't understand him, Frank thinks, or they would have named him Chupcake.

It's his last night of food duty for the week, and the pickings are getting slimmer. He doesn't want to alarm them, but they may have to risk more extreme measures in a few weeks.

Though they have no leader, Roxie is often the one to make new initiatives. More than once, members of the Crew have asked about their relationship.

"She seems to like you," Popcorn teased occasionally.

Frank knew this. But every time he came close to thinking of Roxie as more than a friend, Mallory's face would appear. Haunting him. And all feelings shut down.

If his apparent rejection hurt Roxie, she didn't show it. She took Frank under her wing from day one. Showed him how to borrow electricity and even Wi-Fi. Taught him about scavenging and what dumpsters to avoid. Even showed him how to do basic first aid. Luckily they hadn't needed it in months.

Frank shifts restlessly. His mind won't settle. He thinks of the stores of food, dwindling. He thinks of Roxie, bold and alive. Here now. And inevitably, thinks of Mallory, whose face is a continued specter he can barely remember in detail.

I need to sleep.

Tomorrow will be another busy day. Popcorn stretches and crawls along the floor silently, but Frank still feels him pass by. The critter curls up by his knees. He pets the possum with one hand, something Popcorn usually shies away from but now seems to enjoy.

As he drifts to sleep, a memory fills his mind. Shortly after he joined the Possum Crew, in a rare moment of extraversion, Lia approached him, a velvety pouch in her hand.

"Want a Tarot Reading?"

"You mean like they do on the boardwalk?" Frank asked.

"Yeah, maybe. I don't know. Never been to the boardwalk."

"Sure," Frank shrugged. Lia removed long, gilded cards from the pouch and shuffled them in what appeared a random style before laying them on the floor at his feet. Not wanting to hover above her, Frank dropped to the floor as well. Even Popcorn, who had been snoozing in a corner, came over to check it out.

"This card represents you," Lia began. Frank saw the name Jongleur on the bottom of a picture of a clown. Behind the clown, a dog.

"Um, thanks? So, I'm a clown?"

"The Fool, the adventurer. The blank slate. The world projects its wishes onto you. But you can take or leave anything you choose. You are clear. Open. The Wanderer."

He flashes to another memory. Mallory smiling at him, "You're a fool." How many times had she called him that? He pushes the tears down. Buries them.

"Yeah, I guess. I like the dog." Frank points to the terrier at the Fool's feet.

"Yes, you have more companions among the animals than among your comrade humans. It is one of your gifts. Because you're open. You must listen to them. They always walk with you."

She placed another card and another. Even said something about Roxie, "One admires you now, one love is lost. The Fool's path is complicated. You must be unencumbered by attachment, so you can truly love."

Frank nodded, not sure he understood, but suddenly wanting this to be over. Another card, this one a tower devoured by flames.

"Yeah, that looks like my luck," Frank joked. She didn't laugh.

"This year you enter the Twelfth House. The place of Self-Undoing."

Frank's stomach tightened.

"The place where you lose yourself and find yourself. Where you find confinement in jails, institutions, and hospitals, only to find freedom. True freedom. Don't despair when you are confined. The darkest moment is before dawn."

Frank shudders, remembering the cryptic message. He wonders as he did then, how seriously he should take Lia. Maybe she read his past. His father's house was the 12th on their street, and it felt like a jail. Then there was the cabin, which was like a hospital. A place he went to heal. Maybe she got her signals confused.

He yawns and stretches. Feeling Popcorn snore behind his legs. His eyes close and he joins his friend in sleep.

CHAPTER 61

Frank

Frank understands the importance of consensus, but as the meeting spills into its fourth hour, he wishes some things could just be majority rule. Roxie and one of the founders of the Crew, David, have been debating for what seems like forever.

"We don't currently have the infrastructure to do what you're suggesting." Roxie keeps repeating. "It's a good idea, and I do agree it's needed, but that kind of eviction defense squad requires a lot more people willing to risk arrest than what we currently have."

Frank looks around. Less than a dozen people in attendance, and this is normal. She has a point.

"The more actions we do, the more word gets out. The more people will join us. We have an encampment of recently displaced people a few blocks away, some of them may be willing to help."

David is their liaison with a few of the local encampments. At first, there was one, now there are half a dozen within walking and bicycling distance. Frank understands his point. The problem of mass evictions is only getting worse.

"We can't expect people living in the encampment to risk arrest, they're already in too vulnerable a situation," Roxie responds.

"We shouldn't speak for them. Why not raise the question? Let them decide?"

The argument is getting off track. Frank raises his hand.

"Frank is on stack," Iria, one of the quieter original members points out. All eyes on him, Frank stumbles to put his thoughts into words. Even after all this time, he hates the attention. He averts his gaze to a corner of the room where Popcorn is shredding magazines to make a nest.

"We need to build up capacity. We also definitely need to do more for eviction defense. So why don't we do an action that leads to both?"

"What do you have in mind?" David looks curious.

"What if we do a massive art project, bring people together from different groups, and as we're planning and leading up to that action we can do some coalition building, get a pulse on what others are open for?"

"We've already dealt with the other groups, they're all problematic," Sophia responds.

"Every group is problematic. We can have perfect activists, or we can have enough people to get shit done. I'm all for getting shit done," Cal adds, frustration showing in his voice.

The conversation has devolved close to an argument, rather than waiting his turn, Frank jumps in again, "the anniversary of the mass evictions from last year, the one where police came down and killed someone," he stops short of saying Mallory's name, but they all know who he is talking about, "it's coming up. We can do an action to keep that on peoples' minds. As a rallying cry. To show Bernardoni he isn't going to win and to send a sign to others like him."

He hasn't referred to Pat Bernardoni as his father in months. Some of the newcomers to the Crew don't even know there is a connection. Some seem to consider this idea, nodding silently. Others seem on the verge of falling asleep.

"Okay, but if we put resources into the action to plan for an eviction defense squad, and shit goes south, there goes our people power for future actions for like, months," David mentions.

He's not wrong, Frank knows.

"Well, then we have to make sure shit doesn't go south."

A few people groan. "Be realistic," Cal interjects. "I want to get mobilizing as much as the next person but unless we do some extreme planning on this, like knowing the security information from jump, it's not going to happen. Not the way you're thinking."

"Yes and No," David adds, beginning to contradict himself. "Assuming the standard alarm response time, the more people we have, the easier we can decorate the place and split before the pigs arrive."

The conversation shifts to what groups they should involve and details of who can fill each role needed.

Later in the evening, after the crowd has subsided, Roxie paces the flat, a troubled look on her face.

"You're in the doghouse now. What did you do? Leave the seat up on the bucket?" Popcorn teases him, waving his tail in Roxie's direction.

Frank was trying to ignore her apparent bad mood but decides against maintaining his silence.

"What's wrong?"

She turns to him, pulls up a plastic chair, and sits hard, huffing her breath out in a sigh.

"Why do you really want to do this big action at your father's place?"

He winces at the reference to his father.

"As I said, it's a rallying call. It sends a message."

"Is that all?"

Frank lets the question hang in the air momentarily.

"And because he can't think he's getting away with what he did."

She rolls her eyes.

"What?"

"We're trying to help entire communities. This can't be about your vendetta with your dad."

Her words sting. Frank sits back as if he's been slapped.

"It's to rally people together. I think someone being murdered by police warrants a memorial..."

"Yeah, I do too. But guess what? Not to sound like an ass, but people are being murdered by police every minute."

She crosses her arms over her chest. Her foot shakes, tapping on the floor. She takes another long slow breath and when she speaks again her tone is level.

"I'm fine going forward with this. I just want to make sure you're doing it for the reasons you think you're doing it. Because if you're only there to get back at your dad? Then you're not going to be thinking- and acting- like part of the team."

They both sit in silence for a moment. Eventually, Roxie rises from the chair and heads toward the door. "I'm going to go check on the encampment on South and Port Streets. Be back later."

"So moody that one, am I right?" Popcorn jabs at Frank's arm with his long snout.

Frank wants to believe it's just jealousy. But he's heard these words, or something like it, before.

CHAPTER 62

Narrator

As you can see, Frank wasn't sad to leave the cabin behind after all. Before long, he had found community in new and unexpected places. The wolf couldn't follow him into the city, and Frank didn't fault him for it.

Instead, he was accompanied everywhere by a possum and a trail of stray dogs, cats, the occasional skunk, and an adoring cadre of squirrels to say nothing of pigeons.

Throughout the Old Neighborhood, there was plenty to keep someone like Frank busy. Murmurs vibrated along the cracked pavement. Whispers traveled in the caw of crows.

Beneath the bedrooms where children lay sweltering in the summer heat and never warm enough from September to April, pangs of hunger gnawing in their bellies, the midnight shadowed sidewalks and alleys, stairwells and corners became meeting places.

A different kind of hunger was spreading in the Old Neighborhood. And not just in New Jersey. In Pough-keepsie, New York, and Allentown Pennsylvania. Birds carried word from abandoned warehouses in Ohio, where weeds grew wild and clusters of rustbelt travelers cultivated gardens of whatever would grow. Raised beds made of old tires, wood pallets turned to box springs, sleeping bags passing for bedding.

When the crows cavorted on telephone wires with their comrades, they were told of secret meetings in Gary, Indiana. Of feasts of plenty springing up in the forgotten corners of Albuquerque and Houston, Rutland Vermont, and Portland Oregon. Of people in hidden places offering tables of vegetables, rice, grains, and more to all who came.

Even the crows.

And whenever a gullible pigeon would butt into the conversation, asking why they hadn't heard such whispers or seen such displays of bounty, the crows would caw, pecking at the scrawny grey bird.

"You're vain," the crows were known to say. "You still hover around the parks uptown. The places with sulfurous bright green lawns, all cut down the same, and man-made lakes reeking of bleach. No wonder you're starving."

And the vain pigeon, of course, would raise his proud head and fly away, promising to visit the places of cracked pavement in search of such sights and of course food.

But they never would. Because pigeons are creatures of habit.

Yet they carry word of this gossip. These fables. And the cardinals and blue jays lining the trees in suburban orchards would hang on every word.

Pat Bernardoni was hungry, too. For days he brought machines to dig their teeth into the ground and pull roots from the earth. A feast that sent squirrels and chipmunks running for cover. An aged mole, having survived two hurricanes and a historic drought, was shredded limb from limb as the carnage continued.

The ground shook with an ominous warning that rattled all creatures for miles around. But their vision was limited.

Rather than abandoning their burrows and nests and resettling miles away, those who survived rebuilt where it was convenient. Amidst turmoil, they couldn't sense nor imagine.

Long before anyone else, the birds knew something was coming.

CHAPTER 63

Anniversary of Mallory's Death June 2023

Frank holds the remnants of a sandwich he scored from the bistro's dumpster, waving it into the darkness. The crow, eager eyes illuminated by one of the few working streetlights, swoops down and snatches it away.

"You're welcome," Frank speaks to the air in jest. Even in this early spring, the streets are vacant. It's been hours since tired feet pedaled home from the second shift on bicycles and harried parents exited the bus, tired children in one arm or trailing behind and bags of groceries slung over their shoulders.

In the months he's lived among the abandoned buildings near the port, Frank has grown used to the late-night sounds of fall and winter. But in spring, the rustling of squirrels and chatter of nocturnal birds and insects create a new chorus he hasn't gotten to know.

Whether winged or on paws, or skittering along the edges of walls in the dark, the creatures here have one thing in common. They're all hungry and there's never enough.

The flip phone Roxie gave him when he first joined the Possum Crew buzzes in his pocket. He takes a quick bite of what remains of the butt of his sandwich and then leaves the rest on the ground to be gobbled down by a thrifty raccoon or desperate rat.

Swallowing his half-chewed dinner, Frank brushes crumbs from his now sizeable beard and puts the phone to his ear, turning down an alley to take cover out of habit. No one is watching him tonight.

"Yeah," Frank begins, his voice hardly a whisper.

"We have the team together. You sure you want to do this?" A cigarette-cured voice asks him.

"Yeah. Of course. I'm ready."

"You don't have to," the voice tries again as if talking him out of the commitment that has been weeks in planning.

"I need to. I'm ready."

Frank makes a mental note of the directions Roxie gives him. The meeting place where others will be dressed from head to toe in black, spray paint ready. He hangs up the phone and looks over both shoulders.

As his eyes study the night, a loud clanging makes him jump. His head jerks to his left, following the direction of the noise. A cat strolls casually from behind a trash can now knocked to the ground. Frank lets out a breath he didn't know he was holding.

He glances side to side again before slipping between wooden boards loosened from the doorway they were intended to seal off to the world. The abandoned house was infiltrated long before Frank's time. This building isn't one of the apartments he occupies with Roxie and the others. Instead, it's used just for storage. No identifying information. Just stashes of clothing, water, and provisions.

Frank walks through the abandoned kitchen with its mid-20th century countertop and crumbled plaster tracked across the floor. Wires hang from the ceiling. No one has rigged the electricity here. There has been no need. He finds his way to the dry closet.

The door sticks at first and he has to pull to loosen its grip. The sound disturbs a rat who chitters angrily at him, running past his foot.

"Sorry," he whispers.

Inside the closet, he grabs an old backpack sprinkled with dust that has fallen in snowdrifts since its last use a few weeks ago. Frank swaps out his street clothes for black sweatpants, black socks and sneakers, and a black hoodie. A black balaclava and gloves finish off his outfit. He fishes around in the backpack with one hand and finds a heavy-duty flashlight and a can of spray paint. He won't be using the flashlight to find his way in the darkness, but no one has to know that.

Stuffing the supplies in his ample pockets, he thinks of Chili, then Kevin and Bread and the others from the cabin. He wonders how they are from time to time, but aside from seeing Chili across a sea of faces at an action in the winter- or at least he thought it was Chili, the face disappeared in the crowd before he could take a second glance- he's been out of contact.

Shoving his clothes into a dark corner of the closet, he remembers the adrenaline rush the first time he tagged a building. How green he had been then. The Possums are different from the people at the cabin. Back then, he had been naïve. Just a boy running away from his problems, stumbling in the dark.

Frank hardly recognizes the boy who comes to his mind through memory. He tries to forget.

He tucks his bushy, long hair into his hoody. Exiting the building through the same covered back door through which he entered, Frank heads toward the familiar intersection where he will meet the others.

A place he also has tried to forget since the last time he was here one year ago.

On the way, he passes a dumpster. He takes the card out of his phone, drops it to the ground, stomps on it, and then throws it away, before continuing on his way.

When he arrives, Frank can see three bodies covered in black clothing trying to blend in with the alley across from his father's storage building. The place that had once housed Mallory, her grandmother, and an elderly lady who was pleased as punch to receive a new electric wheelchair, courtesy of her neighbors.

The place where only weeks later, he watched police descend on protestors. The sidewalk where Mallory's blood spilled after police fired on the crowd is now buried, like Mallory, for all eternity. Her blood is washed over by blacktop that has long since dried and rests smoothly under a warehouse-like building. Row upon row of identical steel doors. Barbed wire fencing wraps around the sprawling building so that it looks like a prison. He can see security cameras pointed at various angles in the distance, just as Roxie described in the map she drew for the group.

In contrast to the neighboring apartment buildings, neglected by landlords whose rent checks finance their mansion by the coast in Maryland and North Carolina, the storage building seems an imposition. A giant's dirty footprint amid homes. Even more awkward, the grounds surrounding the storage building are marked by a stone sign that reads "Bernardoni Realty" and an assortment of bright pink and yellow flowers resting in manicured heaps of manure and set against a lawn that, according to little yellow flags, has recently been treated with pesticides.

Frank shakes his head. He feels his heart pound.

Don't think about it.

He reminds himself to stay in the moment. He can't lose control today. Not like he did last year. He'd barely known the crew at the cabin and leaving them had been hard enough. The Possum Crew is like his family. He can't fuck things up with them.

Frank turns his back on the building and creeps along the rows of apartments and multistory houses nearby, greeting his comrades with a wave.

They murmur to each other, reviewing plans in clipped, whispered phrases, wary of the surveillance equipment feet away at the gates. Frank tries to listen, but a louder sound interrupts the cluster of figures in black. A high-pitched hiss makes him wince and turn to a newly arrived comrade, finger to his lips, ready to chastise the interloper.

He turns in the direction of the intrusive sound piercing the quiet night only to find the street behind him empty. Lowering his eyes, a possum, one of several who has followed Frank for weeks, stares up at him.

The creature repeats herself.

"Are you ready for what's coming?" she hisses again.

"Why wouldn't I be?" he whispers back, aware now the others can't hear her. The security cameras won't register her words.

"Mistake. Go home. You're not ready." Her voice was shrill and high-pitched. He raises a finger to his ear, throbbing with the noise.

"Who is that guy talking to?" He hears one of the small crowd whispers to another figure standing nearby. He doesn't recognize the voice.

"Oh, that's Frank. He talks to animals. It's cool." He recognizes Janis responding and can now imagine their iridescent purple hair, shaved in patterns in an undercut, their friendly brown eyes, one brow pierced, beneath the mask and hoodie.

"Dr. Doolittle?" The original inquirer asks as if he's not standing nearby.

"Sort of," Janis responds.

"Put a pin in this for later, folx, we need to get ready." The third figure chimes in. Frank recognizes this voice as well. Marcus, the lead organizer for this action, motions toward an alley to their right. In the dim lighting, a silent parade of silhouettes walks toward them. All were concealed beneath different shades of black, some carrying backpacks, others with heavy nightsticks and flashlights resting against their shoulders, as if carrying weapons in a military march.

They close in for one final huddle. In the distance, Frank hears the possum hiss one last time.

"You're not ready. Mistake."

CHAPTER 64

By the time a dozen figures in black have arrived, Frank no longer thinks of the building that used to stand across the cracked street. He no longer hears the echo of laughing, singing, and encouragement to fill another plate from the ghosts of those who called the lot home only a year ago. He pushes the memory of Mallory's face from his mind, focusing instead on scanning his surroundings.

Like clockwork, a tall figure emerges from the crowd and approaches the building. Two others follow. He keeps his eyes fixed on the first figure, moving casually in the direction of the nearest security camera. He recognizes Roxie despite the anonymous black bloc. Sees her pull out her phone, on airplane mode for security, she pretends to read messages as she strolls up the block. He grips both hands in fists, feeling sweat beginning to trickle down his back. With one swift movement, Roxie aims something small at the camera. Within minutes, the camera lens begins to smoke. He shifts his eyes toward the far corners of the gate where others are doing the same, then glances back at Roxie.

Arm extended, she holds up three fingers toward the crowd gathered around him, waiting for the sign. She drops one finger, then lowers the other, then gestures with her hand, beckoning them forth. They advance toward the fence in continued silence. Frank follows, his shoulders back and head high and resolute. Today is the day they've been planning for weeks.

The sound of hands and feet rattling the chain link fence echoes in the dark. One body ascends and in a moment, the figure uses bolt cutters to cut away a section of razor wire, leaving an opening through which this figure can easily jump the fence. Two others repeat this process several feet away on both sides. Frank watches a petite person in front of him scale the fence before it is his turn. He climbs easily, hurling himself over the top of the fence and landing hard on his feet. The shock only stings the soles of his feet for a moment before he springs again into motion, running, with the others, toward the building.

Adrenaline surges through his body. His eyes are more alert. He hears his heart beating louder than the sound of boots and sneakers slapping against the pavement. Someone ahead of him hurls an object- a brick or a rock- over their head and before he can release the breath he's been holding, a window collapses, and splinters of glass cascade to the ground. Most of the shattered glass falls inside the building, but he raises an arm to block his face just in case. Several people rush into the building's office, ignoring jagged teeth of glass that frame the opening.

Frank's heart races. A flashing red light above the Axle alarm system signals their time is limited. He raises the can of red spray paint and goes to work. The fumes waken his sinuses, and he squints back tears, it's been months since he's gone to an action like this. His hand remains steady.

Stick to the plan.

He hears Roxie's words in his mind.

He finishes tagging one side of the wall and runs to the next.

"Cops!"

The shout breaks his concentration. He turns to see a figure in black running toward the building, arms waving.

"Get out, go! Get out through the back!" The shouting continues.

Too soon for it to be a response from the alarm. Someone snitched.

Frank's feet freeze to the ground. He turns his head looking as chaos ensues. Some are ignoring the warning. Inside the office, someone continually smashes a computer against a wall before taking a crowbar to what's left of another wall.

"Hey!" Roxie yells now. "Hey! Get out, around the back!"

Others grab the arms of comrades who continue spray painting the outside.

Frank wonders if it was a false alarm.

Is that guy fucking with us?

A siren in the distance tells him otherwise. Roxie pulls the figure from inside the office and leads them back out through the broken window and around the corner of the building, gesturing for them to follow others fleeing toward the back of the parking lot.

Frank runs to follow them. One after another, his comrades scale the back fence and launch themselves through an opening cut in the razor wire, escaping into the dark alley.

He throws his can of spray paint and flashlight over the fence, planning to retrieve them once he's on the other side. As he reaches to grab the fence with both hands, a scream followed by a thud stops him.

He turns to see one, then two sets of flashing lights as patrol cars approach the building. His gaze drops then, and he sees Roxie on the ground.

And blood gushes over the curb while police stand by with shields.

"No!" he closes his eyes, willing the scene to disappear. He opens his eyes again, returning his focus to Roxie, not Mallory, not bleeding, but hurt from tripping on debris on the ground.

"I got you," another voice whispers. Frank recognizes it as belonging to Jayton, who hovers over their hurt comrade, pulling her slowly to her feet.

"Stop! Put your hands where we can see them!" A voice calls out from the other side of the fence, through a bullhorn.

"Fuck!" Roxie whispers, staggering to her feet. "I'm too slow, you both get out of here!"

"No!" Frank whispers back, "I got this, you both run."

"What are you doing?" Jayton begins to ask, but Frank interrupts him.

"I got this. Fucking run."

Roxie says something in reply, but Frank can't hear it. He's already walking in the direction of the flashing lights.

"Put your hands where we can see them!" The officer repeats, impatient.

Frank walks steadily forward, and slowly, he lifts both hands. He walks several feet to the side, making sure the flashlight beam remains on him as the others get away.

"It's just me. I'm not armed." He yells back. The light is fixed on him now. As if he's on a stage. He squints his eyes, hands still above his head.

"I surrender!" he calls into the beam of light. He resists the urge to look back over his shoulder. Trusting instead that the rest of the group escaped.

"I surrender," he says again, this time his voice serene.

He feels hands on each raised arm, jerking him forward, slamming his hands behind his back. Feels the metal cuffs clench tight around each wrist.

"I surrender," He repeats as someone pulls the balaclava from his head, pulling a tuft of hair from the roots in the process.

The flashlight dances around his face once, then again, and another time, as if searching for something. Then he hears a familiar voice.

"Jesus fucking Christ. It's the Bernardoni kid."

CHAPTER 65

Narrator

You can't always believe what a possum tells you. This is not to disparage possum. They do a lot of good.

But they aren't much on confrontation.

They mean well, it's just that a creature whose defense involves playing dead isn't the best one to help face the Dark Night of the Soul, now are they?

Frank was most definitely prepared. Even if possum didn't realize it. Even if Frank didn't realize it.

CHAPTER 66

Frank

Officer Dimples removes the cuffs from Frank's wrists, yelling to another officer, "Call off the rest of the cars. We're not making any arrests until we talk to Pat Bernardoni."

"What the fuck?" an officer shouts back as others groan.

"Do what I said! Now!"

Frank isn't listening to them. He squints through the glare of flashing lights, focusing on a crow perched on the newly cut fence in the distance.

A bird caws a warning before flying off, leaving him to the sounds of police radios and the cursing and grumbling of officers surrounding him.

Dimples puts his hand on Frank's back, walking him slowly to a patrol car.

"We're going to get you home, don't worry," he tells Frank, "and we're going to find who is responsible for this."

CHAPTER 67

The house Frank grew up in is illuminated by early morning light when Dimples pulls the patrol car into the driveway. The officer spent the drive talking reassuring gibberish.

Frank remembers the story Chili taught him. The wealthy heiress and her kidnappers. He thinks this is the deduction the police made as well.

He sees his father standing in the doorway as Dimples puts the car in park. Something is different.

Pat Bernardoni, the man who had always loomed large and ominous in Frank's life, who, even on Christmas and birthdays had seemed an imposing figure to be feared and appeased, now looks like a mere mortal. The old man's eyes sag. Lines cut deep throughout his face. His mouth, a perpetual frown except for a smile he saved for the camera, weighted down in exaggerated sobriety.

He looks old. Frail. Weak. The power that seemed to emanate from his being for all of Frank's life, threatening to cut him down at any moment, drained. Leaving behind a shell of a man whose hair was now more salt than pepper.

"Mr. Bernardoni," Dimples rushes to explain himself, leaving Frank in the back of the patrol car, "we didn't find the people responsible, but we did find your son. As soon as I realized it was him I had him uncuffed. There won't be any arrest, sir, and I apologize for our hasty actions."

Frank sees it now, in Dimples' eyes, the fear and anticipation so familiar to him. He can tell the officer is hoping his excuse is acceptable to the man before him.

Pat Bernardoni looks at Frank for a moment, then returns his gaze, face set in a scowl, to the young officer standing in his driveway.

"Someone broke into my property, and when you got there, you found my son?" Pat Bernardoni asks, his voice betraying no hint of emotion.

"That's correct, sir."

"Then an arrest will be made."

"Yes, sir, as soon as we find the responsible party."

Bernardoni gestures toward the car, "it looks like you already did."

"Excuse me, sir?" Dimples blinks. Frank can tell the officer can't comprehend what is being asked of him let alone why.

"Arrest my son for criminal trespassing."

"But…" Dimples shakes his head in disbelief.

"He was trespassing. He committed a crime. Arrest him. Then bring him back here."

Dimples' mouth drops open. He stares at Bernardoni for a moment, before the older man turns his back, walks into the house, and closes the door in the officer's face.

CHAPTER 68

Chili

The insides of a flying bug smear the windshield of the van as Chili pulls into the driveway. They turn on the windshield wipers and pull the lever. Instead of the needed splash of windshield wiper fluid, a pitiful spout of liquid mixes with the insect's guts, creating a grey watercolor skyscape across their visual field. They turn the keys, putting a stop to the carnage and the whining that accompanied the tired wipers.

Chili is also tired.

No sooner did I tell you… and now this.

They push the creaking van door open, hauling out from the driver's seat. It had been a relief to see the kid, Frank, not so long ago. Chili was sure it had been him. Truth be told, it would have been nice to catch up and see how he was doing, but it seemed as soon as the young man's eyes caught theirs, Chili had been pulled away by the Safety Team to handle some logistics at the protest.

The kid looked good. Hair shaggier, growing a beard, not quite like Bread's, but then again, not many could boast that accomplishment. Chili runs fingers through the hair growing from their own chin at the thought.

Up ahead, the door swings open. Kevin waves them in, standing with what looks like a glass of iced tea in his hand.

"Looking forward to the weekend?" the younger man smiles.

Chili's heart sinks.

Bread sits on the couch, lighting a bong. Kevin is already making jokes with the others. Everyone seems to be in a good mood.

And that is how Chili knows they haven't gotten the news.

They ease into a metal folding chair, slipping both sandals off and looking down at their toes for a moment before speaking the words that will change the mood in the room.

"Have you heard about Frank?"

The others freeze. The kid's name only came up a handful of times since the fall, when he returned to the city. Other business to tend to, and perhaps some degree of guilt. Whether he should have had a second chance or not, Chili took comfort in the thought that Frank connected with Roxie's crew.

I wouldn't have told you, otherwise. If I didn't think he was safe.

Chili shakes the thought away. They can send that message later.

"What happened to Frank?" Bread scoots forward to the edge of the couch. It creaks as Kevin drops down beside him, leaning on both elbows.

"There was an action. His dad's place."

"Jesus fucking Christ," Miles begins, shaking their head.

"No, it's not what you think." Chili continues, "word is they were sold out from someone on the inside. Police showed up too soon for it to just be the alarm."

"Who else got arrested?" Kevin asks.

"Just Frank. I heard it from Roxie. She fell. Trying to escape. Frank went to distract the cops, basically handed himself over to buy the others time to get away."

Chili can't resist looking Miles in the eyes as they say this. Miles drops their gaze and fidgets with a loose thread on their shirt.

"So, what happened? His dad is loaded. So, he should be okay, right?" Bread asks.

"Not necessarily."

They've been tracking people like Pat Bernardoni for some time. They understand him as a businessman, but not as a person. Only Chili has that insight.

CHAPTER 69

Jonathan

Jonathan wakes to the sound of pounding on his bedroom door. His head throbs. The Screwdrivers tasted good last night. But after a while, he'd forgotten to add the orange juice, and this morning the inside of his mouth is coated with sour film.

"Jonathan!" his mother's voice barrels through his throbbing head.

"Just a minute," he groans into his pillow, kicking a foot on the bed. "Fuck," he whispers as the knocking continues.

She doesn't wait for him to open the door but has also given up on barging in. "Jonathan, I gotta go to work, you're going to be late if you don't get your ass moving, so get out of bed, this is the last time I'm going to come to wake you."

He can tell by the fading sound of her voice that she's heading back down the stairs. Hears her grumbling something about him being fucking drunk already, like his no-good sonofabitch father.

She leaves the house, closing the front door hard enough to rattle the floor beneath his bed. Turning away from the morning sun sneaking through his bedroom window, Jonathan forces himself to stand, hand over his eyes.

Bella follows him to the bathroom, sitting at his feet like a sentinel as an arc of urine springs through the air and lands, mostly, in the toilet.

With one eye open, he reaches into the medicine cabinet, fumbling for something to make the headache better. He should wash his hands. But what's the point? He may go to work today. He may not. He may lose his job today. He may tell his boss to eat an entire bag of dicks. He may sit at home and watch cartoons.

"Live in the moment, right Bel?"

The dog lowers her face, shoulders hunched.

"Crap, Bel, don't do that. You look at me like I'm a douche or something."

As if to confirm this, Bella maintains her focus on him lifting one eyebrow, then the other. She tilts her head to the side slightly and whimpers.

"Sorry, Bel. I know you're hungry. Let's go get something to eat."

Bracing his still-sensitive eyes with one hand, he shuffles through the hall and down the stairs, the dog trailing close behind him.

He starts to reach for a can of dog food from the pantry, then reconsiders.

"You don't want to eat that slop, do you?" he asks.

Bella looks at him, then turns toward the fridge. He follows her gaze.

"Right. Fuck that shit. Let's have leftover pizza. And spray cheese. Right out of the can."

He should at least microwave the pizza. If not for himself, then for Bella's sake. But he doesn't.

Jonathan slinks into the couch, springs bounce beneath him, not quite stabbing through the cushions, but not far off. Bella jumps onto the couch and tries to push the cold pizza away, edging closer to his lap, wanting his full attention.

He shifts to the side, biting into a slice of pizza as chunks of pepperoni fall to his lap.

"What's the matter, Bel? You don't even want to share with me?" he asks when she doesn't move to gobble the tumbling bits of leftover dinner.

"Okay, guess I have to clean it up then." He reclaims a fallen piece of food, stares momentarily at a piece of fur now stuck to it, and pops it in his mouth anyway.

Bella starts whimpering.

"Here, have some, don't let me have all the fun," he hands her a slice of pizza. She turns her snout away, rejecting the gift.

"Well, what then?"
Bella paws at his arm, groaning and whining.

"What is it?"

She hoists her front paws onto the back of the couch. He turns to follow her gaze out the window, squinting.

"No one out there, Bel."

She barks.

"Here, have some pizza." He holds a smaller slice of crust out to her. She jumps to the floor and begins circling around the room, barking, and whimpering.

"What is it? What's wrong?"

She sits at his feet, her eyes pleading with him to solve some unspoken woe.

"I don't know what you want, Bel."

Jonathan's eyes begin to well up with tears. He takes another bite of pizza. It feels dry in his mouth. He forces it down, almost choking.

She starts pacing again, then howling in a way he's never heard.

"Jesus, Bel, what is it? What's wrong?"

And I actually expect her to answer, he thinks. I've lost my fucking mind.

"I'm sorry, Bel. Sorry your life with me is so shitty. Sorry, I don't know how to understand you. Sorry for everything, Bel."

He wants another drink.

Shuffling to the kitchen, Bella runs for the front door and begins scratching.

"What? You gotta go out? You gotta shit or something? Well, okay. Gimme a second, okay?" If the day is going to start, and it looks like it is, he can't keep drinking. He grabs a vitamin drink from the door of the fridge and chugs it until he feels like vomiting.

Please make me feel like a human so I can make it through this fucking day.

Jonathan hasn't brushed his hair or his teeth. He hasn't showered today or yesterday. He can't smell his own sweat yet. When he does, that's when he'll make himself shower. Maybe tomorrow. Or the next day. He opens the door, expecting Bella to relieve herself on the front lawn and return.

Instead, she starts trotting down the block.

"Fuck, Bel, wait!"

Jonathan follows.

PART 4 THE HOUSE OF SELF-UNDOING

CHAPTER 70

Frank

Frank's room has never felt so much like a prison. He was released from jail after forty-eight hours. Officer Dimples insisted on driving him home, Frank thought he seemed guilty for going through with the arrest his father demanded.

When he returned home, his father played happy to see him. But as soon as Dimples was gone, his father's tone changed.

"I'm going to schedule an interview with the news. You're going to recant your actions and help me find the people responsible for kidnapping you!"

"I wasn't kidnapped!" Frank walked up the stairs, turning his back on his father, who began ranting.

"You'll do what I say, young man, or I'll make your life miserable!"

It already is, Frank thought but ignored his father. He shut himself in his room where he now paces, trying to figure out what to do.

But Frank can't think. If he returns to the neighborhoods with the Possum Crew, he could lead the police to them, now that his father would be on his trail. It was too risky, at least for now. His thoughts jump from Roxie to the police to his father's lecturing, "First thing, get rid of that beard, you look like a street person! You're getting a haircut…" to his mother's tears.

"Thank God you're home! I thought you were dead!"

Yet even in his mother's relief, he thinks now, there had been little on her face that resembled happiness. Just a weary smile made less haggard by the sight of him.

His room was preserved like a shrine. He heard about people doing this when their family members or kids died or went missing, but the effect remains eerie. A slight coating of dust on the top of his dresser, his mirror and night table, and the game console on a stand in the corner is all that has been added. He feels like a stranger lying on a bed amidst a museum display, a temple to a boy who no longer exists.

There is one thing missing.

His eyes fix on a rawhide bone tangled in dirty clothes on the floor. The Chorus told him Bella was still alive. But his parents had said nothing, and she's nowhere to be found. If she survived the police, his father probably dumped her on the side of a road somewhere. Or worse.

Frank closes his eyes tight.

His stomach rumbles, but food doesn't interest him. He doesn't want to open his eyes to crisp, professionally painted walls with perfect trim around the windows. He doesn't want to sit inside, breathing conditioned air. He doesn't want meals prepared by… what had her name even been? Had he really been served by a maid once?

And had he ever thanked her, even one time?

He shakes his head, ridding himself of the memory of Francesco.

The television has been disconnected, his father said, "On doctor's orders to not upset you."

Frank hadn't had to wonder what kind of doctor. He doesn't care about missing shows but wants to check the news. To see what is being broadcast about the action at his father's building.

In the distance, a clamoring of voices, heavy breathing, and feet pounding on the ground in a steady run draw him from his thoughts. He hops out of bed and onto his feet, running for the window facing the street in front of the house.

The smaller roof over the porch blocks his view, but he can hear knocking escalating into desperate pounding on the door, along with scratching and then a familiar howl.

CHAPTER 71

Frank throws open the front door. The smell of a sour hangover forces him to choke, before he can process the image of the man standing before him, he's knocked to the ground by a brown, furry mass.

"Bella!" He tries to say her name out loud, but her tongue is lapping up his beard, inching into his nostrils, sweeping the inner corners of his eyes. Her paws, heavy on his shoulders, keep him pinned to the ground.

Tears escape his eyes and the dog licks at the salty streaks, stopping only to shove her nose into the side of his neck.

He laughs through tears, hugs her tight, and eventually regains his balance, leaning up on his hands. He turns his face back to the man standing in his doorway.

Frank thought he looked bedraggled after his time living rough. But the sight of his once best friend, Jonathan, sends a stabbing through his heart.

"What the fuck happened to you?" Frank asks, rising to his feet as Bella hops side to side, nudging his legs and pawing at him.

Jonathan blinks at him with red eyes. Not the red of tears, Frank thinks, or not only tears.

"What happened to me?" Jonathan repeats, seething. "How about what the fuck happened to you?"

And now it's the man who lunges for him. Jonathan's fist lands on Frank's shoulder, a poorly aimed blow with no force behind it. Jonathan hits him again and slaps his face. Frank lifts both hands, catching his friend's wrists. Jonathan continues to swing, but can't land a blow.

"You sonofabitch! You fucking left me here! With nothing! What the fuck?"

Frank stands his ground, Bella barking and whimpering behind him until Jonathan wears himself out and collapses into his arms. He hugs his friend, who reeks of sweat and booze.

"I'm sorry," Frank whispers to his friend, whose heavy sobs drown out the sound of his voice.

When Frank is finished relaying the story, in as much detail as he safely can, it feels like he's been talking for an eternity.

Jonathan, who had been quiet for the duration, sitting on his bed beside Bella, now stares at him. The scene is surreal. Like the old days. His best friend. His dog. He's home.

But this illusion is shattered when Jonathan finally responds.

"You're out of your fucking mind."

"Jonathan," he begins, but Jonathan's bellowing voice cuts him off.

"No! It's bad enough you fucking abandon me here and go off and do all this crazy shit but you fucking lie to my face about it?"

"I'm telling the truth."

"What? That God talks to you? Or fucking trees? Or animals? Or what? Dude, you always do this to me!"

"Do what to you?" Frank can't hide the shock. His voice cracks.

"You always have to make yourself better than me. At school, with girls, and now this? Really dude?"

"That's not what I'm doing. I'm not better than you, in fact, I'm a fucking asshole. Or I was. But I'm trying to be better."

"So, now you're better than me because you smash windows and spray-paint buildings but it's okay because God told you to? You've been all over the news, you know? You're hurting your father!"

"Since when do you care about my father's reputation?" Frank scoffs.

"Your dad does a lot of good for a lot of people!" Jonathan's nostrils flare with anger, he launches himself from the bed, hands clenched in fists. Bella watches him, hunching low, licking her lips in anxiety.

Frank steps back, squinting, trying to process the words coming from his friend. "What? You never liked my dad."

"That's not true!" Jonathan yells back, "I listened to you moan and bitch about what a bad guy your dad is, it's all you ever did. But you know what? Your dad is there for you!"

Jonathan pounds his fists onto his thighs as he yells this.

"Do you even realize that? All that time I listened to you bitch because your dad is strict? Dude, I don't have a fucking dad at all! So yeah, you fucking abandoned me because you're a spoiled, selfish bastard, and you're ruining your family and too selfish to even care. I'm done with you, Francesco!"

"It's Frank, and fuck you! Fuck off and run to my dad if you're that much of a pussy!" Frank hears the words, but it's too late.

His best friend's face has gone from pale to grey, then maroon. He can tell Jonathan is fighting tears. Before he can respond, Jonathan slams the bedroom door behind him. Frank hears him stomping down the stairs, hears the front door to the house slam. Feels the floor under his feet vibrate.

Bella looks at him, whimpers then looks to the bedroom door and back to Frank. She lifts one sad eyelid, then the other.

"I know. It's ok. He needs you now." Frank tells her.

She climbs down from the bed and runs to him. Climbing up his leg with her front paws, she stretches, pushing into him, then extends her face forward, licking her lips. He leans down for a kiss.

Happy you're back.

He knows she isn't just referring to his return home. Memories return in foggy waves. Looking into her eyes, he knows now the dream of a time when he talked to his dog was real.

"I'm back, Bella. And I know you have a job to do." He opens the door and they walk in silence down the stairs. He opens the front door and watches as she bounds down the steps.

She turns back once to say, "I love you," and then continues in the direction of Jonathan's house.

CHAPTER 72

Pat Bernardoni

Pat Bernardoni deletes another voicemail from yet another reporter. "Fucking vultures, that's how many today?"

Pat Bernardoni wanted the news involved, but only so his son could set things right and save his reputation. Instead, they were swarming around, prying and calling him all hours of the day.

He didn't know his mailbox was full until he heard from his lawyer, who had been trying to get through to him about the closing on a new property. After deleting a dozen messages, with more to go, he returns to the keypad and punches in the number for the police.

"This is Pat Bernardoni. I want my son arrested."

"Has he committed a crime?" The man on the other end of the phone asks.

"Don't get cute with me!"

"Sir, what crime has he committed?" the officer asks.

"I already filed a report. He was caught by your police department vandalizing my building. Frank Bernardoni. It's been all over the press and I know it was someone from your office that leaked it!"

"Sir, please calm down…"

"Don't fucking tell me to calm down!" Bernardoni screams. His wife tiptoes into the dining room, takes a glance at him, and then retreats toward the stairs.

Bernardoni lowers his voice and tries again, in a near whine, "You just can't understand what it's like. My son has always been troubled. Because of him, his sister left home, and we haven't heard from her in years. And I'm a prominent businessman. I give to the community. I've received awards for my charitable work. And here he is trying to ruin all I've worked for…"

"Sir, I understand, but if you've already filed charges, then a court date is pending. Are there new charges?"

"What? No, I want him arrested. He committed a crime. I want him in jail. All these reporters are calling my phone, I'm missing business calls…"

"Sir, I'm sorry, but that is not a crime."

"Can you at least get these reporters to leave me alone?"

"I'm sorry, as long as they are only calling you it is not a crime."

The officer begins to speak again, but Bernardoni doesn't wait for him. He pounds his finger against the red button disconnecting the call.

His chest heaves with deep breaths as he paces the floor. One hand on the back of a chair to steady himself, Bernardoni waits for a moment before storming up the stairs toward Frank's room, almost shoving his wife out of the way.

He stops partway up the stairs, a new idea occurring to him. Racing back down to the living room, Pat Bernardoni ignores his wife's pleading voice- what's wrong with you?- and shuffles through the papers on his desk.

He finds a business card and ignores his wife, who is now hovering behind him, looking over his shoulder.

"Pat, no! What are you doing?" she shrieks.

He raises a hand and slaps her, hard enough to knock her back a few steps.

He dials the number on the card.

CHAPTER 73

Jonathan

In the hours after Jonathan fled his room in anger, Bella following behind him, the sun had grown sweltering. Frank felt like an intruder inside his childhood room. The laptop, games, and clothes he outgrew all relics in a museum for him to see but not touch.

I can't stay here.

His heartbeat quickening, he felt the walls closing in. Saw himself rise from the bed, bang on the window, begging for escape.

His vision hazy, the room distorting in pre-syncopal waves, then clear again. There is a banging on the window. It is not him. Frozen in place on the bed still, Frank feels himself return to his body, lightheaded and dazed.

The banging resumes. The tapping of a beak, not the banging of a fist.

He rises from the bed, in his body, not just his mind, and approaches the window, feeling the heat coming in from outside. A creature on the other side a pigeon, iridescent neck, and plump grey body. Frenetic tapping of its beak.

He opens the window, then the screen.

You'll let the air out, he hears his father's voice scolding in the back of his mind.

Frank furrows his brows, feels pressure on his forehead, then relaxes. Don't try so hard, he reminds himself. Let it come to you.

The pigeon flaps its wings close to his face, looking right at him, before landing on his dresser. Head bobbing, he hears the bird.

They're coming for you.

"Who? Where should I go? What should I do?" Frank asks aloud.

They're coming for you, the pigeon repeats, head bobbing in cadence with the words filling the room, *and you go, you go, you go. Where they take you, you go. You have work to do, where they take you. You go.*

Frank lowers his eyes for a moment, and when he returns his gaze to the direction of his dresser, the bird is gone.

When his father bursts through the door moments later, he ignores the open window. He doesn't remind Frank about the electric bill or the air conditioning.

Frank regards his father with a stiff spine. No longer cowering in the shadow of the older man standing in the doorway. He stands calm, accepting. His eyes are soft.

He sees the lines etched on his father's face, heavy and deep. The bend of his disapproving mouth. The fury in his eyes. He feels a fever of anger emanating from his father's body.

Pat Bernardoni, fists clenched at his sides, jaw set, shouting words Frank doesn't hear.

I am you.

The Chorus whispers louder than his father's bellowing. Frank can barely hear words forming. He smiles. His father's face is the shade of grape juice, his jugular vein looks ready to explode.

"You're going to obey! You're coming with your mother and I and you'll obey, Francesco, or you're out of the will! Disowned! Out on the street!"

Frank finds this amusing. He was already on the street, and happier there. He wants to throw his head back and laugh, but a refreshing peace has settled over him.

Arguing is too strenuous, he realizes, slinking down onto the bed. He stares at his father who seems more perplexed by his silence.

"They're coming! They're going to be here soon! Get ready." His father repeats the words and Frank realizes he doesn't know what he's getting ready for. His father finally leaves him alone, slamming his bedroom door as he stomps his feet down each stairstep.

Frank turns his head, and sees his reflection in the mirror over his dresser. His beard is long and shaggy. He's never grown it so full. He pulls at the ends of the coarse hairs. His hair stretches far past his shoulders. All this time he knew it was getting longer, but had no reason to find his reflection in a mirror. His eyes look tired, years older than his age.

He smiles. Whoever is coming must be important. His father is heated. Anxious. Up to one of his schemes and counting on Frank to look his best and behave.

They're coming for you.

The words echo in his mind as Frank tosses his t-shirt on the floor in exchange for a crisp, ironed suit shirt hanging in his closet. He puts it on and buttons the front, concealing the tattoo he acquired living rough. The shirt sags on his frame. He's far from emaciated but has lost the little bit of padding that used to bulk up his school uniforms.

He watches as his reflection slides out of shorts and into khaki pants, tightening his old belt two notches. His father will be pleased, he smiles.

Something- someone- is coming. And he'll be ready.

CHAPTER 74

Frank

Moments later, a sharp rap on his bedroom door brings Frank back from a daydream of wolves, brilliant sunshine, and glistening water.

His father doesn't wait for him to respond before pushing the door open. He looks surprised to see Frank waiting for him, dressed to receive company. Pat Bernardoni looks his son up and down and scowls as his eyes meet Frank's.

"That hair! You look like a caveman!"

Frank doesn't respond.

Pat Bernardoni disappears for a moment, returning with something strong and Old Spice-smelling between his hands which he rubs together. Frank stands still, staring blankly at the wall as his father covers his long hair in the oily, smelly stuff. A gel or mousse meant to tame his mane.

I won't be tamed, Frank thinks, but he lets his father think he's won.

CHAPTER 75

Pat Bernardoni

He sizes up his son, deciding the younger man looks less like a derelict- slightly- with the flyaway hairs slicked back. Doesn't change the ponytail or the redneck beard.

Disgusting.

Then again, this could work to his advantage. Everything always did. Francesco isn't smiling anymore, Bernardoni notices. Just staring at the wall, like a fool. At least he put on some decent clothes.

"Come on, Chet is on his way."

Bernardoni turns his back on his son, heading down the stairs. He's ready to threaten to knock the young man down the stairs if he doesn't obey, but there is no need. He hears Francesco shuffling behind him.

"Is this really necessary?" his wife asked when he told her Chet was coming with a camera crew.

"He owes me a favor. I got him that job at WAJX."

"That's not the point, this is personal, Pat, it's our son!"

"It's my reputation!" he snapped.

She locked herself in her room, refusing to be part of the press conference. Just as well. Liable to run her mouth and make things worse. She always babied Francesco. No wonder he turned out like this.

It would be just the two of them. A last-ditch effort to turn things around. Pat hears something rustle behind him and turns to see Francesco sitting on the couch.

"Not so fast, out on the steps." He motions toward the front door. Francesco doesn't talk back, to his father's surprise. He stands and follows him.

Pat thinks it's about time. This will be quick, painless, and he can get back to business as usual once he deals with his son.

CHAPTER 76

Chet Brewster was on his way to his granddaughter's dance recital when Bernardoni called.

Dammit.

"Chet, what is it?" his wife, Matilda, asked.

"I gotta take this," he pulled the car over despite her protests and answered the phone.

His wife was stony and silent when he dropped her off at the dance school and broke the news.

"I can't come in. Tell Bethany I'm sorry. I have to go to a press conference."

His wife stood outside the car, hand on her hip, and scoffed, "Who called a press conference and you have to miss your granddaughter's recital? The president?"

Chet would have told the president to fuck off, he thinks, as his hands grip the steering wheel. But he doesn't have the luxury of telling Pat Bernardoni.

"We've had a lot of deals." Bernardoni reminded him, needlessly.

"I know we do, but…"

"And some of those deals would not look good for you if word were to get out."

Sonofabitch!

He slams his hands on the wheel, acid churning in his stomach. He hates himself for being weak. For giving in.

Again. He sees the WAJX van up ahead, already parking in front of the sprawling Bernardoni estate.

He heard about Francesco through the rumor mill. Chet recalls as he pulls in behind the van. He checks the rearview mirror for any stray pieces of food in his teeth before emerging from the car.

His son had run away. Or was he kidnapped? He can't recall. Chet wouldn't blame Francesco for running away if that was the case.

But his kid was home now, and the old man was throwing a press conference because that's the kind of thing Pat Bernardoni does. Chet grabs his notebook, recorder, and a pack of batteries from the passenger seat in the car.

The last thing he sees on his phone is a text from Matilda, "Bethany is heartbroken… asshole!"

He shoves the phone in the glove box, slams the car door shut, and turns to meet his camera crew.

Chapter 77

Frank

They're here! They're here! They're here!
The crows call out as they circle ahead.

Frank remains stoic, watching the birds. He ignores the camera crew assembling on his father's front lawn. His father greets a man he vaguely recognizes. Chet. He's been over for dinner a few times. After dinner, Chet and his father had retreated to his father's home office for drinks and to "wheel and deal" as his father would joke.

Chet isn't loosened by wine and a three-course meal today. He looks frazzled, and something else.

Angry.

Frank sees his anger. Sees his camera crew, a young person, indifferent to the family drama they will soon capture for posterity. Another running frantically to and from the van, wires dragging behind him.

Another van pulls up, and another. Were Frank paying attention, he would recognize the names of local newspapers, radio stations, and television news. The reporters gather around, setting up recording devices and microphone stands at the bottom of the steps.

"Test," a young woman speaks into a microphone, tapping it, and replacing it in the stand. A man carrying a camera hovers behind her.

Lenses zoom in and out, focusing on the Bernardoni house and garden, the velvety-trimmed lawn, and the men standing on the steps. One as finely manicured as the grass, wearing an Italian silk tie. The other as wild as the woods beyond this development, not so much wearing a button-down shirt as restrained by it. Eyes as vacant and dreamy as the older man's are intense and determined.

"Test," another voice adds.

"Set that up over there," a reporter instructs their crew.

"I need a triple-A battery…"

"Okay, we're all set…"

The birds cease their circling and cling to tree branches, watching him from above.

His father, who had a moment ago stood dictating instructions to the assembled reporters, resumes his place beside Frank on the broad steps in front of the house. A boom microphone hovers before them, intrusive and probing.

"Do the right fucking thing," Bernardoni hisses to his son as the cameras again focus on them. Chet, who has been given the role of lead interviewer, tests a large microphone with the label WAJX and then begins.

"I'm here at the home of local businessman and philanthropist Pat Bernardoni who, after over a year of grief and anxiety, has finally been reunited with his son."

Chet turns to Bernardoni, "Can you tell us how you and Mrs. Bernardoni are feeling to finally have Francesco home?"

Pat Bernardoni smiles for the camera. He looks like a child visiting a mall Santa, Frank thinks.

"We are just overwhelmed with joy and so many feelings. My wife wanted to be here, but she has been so overwhelmed with emotion, the trauma of Francesco's abduction…"

"So, Francesco, you confirm you were abducted..." Chet begins to ask when Bernardoni nearly grabs the microphone from his hand.

"Yes, yes, he was abducted. It's very traumatic, and we want to be clear, whatever behavior my son," he puts a hand on Frank's shoulder as he says this and squeezes, "whatever my son has done in the duration or recently, these actions were not his doing. He was forced by a mob of violent terrorists and the police are currently looking for the people who did this."

Solemn-faced reporters rush to scribble every word on notepads. A man with glasses and a partially shaved head leans closer, his recorder extended, monitoring the volume to ensure he captures every word.

Chet turns to Frank, holding the microphone in front of the younger man's face, "and Francesco, how are you feeling to be home? And what can you tell us about who is responsible and what happened to you?"

Frank smiles, but not for the cameras. His eyes are on the birds, lining the tree limbs. Had Chet thought to turn around, he would have no doubt pointed in awe- or fear- and the crowd would have witnessed the scene. There were several dozen now. Crows. Pigeons. Cardinals. Blue Jays.

"Francesco?" Chet prompts again.

Frank blinks, looking at the older man for the first time. "Frank."

"Frank," Chet repeats.

"It's Francesco," Bernardoni pulls on his son's shoulder, his hand there as if to restrain the younger man. His voice barely concealing impatience.

"Frank, from Jersey." The young man repeats.

From the periphery of the front yard, behind the huddled crowd of reporters, squirrels chase each other. They stop one at a time to witness the spectacle.

"Frank, glad you're home safe, can you tell us who is responsible for this and what happened?"

Frank answers; his voice calm. As if placing a lunch order. "I am responsible. You are responsible. We are responsible."

"Excuse me?" Shock falls over Chet's face. Frank doesn't notice the confused glances exchanged through the crowd in front of him.

He hears his father mumble something but ignores him and continues. "You want to know what happened to me? I will tell you. I was led into the woods, compelled only by the call of wolves and the magic of the Moon, my sister."

Frank doesn't recognize the words he speaks. He feels lighter and more expansive as if he no longer just hears the Chorus but speaks their words. He begins to panic, then feels his muscles constrict.

No. The birds remind him. *You have work to do.*

He closes his eyes, opens his mouth, hesitates, and then speaks again.

"I was found by strangers, who welcomed me, by animals who spoke to me, by myself, who returned me and repaired me."

"Clearly," Bernardoni manages to grab the microphone now, "my son has been traumatized and he is very disturbed. I thought he was in a better frame of mind, but as you can tell by his appearance, he is still troubled by his abduction."

Chet gently retrieves the microphone from Bernardoni's hand and tries to salvage what could possibly be left of this press conference from Hell.

"Francesco- Frank, your father is clearly very worried about you...."

"I have no father," Frank observes casually.

"I beg your pardon?" Chet takes a step back, trying to make sense and wondering if Bernardoni has propped up a psychotic young man as some type of stunt.

"Nonsense! Stop sputtering nonsense! You are Francesco Bernardoni!" Pat Bernardoni interrupts, his voice escalating.

Pages turn as reporters jot notes, their brows furrowed in confusion, some smirking, others concealing excitement, anticipating the headlines to come.

Frank's soft voice interrupts the older man, "Up until now, I have called Pat Bernardoni father, but now I am a child only of the Earth. I am the servant of the Earth and beyond this I am fatherless."

Chet's face is frozen in a stunned expression. The birds, squirrels, and a few straggling pedestrians who stopped in curiosity stare silent, like human-sized suburban lawn ornaments.

Frank feels himself in a different kind of trance. He continues, "For there are no gods and no masters. Pat Bernardoni, and all like him, will receive what they have earned. All that he has earned will be delivered to him."

Frank's hands move to tear at his shirt. "Even the clothes that were his," the young man's voice now elevated in a frenzied passion, "he shall have!"

Someone gasps. Frank tears the shirt in two and throws it to the ground. His father, Chet, and all the major news networks assembled on the lawn have only a moment to register the sight of the bright red A tattooed across his chest, enclosed in a circle, the symbol for Anarchy, before the young man unbuckles his belt and pushes the khakis to the ground as well. A horrified scream from one of the onlookers, a reporter drops pen and notebook, another shakes her head, smiling, a flurry of gasps and pens scribbling are eclipsed by Pat Bernardoni screaming "Turn these goddamn cameras off!"

Frank stands completely nude, unmoving now.

Cool air consecrating all the parts of his body heretofore hidden.

He watches the birds. They stare down at him. Brother Sun, he thinks, before thinking of Chili and correcting himself, Comrade Sun. Warm rays encircle his body.

His father screams at Chet, but the old man's words are indecipherable. The cameras stay locked on Frank from Jersey, in the nude, Pat Bernardoni rants frantically around him.

Frank steps one foot, then the other, out of his shoes and pants. He walks off, eyes on the sky, following the birds.

The cameras turn to follow him. Reporters call out questions that go unanswered.

"Are you part of an environmentalist group?"

"Was it a cult?"

"What did you mean by…"

A Blue Jay launches from the tree passing over the crowd, leaving thick, pasty droppings on the boom microphone.

Frank keeps walking. He doesn't hear the commotion. Doesn't hear the laughter as reporters contemplate whether Blue Jay shit is good luck or only Pigeon shit. Doesn't hear Pat Bernardoni screaming at Chet.

He doesn't hear the sirens.

When he is tackled to the ground by seven officers, running from numerous cars, he is too elated to feel the pain.

Doesn't feel the blood trickle from a wound on the side of his head.

Hardly notices when Comrade Sun disappears, leaving him wrapped in a blanket of darkness.

CHAPTER 78

Frank's roots stretch deep into the soil. He feels the darkness, smells the rain saturating dirt, tastes minerals. The darkness refreshes him after so much sunlight.

Earthworms glide along his roots, their bodies form tunnels allowing more water to quench his thirst. He is growing.

Sister Moon shines overhead, then flickers. Voices crowd his solitude.

"He has a history," one echoes, "runs in the family."

A shadow blocks Sister Moon now, she flickers again.

The voices echo through worm tunnels but another voice is closer.

The Earth is Our Mother, we shall not want....

He smiles and stretches roots in all directions, drinking heartily.

"Self-harm. That tattoo, self-inflicted." The voice echoes. "Francesco..."

He recognizes it now. Pat Bernardoni's voice. Sad man. Going on about someone who no longer exists.

You have to open your eyes now...

The Chorus instructs him. The words vibrate through the ground, in the sky.

Frank's eyes remain closed. He's savoring the darkness.

Look at me.

He smiles at Sister Moon. Her glow intensifies.

The whiteness stabs deep in his head, behind his eyes, he tries to close them but it's too late. The whiteness expands, it fills the room.

He's not outside. The orb above his head, a fluorescent light, coating the hospital room in perturbing brightness.

Pat Bernardoni stands near the door, back to him, talking to a man Frank thinks is a doctor. Bernardoni's hands wave in animated gestures, his voice like corn syrup.

"We've just been beside ourselves, we tried our best to take care of him at home," Bernardoni pleads with the doctor, "we have no choice but to commit him. My lawyer is ready to look at the paperwork when you have it ready."

The doctor looks over Bernardoni's shoulder, looking Frank in the eyes. "I see you're awake." The lanky man with a ring of grey hair surrounding a bald head.

"May I meet with Francesco alone, Mr. Bernardoni?" the doctor asks.

"Dr. Stanley, I insist on observing. My son is a dangerous man. You're not safe alone with him." His father lies and Frank understands.

"Mr. Bernardoni, we have a full professional staff prepared to handle people who have dangerous outbursts, I can bring in some techs for backup but I assure you we are capable of...."

"My son needs me!" Bernardoni responds, a theatric display of fatherly sentimentality.

Dr. Stanley steps back through the door, into a hallway, and returns a moment later with three young people in scrubs. He nudges past Bernardoni and enters the room. "Please excuse us," he repeats.

Bernardoni doesn't move. "He's my son! I have a right to stay here."

"Very well," Dr. Stanley caves, you can remain here for the initial interview, but we will need to speak to your son privately before admitting him."

Admitting him? Frank tries to remember what happened before Sister Moon lured him here. Is he sick? He thinks hard. His head hurts. He raises a hand to touch the corner of his forehead and feels a ridge of crusted blood.

I fell. He begins forming a memory.

Was pushed. The memory is clear now. A press conference. They all came to bear witness to his rebirth. He shed his skin and denounced his father and followed the birds.

You have work to do.

He understands. He's not sick. He just refuses to obey.

"Your father is worried about you."

Frank watches the man, his face placid. Dr. Stanley's eyes pass over Frank as if looking for clues. Frank returns his gaze, betraying nothing. Feeling no reaction. Just observing.

The doctor stammers then continue, "I understand you disappeared for a while. And you got involved in some, um, dangerous behaviors?"

Frank remains silent, watchful.

"Francesco," the doctor begins again, but Pat Bernardoni interrupts.

"He's playing one of his games. My son is a danger to himself and others. He's been associating with violent criminals and he threatened my life and his mother's life just this morning!"

Frank blinks at the audacity of the lie. Dr. Stanley steps back, eyes wide.

"You lie." Frank calmly asserts, staring at Bernardoni.

"Young man, your father is concerned about you." Dr. Stanley's voice is patronizing. Frank tries to interrupt, but the older man lifts a hand to silence him.

"Tell me about these thoughts about hurting your father. You're not in trouble. I want to help."

Frank opens his mouth to answer, he tries not to yell "It's a lie," but now his father's voice drowns out his protests. "Of course, it's true! Are you calling me a liar?"

"Mr. Bernardoni," the doctor begins.

"He's always had a condition." His father says it decisively. "We didn't like to talk about it because of the stigma, but he has a long history, doctor. Violence, cruelty to animals…"

"He's lying," Frank raises his voice for the first time, breaking his composure, "none of that is true. Ask me whatever you want, he's lying."

"Dr. Stanley, my son suffers from psychotic breaks. He often doesn't remember these episodes. But I can tell you, and so can my wife and our friends, he's often had violent outbursts."

Before Frank can respond, Dr. Stanley has raised both hands in a gesture of silence. Frank holds his tongue, but his father continues, "I have written statements from several family members and friends, they will no longer visit because of Francesco's behavior."

"I would have you speak to my wife, Joann" Pat continues, "just this afternoon, I hate to even say it, it's so embarrassing, but just this afternoon this young man," he gestures toward Frank, "slapped his mother clear across the face. Left a bruise on her face. You remember her delicate condition."

"Have you thought of pressing charges?" Dr. Stanley seems more concerned now.

Frank jumps up, heart pounding. "That's bullshit! He's full of shit!"

"Young man, if you can't control yourself…"

Frank sees there is no reason to argue. He settles back in the bed, ready to accept whatever comes next.

They're coming for you… you have work to do.

CHAPTER 79

Tabitha Whitaker, Anchor at Pompton Lakes Regional News

Tabitha steps off the elevator, feet from the entry to the greenroom when she hears the commotion.

She walks faster, and drops of coffee splash her hand, thanks to the stormy seas inside her PerfectGrind cup. She hasn't been to her desk yet this morning and doesn't remember who their scheduled guest is. The last time a guest made a commotion it was Bill Merlick, a local school board candidate whose unusual beliefs led to a flurry of attention. And votes.

"Tabby," her boss, Rebecca, calls from a side office. Tabitha turns, momentarily distracted by the racket coming from the green room.

The older woman pulls the glasses from her nose and squints her eyes, lined with crow's feet. "It seems we have a high-profile guest today, I'd like to talk to you briefly in my office."

Tabitha follows the grey-haired woman into a small office, closing the door behind her.

"Pat Bernardoni is here," Rebecca begins.

"Who?" Tabitha asks, then panics, wondering if she sounds like an amateur.

"Pat Bernardoni. The real-estate developer. Didn't you see the news story the other day? WAJX is ahead of us on this, hell every other station is ahead of us, but today we have an exclusive interview since his son was committed."

Tabitha bites her bottom lip. She nods, not wanting to sound uninformed. "Of course, right." She'll Google his name as soon as she leaves her boss's office.

"His son, Francesco, was captured by radical extremists. He was found recently. His son has been using the moniker 'Frank from Jersey' to tag all those condos and then tore off his clothes at the press conference we weren't invited to the other day."

"Oh, right," Tabitha raises a hand to her head in recognition, forgetting all about her coffee until a splash from her cup burns her hand.

This day keeps getting better.

"I just want to remind you," Rebecca continues, "this man is a very influential, high-profile businessman with a lot of connections. He's already had some... difficulties... with staff, but I hope you can keep his circumstances in mind."

Rebecca pauses, eyeing Tabitha, who thinks her boss is trying to use her stare to impart some unspoken message.

"Of course. Understood," Tabitha lies.

"I knew I could count on you," the older woman smiles, reaches around Tabitha, and opens the door, dismissing the anchor.

In the hallway, Tabitha again hears a loud voice booming from the direction of the green room. As she approaches, she gasps in horror.

Did I really just hear that?

She hurries to pull the door open with her free hand.

"Miss! Miss come over here!" An older man not much taller than her spins his swivel chair to face her, knocking a makeup artist out of the way in the process.

"Will you tell this *fairy* I am not wearing makeup?"

She now knows the word she thought she heard a moment ago wasn't a trick of her imagination. And it wasn't the word "fairy."

Her mouth drops open. She pauses in shock.

"Miss! What are you? The cleaning service? Get me the anchor. Mr. Whitaker!"

She swallows hard, coming back to her senses with a quick shake of her head. This, she understands now, is Pat Bernardoni.

"Sir, I am Tabitha Whitaker. I am the anchor and this," she motions toward a befuddled makeup artist who looks to be near tears or violence, "is part of our professional staff. He is an excellent makeup artist."

"I'm not wearing any makeup!"

"Sir, if you don't wear makeup on camera, your face will be washed out and you'll look like a ghost. You want to make a good impression don't you?" She tries an appeal to his vanity.

Paul, the makeup artist, looks at Tabitha. His eyes say, "get me out of here." But she ignores his plea and raises a dismissive hand.

"We're almost ready for the interview, Mr. Bernardoni. The makeup is minimal. Just enough to make sure your face doesn't get washed out by the lights. And you can wash it off as soon as the interview ends."

She exits the green room before he can protest. Unfair to Paul, she thinks, but this morning is already an entire soap opera and she needs to prepare for the interview.

In the newsroom, Mr. Bernardoni allows the assistants to attach his microphone and seat him at the table in perfect view of the cameras. No profanity, no insults, Tabitha wonders whether he was just stressed. His son was kidnapped, she reminds herself.

The lights dim, signaling the interview is about to begin.

Thank God, Tabitha thinks, sipping her now lukewarm coffee. Let's just get this over with.

She places the cup under the table at her feet and dabs at the corners of her mouth with her fingers to clear any trace of the liquid. She clears her throat and smiles, noticing her guest staring at the camera like it was water on a hot day.

It was something all the newbies did.

She glances down at her notes.

Pat Bernardoni. Son: Francesco Bernardoni. Missing/believed kidnapped last year. Found recently. Mentally unstable. Plea for help to find his captors.

When her cue arrives, she plasters an enthusiastic smile across her face. Her voice in an artificially low register as she begins her introduction.

"Thank you for joining us today, I'm Tabitha Whitaker, John Dunne has the day off. We're joined this morning by well-respected businessman and philanthropist," she tries to recall her notes, "Pat Bernardoni. Mr. Bernardoni," she turns to face him, "you're used to making deals but now, it seems you're in the headlines for a tragic reason. Tell us about the horrible situation your family has had to endure."

She watches his face transform. His cocky smile fades. His eyebrows furrow more than they should. She's sat across from many grieving families and knows trauma manifests in different ways. But as he begins to speak, something about his demeanor seems contrived.

"Yes. My son, Francesco was kidnapped. His mother and I spent months fearing the worst. Every time the phone rang, we thought this would be it, the call that our son was dead."

She leans forward, fixing her face in a carefully contrived mask of grief. It was an essential skill on this job and part of the reason she could tell when someone was faking. And faking badly.

"But you've had some good news. Tell us about how your son was found."

Something passes across his eyes. Anger? She wonders.

"Well, it wasn't bad enough that my son went missing. Was kidnapped. But to make matters worse, whoever did this… the person… or people… who took Francesco, hostage, they began a campaign of terror."

Her eyes widen in genuine surprise. She resists the urge to check her cue cards.

I wasn't briefed on this.

"What happened?"

He looks indignant as if she should have already known. "My buildings were vandalized. Several of my properties. Brand new condos among them. The terrorists had the nerve to spray-paint a message to me from my son."

She pauses, unsure if she missed something or if he is referring to spray paint on a building as an act of terrorism.

"So, your son was returned home, how was he found?" She decides against venturing further into a line of questioning related to said terrorism. She just wants this over.

"Whatever criminals were responsible for my son's disappearance, they attacked again. A new condo downtown. Neighborhood was all blight. I could've invested anywhere, but I chose there. And this is what they do. They bring my son there, ransack my building, and then drop him off. And that's where the police found him."

"Bizarre."

The word escapes her before she realizes her face is crooked in a look of disbelief. Nothing this man is saying makes sense, yet she doesn't want to turn over any stones, who knows what he may say next?

"Are there any leads, any ideas as to who was responsible for your son's disappearance?"

"That's why I'm here. I need the help of your viewers. We're very disappointed in the police. Not only did they not find who did this, they've been disrespectful to me. And I give every year, generously, to the PBA."

She cuts him off when he stops for a breath, "So, you are asking for viewer tips?"

He looks annoyed, but continues, "I'm offering a reward of $10,000.00 for any information that leads to the capture and arrest of the people responsible for brainwashing my son."

"Brainwashing?" she blurts the word out.

"Not only was my son kidnapped, but he was also in-doctrinated. I believe it was a radical left-wing cult," Pat Bernardoni pauses, then chooses his words carefully. "My son has always struggled with... severe... mental illness. Suddenly, he's delusional. Thinks he's some kind of prophet, all kinds of religious ramblings."

"Oh."

"It's something my wife and I have done our best to keep out of the spotlight. The stigma and all. Especially," he pauses for effect, sighs heavily, and continues, ", especially the self-flogging. We learned our son was involved in some self-harm. We think it was part of the cult. We don't want him treated any differently by society. But the truth is, he goes into fits. I've had to have him committed many times. He has... psychotic rages. Thinks he can talk to animals. It's sad, really."

Silence hangs in the air. Tabitha finally takes the oppor-tunity to wrap up the interview. "Well, I'm glad your son was found and is alive. And yes, viewers, if you have any tips that can help this family finally find some peace, please notify the authorities."

Tabitha is about to turn on the television and sit back with a well-earned glass of wine when her phone rings. The familiar ringtone tells her it's Rebecca.

What the fuck?

It's not like her boss to call at 9:00 P.M.

"Hello?"

"Tabby, I'm afraid I have some bad news."

She waits as her boss clears her throat.

"This was not my decision, I want you to know that. And I'm happy to give you references."

Tabitha barely hears the rest. Her boss's voice sounds like it's coming through a wind tunnel.

"Bernardoni called Rick and Vincent... he knows someone in the upstairs office.... Complained.... Didn't like the way he was treated.... Something about 'that woman anchor didn't ask the right questions...'"

"What are you saying?" Tabitha finally interrupts.

Rebecca sighs. "I don't want to do it. But they're firing you. I have to tell you... I have to let you go. Effective immediately."

When the call ends, Tabitha throws her phone onto the floor. She gulps down the wine in her glass, then puts the glass on an end table and grabs the bottle.

CHAPTER 80

Frank

In the dream, Frank walks through the park downtown.

"Will we walk long?" Bella asks, looking over her shoulder.

"Just long enough to find a girl," Frank hears himself answer. Some part of him recoils. Bella's voice has never sounded clearer. He answers her aloud in broad daylight, and in the way of dreams, it doesn't matter.

"And they call me a dog," Bella teases him, pawing at his leg and then darting a few feet ahead.

The scene grows hazy. Must be long ago. He never goes walking in the park anymore. Or is it that he no longer looks for girls?

Barking in the distance returns his attention to the now-darkened evening. The streets he barely knows, except that for the past few months he's found discarded treasure in a dumpster behind a corner store at the intersection.

Bella runs toward him, leaps, paws on his chest, and knocks him to the ground.

He's falling.

Falling.

He never hits the ground. Instead, he wakes up on the pull-out couch. Deep in the woods in a cabin where he once stayed.

"I found a girl for you," Bella boasts, settling by his side.

He starts to wonder if Kevin and Bread know he's brought his dog, but all thoughts of the two men who live here vanish when he sees what Bella was talking about.

"You kept me waiting," Mallory tells him. She walks toward him from the kitchen, wearing a hoodie with a scarlet A which he knows now is not a band symbol.

"You took forever," she continues, mock teasing.

"Am I dead? Are we dead?"

"Yeah. You're dead."

Relief washes over him.

"Why aren't you scared?" Mallory asks him.

"Do you want me to be? I mean I don't know. I'm just not."

Bella licks at his hand. He feels it.

"If I'm dead, why can I feel Bella?" He looks at Mallory. Not an apparition. "Why can I see you? I can hear Bella, clear, not like the chorus. If I'm dead, why are you here?"

Mallory leans closer. Her face is close enough to his so that her eyes merge in his field of vision.

She's real. More real than before.

"If I'm dead, why does this feel real?"

She leans closer.

"I am you."

He wakes in a cold sweat. The blue streaks of dawn barely enough to illuminate this strange place. Not Kevin and Bread's cabin. His heart sinks. Not Dead. But not with Mallory. Or Bella.

Light streams in from the hallway. The interruption caused by the door to a sterile room abruptly opening.

"What the fuck?"

"Hall checks." A young man about Frank's age grumbles, staring down at a clipboard, and then returns the door to a not-quite-closed position.

The bedroom walls gradually brighten from grey to eggshell to white. Not a bedroom, he remembers. A hospital.

He is suffocating in the heavy emptiness of the room. No windows. No breeze. No sounds of cicadas. Only the hum of the hospital's air conditioning. It sounds louder than it should. Volume rising from wind tunnel to jackhammer.

Okay, mice? Rats? Roaches? Anybody here? Wanna talk? Because I'm fucking bored out of my mind.

The fan blasts a steady reply. It's painful.

He tries again.

Hey, if there's a squirrel stuck in the vents, I'm all ears.

"Francesco Bernardoni?" A voice echoes from the doorway.

He doesn't have to look to know it's no squirrel. Not a cockroach either.

He doesn't answer and the man in a lab coat carrying a clipboard walks toward him, standing in his line of vision.

"Francesco Bernardoni?" He tries again.

Frank thinks of the dream. Of Mallory.

"Francesco Bernardoni is dead." He replies.

The man flips pages on his clipboard, a skeptical look on his face, then eyes Frank. In a patronizing voice, he asks, "Then who are you?"

"I'm Frank. From Jersey."

Frank replays his conversation with Dr. D'Lerio, the Pompton Correctional Facility's Psychiatrist, whose visit was the only break in his solitude in what seemed like days.

"I don't belong here." Frank insisted.

"Mmmm." The doctor responded, then fell silent. Frank thought he was waiting for him to flip out. To give away the violent side his father lied about.

"My father was lying. He's mad at me."

"So, you think your dad is conspiring against you?" Dr. D'Lerio raised his eyebrows.

"That's not what I said."

"Do you often have difficulties expressing yourself? Feel like others don't understand you?"

God, there's no way out of this.

The questioning went on for what seemed like hours. Frank felt his pulse quickening. His patience waning.

Fine. You want crazy? I'll give you crazy. Either way, I'm fucked.

"Do you ever hear voices?" D'Lerio asked.

"Only when I'm lucky," Frank replied, his tone nonchalant again.

"Excuse me?"

"I can't grant pardons. I'm just a humble servant."

D'Lerio eyed him as if wondering if he was being toyed with.

Only slightly.

"Do you know whose voice it is? Can you tell me more about it?"

"It's not just one voice. It's all of us. A collective. It gives …. Guidance."

D'Lerio stopped scribbling on his clipboard and stared at Frank.

"Does anything in particular trigger it?" Dr. D'Lerio asked.

Frank furrowed his eyebrows, "It mostly comes when I need help."

D'Lerio begins scribbling notes on his paperwork again.

"And animals."

"What?" D'Lerio looked up at him.

"Animals. The voices usually come through animals. But … not always."

"Has the voice ever told you to hurt anyone?"

Frank considered this. "No. It made me aware…" he answered slowly, "that I'm already both dead. And alive."

Looking back, he can't tell if the doctor was satisfied to have something substantial to document, or disappointed that Frank's description of the Chorus wasn't dramatic enough.

Fuck him.

Frank could play along with this little game long enough to find a way out of here.

CHAPTER 81

Frank

After the show he put on for Dr. D'Lerio, Frank is not surprised when a nurse, a man who can't be much older than him, approaches his cell that evening.

"Francesco Bernardoni?"

"No."

The nurse looks confused, then eyes his clipboard.

"It says here your name is Francesco Bernardoni."

Frank avoids the man's eyes, staring straight ahead.

"My name is Frank. I denounce my family. I don't answer to their name."

"Frank, then, I have your meds."

The nurse holds the cup toward him. Frank's eyes glance toward the side. He sees a blue and white capsule and two tiny yellow pills. Frank asks the nurse for water and the young man produces a Styrofoam cup and slides it through the opening in his cell.

He eyes the nurse, *Paul,* his nametag reads, and makes a dramatic gesture of emptying the contents of the cup into his mouth, then chugging water.

He expects the nurse to check his mouth for pills and is relieved to see the man turning away from him and continuing down the hall, no doubt many other deliveries to make.

He waits to hear the nurse's footsteps fading as he walks down the hall before spitting the bitter, partially dissolved pills into his hand. There's nowhere to stash the chalky residue, he crumbles it between his thumb and forefinger and shakes it off his hands and onto the floor behind his bed.

Chapter 82

The sound of a door creaking open startles him awake. He's about to curse at the doctor, his eyes adjust to the light- brighter than usual- and he knows as soon as he sees who has entered the room that he must still be dreaming.

He sits up in bed, wiping his eyes, wishing his teeth were brushed, then realizing it doesn't matter.

"Mallory."

She smiles. Radiant. Does death do that? He wonders.

"I miss you," he hears his voice crack, stifling a sob.

"Why?"

"What do you mean, why?"

Her eyes sparkle. She walks toward him and sits on the edge of the bed.

"I haven't gone anywhere. Nowhere far, at least."

Her voice sounds more beautiful than he remembered. He resists the urge to blink, not wanting to miss the chance to see her. Not as a memory, but here. She looks more real than his last dream of her, he thinks. Completely whole.

"You're dead."

"I'm dead, you're dead," she shrugs, "what're ya going to do?" She gets up and walks around before adding, "I'm more alive than you. Sometimes. You've been coming to life, though." She pauses, "You were. But you've forgotten."

Frank feels his cheeks grow warm.

"There's not much life in this place.

Mallory's smile fades.

"You would be surprised."

"What do you mean?"

"This is not a morgue."

"But I'm stuck here. My dad lied, they all bought it. Now they think I'm crazy. I'm stuck here. There's nothing I can do anymore."

"You have work to do." Her voice somber, she takes his hand in hers. He can feel her skin. Not an apparition. She's real.

"You sound like the squirrel."

"Not a game," she chastises him. "You don't understand."

"So, tell me!" He instantly regrets raising his voice in impatience, but he's tired of riddles. Tired of wasting his time. Tired of doing things that go nowhere. Just tired.

"I need your help," he begins, but she raises a finger to her lips to silence him.

"You have all the help you need. You just need to listen."

Frank feels warmth emanating from his chest. It spreads to his arms, throughout his body. He starts to relax, but something deeper, in his gut, erupts. Rage pours over him.

"Bullshit! This is fucking bullshit! I can't do this anymore!"

Mallory disappears and this time, the sound of his cell door slamming is real. Hands restrain him in bed, he feels the jab of another needle. Frank continues to scream.

CHAPTER 83

Frank drifts in and out of dreams for what seems like a week. The dream-induced visions are his new waking life. The brief interludes of reality under the fluorescent lights of the hospital room, an illusion.

The only marker of time is the appearance of aids who check a form on a clipboard once reassured he is still alive, and the morning and evening meds he stuffs in his cheeks like a hamster and spits out onto a corner of the floor when alone again.

Frank is drifting to sleep again one morning when a tech opens the door to his room just enough to glimpse him. The aide, Frank realizes, is a young person. Probably in their early twenties. Their eyes are intense, face serious.

Frank is a young person, too, and yet they scribble their notes, shoulders stooped under the weight of responsibility.

"Hey," Frank addresses the aide, who stops suddenly and looks up in surprise.

"I didn't realize you were awake." They reply.

"I'm always awake. And you're always asleep." Frank winks.

The aide smiles. Braces imprison their already perfect-looking teeth. Frank feels their sadness. Feels their adrenaline, amplified. They run, run, run and never find where they're going. Frank understands.

"Seriously," Frank sits up in bed and looks earnest, he drops his voice so the aid will know he's not the fool they think he is. "You don't need to worry so much. None of this is as important as you think."

The aide steps into the room, eyebrows relaxed, a wave of relief visible on their face. They look like they want to say something, want to confide. They hesitate.

"I know, you don't have to tell me your personal business, just, don't get too uptight about all of this."

"But it's a hospital. People could die."

"Not the hospital," Frank corrects, "The mundane shit. The… the grind."

The aide nods, a spark of understanding comes over their face.

"This is my third job. It's the easiest. The other two are much more stressful."

Frank's heart sinks.

"It's the only way I can afford school. I want to be a therapist and even with my scholarships it's not enough."

"So, you work three jobs, and go to school?"

They smile, "Yeah. I run on coffee. But I'm exhausted all the time."

"You don't need coffee," Frank begins, thinking of the Possum Crew. "And you don't need three jobs. You need one job with a union."

The aide looks from side to side, assured no one is watching, and smiles, "okay, I'll see what I can do."

"Not what you can do," Frank adds, "you and your comrades."

They smile, blush, and give a knowing look before nodding and backing out of the room.

Frank settles back into the bed and sleeps.

CHAPTER 84

A sharp rap on the door startles him awake. Frank sits up in bed, confused, he's already faked his meds, why has the nurse come back? Are they on to him?

"Today's the day." The nurse, Paul, announces.

"What day?" Frank tries to get his bearings.

"Your discharge. You're stabilized, we can't keep you here any longer. And you're an adult so you don't need your parents involved in discharge. Just one thing," Paul checks his paperwork, "it says you were missing and then returned to your parent's house, but again, since you are an adult we can refer you to an apartment program."

Frank feels his chest tighten. More confinement. He has a place to live. A way to live. The Earth is made of many mansions if people only understood how to live.

"That won't be necessary."

"Well, we have to discharge you to somewhere. So, a shelter? A friend's house?"

He can't give the Possum Crew's address.

"Shelter is fine," he replies, not intending to stay.

Paul scribbles on his paperwork, then hands Frank a form to sign.

"I'll give you discharge instructions and a sample of your meds to get you started, but you'll need to do a follow-up at the clinic or get your own doctor."

Frank nods, with no intention of doing either.

"And we can get you some clothes at the donation store on the unit. You can't walk around in hospital gowns."

"Right." Frank agrees for politeness, though he's no longer convinced this is true.

He follows Paul down the hallway to what appears to be a storage closet. The sign on the door is marked "Donations."

Paul unlocks the door, swings it open, and pulls out a plastic container.

"Pick a top," he begins, grabbing another container off a shelf, "These are pants."

Frank rifles through the container and finds an oversized brown hooded sweatshirt. From the assorted pile of pants, he retrieves bulky jeans, the closest to his size.

"Can't help with underwear and socks for obvious reasons, but we can get you hospital socks to wear. We don't have a lot of shoes in our stash, but these might fit you?" Paul pulls a pair of worn sneakers from a shelf.

"Thanks," Franks adds them to his pile.

On the way back to his room he thinks of the free stores the Possum Crew hosted. Racks of clothes like new, tables of shoes and boots. Kids' games and books. Even some furniture.

He remembers one of their last events, set up near an outdoor farmer's market. Someone complained because the free store was more popular than the vendors. They had been driven out.

Back in the hospital room, he puts on the new clothes, sufficient for now. And waits for Paul to return with the discharge instructions he'll ignore.

"Take care of yourself and good luck," Paul shakes his hand before departing to the hallway.

That's it. Frank is free to leave.

As he heads toward the nurse's station to say goodbye, the sound of someone approaching distracts him.

Frank turns to see the young aide. They smile, their braces shine.

"I wanted to wish you good luck," They extend a hand and Frank grasps it and shakes it.

"My name is Tobi by the way. And thank you for what you said."

"Thank you." Frank replies, adding, "You have a beautiful smile, it brings light to the world."

As he leaves the hospital, Comrade Sun warms his face. He stands for a moment on the grass outside the towering institution, basking in the sun. Soaking in the warmth from the light and letting his roots rest deep in the soil beneath the grass.

He feels a shadow pass overhead and opens his eyes in time to see a pigeon land on the sidewalk near his feet.

"They're coming again. You have work to do."

Frank's heart sinks. So soon?

You have work to do.

A memory returns. Even before the men approach from either side and speak the name his father gave him.

Your Twelfth House year.

"Francesco Bernardoni?" He recognizes the voice. Dimples.

No attachments.

"You're under arrest..."

You lose yourself.

"For assault, larceny...."

You have work to do.

CHAPTER 85

Narrator

Spending a week in the psychiatric unit gave Frank a break from the outside world, but it also gave him a break from the news. He didn't see his father lie about him to an anchor named Tabitha.

He didn't see the footage of his father's press conference that went viral.

And if Frank from Jersey had a cult following among rebels and radicals before, well, he was now a household name.

And he didn't even know it.

He had been canonized. A modern-day saint of rebels and revolutionaries. His image, now a meme, is plastered online in chatrooms and social media feeds. Plastered with wheat paste on the walls of banks, real estate brokers, and the like.

Someone even painted a life-size mural on Wall Street showing his likeness with the tagline "Frank is coming."

Even Banksy was rumored to be responsible for a Frank From Jersey "No Gods, No Masters" mural, though the artist has not yet confirmed this.

And it wasn't just his image. Frank from Jersey, the icon, sent a spirit of revolt surging through the country. His image was on shirts, often displaying the possum on his shoulder.

Rumors spread that he had the power to talk to animals, heal the sick, and curse those who escaped justice for too long.

A Bard even changed the lyrics of *Roland the Headless Thompson Gunner* to tell his story and the song of *Frank the Possum Talker from Jersey*, and then that went viral. Chants filled the streets as a backdrop to broken store windows and explosions.

Of course, much debate went into whether Frank from Jersey deserved iconic status, was his presence eclipsing the visibility of marginalized revolutionaries who deserved the spotlight the mysterious Frank was receiving. Others argued that embodying a movement in the image of any person was too cultish and that Frank himself wouldn't approve.

"Are we just perpetuating the tenets of capitalism by branding a movement?" some asked.

But theoretical debates online were drowned out by growing praxis in the streets. For better or worse, the specter of Frank from Jersey was here and growing.

CHAPTER 86

Tabitha

Tabitha stares at her laptop screen as she sits in the cramped office, she now shares with four other people in what InkSword calls a "coworking space." After her first week, she learned to bring headphones to work to drown out distractions.

If she had watched any of the news networks, let alone her own, she would have understood the significance of the man named Pat Bernardoni. But somewhere along the way, between ascending from excited intern to an overworked anchor, the local interest stories and stream of subacute crises all blended together.

She thought it would be easy to get her foot in the door at another network. Weeks went by with no response to her resumes. Job listings remained active. Finally, out of desperation, she called Ben, a friend from grad school who worked at WAJX to see if he had any insights.

"You're poison, Tabitha. I'm sorry. Bernardoni actually called the networks personally to get you blacklisted. Between you and me, the guy is a little nuts."

You're telling me, Tabitha thinks, still scanning through the database on her screen. InkSword wasn't a step down professionally, it was a gaping avalanche. But Tabitha saw more to this opportunity.

"Here at InkSwords," their website's mission statement reads, "we believe in using our platform to create a more just and equitable world. We tell real stories of real people. Our journalists aren't afraid to take down the corporate crooks responsible for injustices and we're not beholden to corporate sponsors."

And there is one corporate crook Tabitha is set to take down. She copies a chunk of text from a website and transfers it to a spreadsheet under a column marked Pat Bernardoni.

CHAPTER 87

Frank has lost count of the days. All he can see from his cell is lit by constant fluorescent lighting. He could time the days by routine. The COs rounding up all the inmates for a head count, or the nurse visiting to distribute meds that he continues to hide in his mouth before crushing the pills against a corner of the wall out of sight of the COs. He could find little ways to keep time. But he's stopped keeping track.

On his first day here, a CO pointed him out in the yard and introduced him as the son of Pat Bernardoni, the millionaire. Some of the men didn't care. They kept lifting weights and playing basketball, talking or staring at the world beyond the razor-wire fence.

But a group of men gathered from around the yard. They circled him. The CO turned his back. Frank's heart raced as he looked from one man to another.

"Your dad's a rich man. He threw me out on the street while my wife was dying of cancer. I got a message for you to give your dad." The man approached him, while the others closed in.

Frank looked the man in the eyes, certain what he said next would have no impact, but said it anyway, "I'm sorry. My father is a liar, a cheat, and a fraud. He deserves to be in a cage more than anyone here."

The man approaching him froze. Frank braced himself, unsure if he'd just made things worse. A moment went by, cold, blank eyes stared into Frank's. He held his breath as a smile spread across the man's face. He began laughing.

"You're a damn fool." The man's eyes bulged as he said it, but the laughter that followed put Frank at ease. The other men laughed. The man reached out his hand. He had tattoos in blue on his fingers, a cross, a pair of dice, and an eye. "Name's Grant."

Frank shook his hand.

The CO seemed perturbed but left Frank alone. At least for the rest of that day.

Frank thinks of this now as he watches a corner of his cell. A spider slides down along a silky thread. Frank watches the spider dance. She sings as she weaves. The sound entrances Frank.

"You're busy working," Frank observes.

"So are you," she reminds him.

CHAPTER 88

Her bags are packed, amounting to a small rolling suitcase. In a bag over her shoulder, Emma Goldman purrs loudly. She's been arguing with Emma all morning, but the cat ultimately won.

She always does.

"It's been a pleasure having you stay with us," the elderly woman embraces her on the steps of the house. The pacific northwest sky is clear that morning. The air is crisp.

"I wish I could stay longer." She's not just being pleasant. Going home isn't her idea. But she can no longer ignore what is happening.

As she heads to the bus station, across from the port, her heart pounds. Chili's words in the signal chat alarmed her more than anything.

"He disowned his father. Publicly. On the news. You know what that will mean. He was in a hospital. Now in jail."

She indulged Chili with a reply that time. The first in decades.

"I'm coming home."

CHAPTER 89

Tabitha

The first four times Tabitha attempted to visit Frank in jail she was denied entry. The reasons ranged from obscure to terse replies. The most disturbing was the report from a younger CO, one of the more polite of the bunch, who told her Frank was in Solitary.

He must have seen the panic on her face.

"Oh, he's fine," the CO rushed to cover his tracks. "He hasn't been eating. Some weird hunger strike or something. So, he's in solitary for observation."

It was less than Tabitha hoped to glean from her visit but enough for her to use as leverage.

Her visit was denied again, and Tabitha pushed back. "I know he's in solitary. And I know he's not eating. I'm happy to print that story, but you can bet the son of a millionaire being kept in jail on solitary and denied visits with no other context will catch some attention you probably don't want …"

It was petty, but she knows how to get access.

She sits in the small meeting room now. One table. Bright, aggressive lighting and pale green walls. She hears the door creak open and the young man, long hair now shaved, is brought in with his ankles and wrists in chains.

"Aren't the bracelets a bit much?" he asks the guards.

They ignore her.

Frank is pushed down into a chair across the table from her.

"Frank," she begins, "my name is Tabitha, I'm a journalist for an indie media agency called InkSword. Your father," she begins, but sees his face change, she corrects herself, "Pat Bernardoni is telling lies. I want to talk to you so I can tell your story."

Tabitha wonders how honest Frank will be in the presence of guards hovering over him. Her worries are unnecessary.

"Thank you for coming. I dreamed about you and knew you were on your way." He then adds, "The spiders told me you tried to get in before but the guards wouldn't let you."

Tabitha freezes, pen above paper. She wonders if he is mentally ill. Or if prison has pushed him over the edge.

"Spiders?"

"Yes. I'll explain. You write."

She follows this instruction and after an hour, she has a generous outline for a story more outrageous than she imagined.

Later that night, as she sits in the office alone, Tabitha outlines her first draft. So much of Frank's story is unbelievable without even touching the whole Dr. Doolittle thing.

But it's part of his story. She argues with herself.

It could be a series, she thinks. And if that's the case, another interview is in order. Taking down Pat Bernardoni means Frank must be seen as credible. Infusing the article with stories of Frank wandering the woods and talking to raccoons only gives credibility to Pat Bernardoni's claims that Frank is unstable.

She decides to wait. To keep digging.

CHAPTER 90

Having seen photos of the Bernardoni Estate, not to mention the infamous video of the press conference on the steps of Bernardoni's home, Tabitha is surprised that this is the home of Frank's childhood best friend Jonathan. Her notes indicate he lives with his single mother. He went to the same Academy as Frank but on scholarship. Eyeing the older home in disrepair as she parks her car, she wonders what their friendship had been like.

A dog barks inside the house as she knocks. She hears the scratching of claws, eager to let her in, and a man's voice in the distance, "All right, Bella, I'm coming."

Jonathan seemed eager to talk to her when she called him the other day. He answers the door in sweatpants and a t-shirt, but Tabitha tries to maintain a poker face. He invites her into the house. She notices a faint smell of alcohol hovering around his face.

The dog is a large chocolate lab.

"Did I hear you call her Bella? As in," she begins to ask, thinking of the story Frank told her.

"Yeah, Francesco's dog."

"You call him Francesco," she comments. They sit on a worn couch in the living room. The room is decorated like the last decades of the analog era. A few books, a television, a few electronics.

"That's his name."

This is not going well. She wonders if he is in a bad mood or if she asked the wrong question. Tabitha decides on another tactic.

"You agreed to speak with me and I had the feeling there's a side of the story you want to tell. What is that story?" She leans close, pen over paper, ready to jot down notes.

Bella jumps onto the couch and curls up beside Jonathan, her front paws and head resting on his lap in a protective gesture.

"I've known Francesco since grade school. At the academy. And you're the first person to ask my side of the story. Yeah, I'll tell you."

He rubs his forehead with the heel of his hand and Tabitha is certain he spent last night drinking and now regrets it. Or will regret it more soon.

Despite this, he manages to tell a coherent story, but one different from the versions she heard so far.

"Francesco was always kind of a bossy asshole, but he was nice to me and a lot of the other kids weren't because I was one of the scholarship kids." Jonathan begins, "I still don't know if maybe he was more compassionate, or if he needed to be around a poor kid to feel more important."

Tabitha doesn't interrupt. She scribbles to keep up with Jonathan as he continues to tell the highs and lows of their friendship. How Francesco kept the other kids from beating him up in middle school. Their nights drinking at the park.

"Francesco was a party animal. All the girls, all the drugs, the alcohol. He didn't care. He acted like a rock star and got away with it because of who his father is."

"What changed?" Tabitha asked.

"He met a girl he liked and for the first time, someone saw through his shit. I mean someone other than me."

Frank told her about Mallory, the girl killed by police at the protest. He alluded to a romance, but Jonathan's take is illuminating.

"I don't think he really even knew her. Maybe he just thought he loved her because it was the first time he didn't just get what he wanted. She kept him chasing her or whatever. Then he's spending all his time with her. Doesn't want to party anymore. Starts talking about how he doesn't need his family. Doesn't need their money. Like he wants to pretend to be poor to impress this girl he just met."

Jonathan shakes his head. He pets Bella's back and continues, "He even got into it with his dad because his dad bought this scummy apartment building downtown and was going to put something useful there and she just happened to live there. So he and his dad have a fight over it because Francesco thought he was going to talk his dad out of a multi-million dollar business deal, like are you crazy?"

"So, what did he do?" Tabitha prompts.

"Typical Francesco. Didn't get his way. Threw a tantrum. Ran off. Took Bella with him to some protest where people were rioting and throwing shit at cops. So of course, they had to protect themselves and it's sad someone died but what do you expect? So, Francesco, I don't know, he just disappeared. I only knew he was there because I saw it on the news. He ran off somewhere. Joined a fanatic cult, or got kidnapped or something I don't even know."

Jonathan looks into the distance. Tabitha gives him a moment before asking, "What do you think happened?"

Jonathan considers this. He starts to speak, then catches himself as if afraid of saying the wrong thing. Then he continues.

"I don't know. It's like him to run off to get attention. But the only thing that didn't make sense, I mean, I thought he was dead. When Bella came back alone."

"He was close with his dog?"

"Close? It was like some weird television show." Jonathan laughs, "I mean, I know it sounds nuts," he looks at Tabitha, "but I swear it's like they could talk to each other."

His words send chills down Tabitha's spine.

Driving home after the interview, Tabitha reviews the two stories in her mind, trying to reconcile the differences. Jonathan strikes her as needy, lonely, and jealous of Frank. Could a son of a millionaire be a total asshole? Sure. The truth, she's learned, is somewhere between these two accounts. Or hovering above it. But something doesn't sit well with her. Of all Jonathan's complaints about Francesco not once did he question his friend's mental health. He even outright substantiated Frank's claim that he could talk to animals. At least, possibly, to Bella.

But weren't people just nuts about their dogs like that?

She replays Jonathan's words, his description of Frank returning home.

"He was trying to act all high and mighty like he doesn't need his family, doesn't need money, had some kind of epiphany out in the forest or something..."

Had his time away opened some new... awareness? Tabitha knows this story won't stand as it is. She needs to dig deeper.

CHAPTER 91

Tabitha stares at the chart that now nearly encompasses her entire living room wall. In the center, three index cards of notes on Pat Bernardoni. To the right, another index card with only a few lines of information she could find on his wife. Spiraling from this, post-it notes and index cards spread layer after layer, so that Pat Bernardoni's name is now the center of a vast bull's eye.

Many of her leads turned out to be dead ends. If Frank had been involved in some kind of underground group, she could find nothing on them. Jonathan had been somewhat helpful, but couldn't lead her to other contacts.

It wasn't until she spent hours on an exhaustive search of local records, birth and death certificates, business deals, and contracts, that she found her next lead. She leans in close to the wall, grabs a pin from the container on her bookshelf, and posts another index card under Pat Bernardoni.

This one contains only a name: Carmen Bernardoni.

Tabitha found little about Carmen online, as if she not only disappeared from the Bernardoni family but also from society before the internet became a pervasive part of daily life. No socials, and no milestones in the paper. She agreed to meet the journalist in the park, by the basketball court. Tabitha is early. She sits on a bench, meditating on the lucky break that brought her to this interview.

Someone called her. Anonymous tips were common when she worked for the bigger network, but she never expected that level of public engagement in InkSword. She still doubts the group has any substantial following.

"I heard you have an interest in Frank Bernardoni?" The voice said.

"Yes, can I schedule an interview with you?"

"Not with me. Talk to his sister."

Her heart fluttered. She found some reference to another Bernardoni child but nothing for years. Tabitha wondered if the girl was dead, but there were no death certificates, no obituary. If she had disappeared, there was nothing in the news, and that would have been a newsworthy story.

"I've been trying to find her. Do you have a number I can reach her at?"

The voice replied and Tabitha scrambled to jot down the number, then read it back to confirm.

So much of her work is luck. Or fate. Was that even a thing?

"Tabitha?" A hesitant voice brings her out of her daydream. She turns to see a woman approaching her. The woman looks much older than Frank. Her dark eyes seem tired. She's dressed in hiking boots, a bag over her side which Tabitha realizes on closer glance is a cat carrier with a furry resident watching her from a screened window.

"Yes. You must be Carmen?" Tabitha stands and extends a hand.

"I was," the woman replies, shaking her hand and joining her on the bench. She adjusts the cat carrier, so it is on her lap. The woman continues, "Please, call me Tania." She doesn't love the alias, but it will be suitable for now. "But anything I tell you can't be cited from me. The family doesn't know where I am or who I am and I need it to stay that way."

"Understood," Tabitha jots the phrase 'a source with knowledge of the family' at the top of the page and leans a hand on her notebook as she continues, "what can you tell me about Pat Bernardoni? Or Frank? He must have been little when you last saw him."

She smiles at the mention of her brother's name. "Frank from Jersey. He's made quite a name for himself. They're talking about him coast to coast in some circles."

"What circles?" Tabitha pushes.

"Revolutionary circles. Anarchist circles. Underground circles. People like Pat Bernardoni are about to get what they've earned. You and I may not live to see it, but it's coming."

"What have they earned?" Tabitha suspects she knows but wants to hear it from Tania. "What about Pat Bernardoni? What was it like growing up with him as a father?"

Tania rolls her eyes and leans back against the bench. "He's a narcissistic, greedy, miserable bastard who tormented my mother and us kids. That's it. In a nutshell. He lies and cheats to get what he wants, then smiles for the cameras."

"And you must have had a falling out?"

"He didn't like when I started taking an interest in environmentalism, of course. I started questioning him. Joining in at protests. One of hundreds of people but he shit a brick thinking my presence there would ruin his reputation. The only thing he cares about more than his money."

Tabitha nods along, writing notes as Tania speaks. She smiles thinking of what will be left of his reputation when she is through with him.

"I had a hard time finding you online. Not many references to you and the family?"

"That's intentional. The old man kicked me out shortly after I started getting involved in the environmental movement, now they call it the climate movement. Same difference. I wasn't out of high school yet. But I found another family underground."

"He kicked you out? Because you went to environmental protests?" Tabitha thinks of Frank, "were you targeting his buildings the way Frank and the others have been?"

"No. Not specifically. We did dredge up some unsavory dirt on one of his business partners, though. He freaked. Probably because the guy has something on him."

"What do you mean?"

"It's the way he does business. All of them. It's as natural to them as breathing. They constantly bribe each other and then pretend to be friends and get more shit on each other so they can keep bribing each other. My father didn't get where he is because he's a master developer or even a good businessman. He's just good at getting dirt on people and then blackmailing and bribing. Occasionally he gets caught up and owes other people favors but he strives to have the upper hand. But anyway we targeted this other business and exposed illegal dumping near the lakes and a bunch of other things, can't remember it's been so long. He was pissed. Said give up that shit and act normal or get out."

"Jesus."

"I felt bad leaving Francesco, Frank, behind, he was little. Like maybe six or eight or something?"

"And you've had no contact with your family since?"

"With the Bernardonis? No. But I found another family and it looks like Frank did too."

They sit in silence for a moment then Tania speaks, "I would like to see Frank. Just once maybe. But not as Carmen. Do you think I can accompany you on your next visit? If you plan to interview him again?"

"Sure. Yeah. I don't see why not. I can say you're from InkSword or just say you're with me and keep it at that. But don't you think he'll recognize you? I mean you look a lot alike."

"We'll see." She stares into the distance.

They talk for another hour and Tabitha fills a notebook with drama worthy of a soap opera. She now sees a pattern, thanks to Tania. Tabitha is far from the only person Pat Bernardoni has had fired from their job when they cross him. And even having his own son hospitalized and jailed is tame in comparison to the way he's bulldozed others who stand in his way. She thinks it's no wonder his daughter was so hard to track. And if Frank is going through some sort of mental health crisis, now that she knows who his father truly is, she can understand why.

Section 5 All Comrades Great and Small

CHAPTER 92

Popcorn

Popcorn crawls along the trashcans. The scent of his favorites, cheesy pizza, stir-fry, and cupcakes, mix in the air, but he forces himself to scurry past, not stopping for a bite.

"You're in a hurry," A familiar voice calls after him.

"Meeting tonight, didn't you get the memo?" he calls over his shoulder, paws maintaining their pace.

Fucking raccoons, they never follow through.

He hears a trash can lid fall to the ground as the larger creature runs to catch up with him.

"That's tonight? I forgot it was tonight, I had a date with this fluffy..."

"Not now!" Popcorn hisses. "No time to talk, this is important."

"What's on the agenda?" The raccoon pads along beside the possum, following him as he darts around corners and into an alley.

"It's about Frank. Hurry, no time."

They run past a stairwell surrounded by cardboard boxes. As they pass, a family of rats poke their heads out into the night air. One of the larger rats gathers the pups and scurries deep into a hole in the wall. The other bounds down the street in pursuit of the possum.

Beneath the full moon, Popcorn can see farther than before. As he reaches the dumpster in the far corner of the strip mall, now dark and mostly empty except for a convenience store and something called an Adult Novelty Shop, he can see others have gathered already. Popcorn weaves through the crowd, ignoring greetings from ravens, pigeons, skunks, and even a rogue ferret.

He climbs to the top of the dumpster and surveys the lot. In the distance, a raccoon, rat, and several stray cats join the congregation. A dog he recognizes, though he's getting thinner, pads over toward the crowd.

A fisher slinks around the perimeter. Popcorn pounds the inner wall of the dumpster with a back paw, calling the meeting to order before any chaos can ensue.

"Order! Attention! Comrades!" All eyes are on him. "We don't have much time. Let me first remind you of the Truce of the Full Moon, predator, and prey gather for the good of all and put aside our instinctive differences."

"Aye!" A squirrel shouts in agreement.

"So theatric." A tabby cat circles twice and then lowers herself to rest in a warm spot in the parking lot.

A few more animals, dogs, birds, and what looks like a coyote, have joined the throng.

"We all know the winds of change are blowing!" Popcorn begins.

"More like the winds of starvation!" A boisterous badger raises her paw in a fist. Animals break out in chatter about the strange weather and disappearance of food."

"Attention! Attention!" Popcorn regains their attention. "Yes, winters are getting harsher. Yes, the class war among humans has trickled down to us, leaving our home places barren and food places empty!"

"The humans call it trickle-down economics," Owl interjects.

Fucking know-it-all.

"Yes, well whatever they call it, clearly, we know it only leads to starvation and homelessness. But even then, we have been lucky. The pigeons will tell you, not far from here animals of all kinds are being poisoned. They're being driven out. They're being killed for sport. And why have we been so lucky?"

It was a rhetorical question, but no one answers, and Popcorn is grateful for small favors. "Because we have lived in harmony with the Possum Crew. They have kept us fed and protected and we have helped them survive. There is one among them, Frank from Jersey, who has done much to improve our diplomatic relations."

"Frank saved my kitten after she was kidnapped by the dog warden!" a dog raises her paw to testify.

"He told me how to cure my arthritis in my wing." A mallard stretches their wing in demonstration.

"I know Frank. He's good people." Raccoon adds.

"Yes, many of us have our stories of mutual aid thanks to Frank. But we need to move on. Listen!" Popcorn raises his voice to restore the crowd to order. "Frank is in trouble."

The animals freeze mid-sentence, he's got their attention again.

"Frank is in jail. The man who put him there is the same one responsible for the extermination of our comrades all around the region. The humans are working on a plan, but they need our help, and we all know how incompetent humans can be."

"It takes them two decades to leave home. Two decades! Imagine having your chicks in the nest for that long?" A raven adds.

"Yes, we all know they are of limited intelligence, but they can be destructive, and if we want to keep their dangerous side controlled we need to work with the humans who know how to advocate for us. People like Frank."

"So, what exactly are we going to do?" Badger asks, folding both paws over her belly in a manner of skepticism.

"We are going to act in solidarity, but each according to their nature."

They gather close as Popcorn lowers his voice. In confidential tones, the animals continue their discussion as dawn approaches.

CHAPTER 93

Frank from Jersey wasn't just on the minds of birds and mammals in the Pompton Lakes region. He was also the subject of much debate and discussion on Signal chats, Reddit, and other online platforms. Those who didn't trust their communications to the ethers met in person in remote locations, far from surveillance cameras, to discuss how they could help their comrade Frank from Jersey.

Kevin peeks into the oven, eyeing the vegan pot roast that has filled the cabin with heat and spicey aroma. Bread comes out of the bedroom, headphones on his ears, wire free-falling, attached to nothing.

"You're not gonna believe what's on The Young Turks."

Kevin shuts the oven door and hurries across the kitchen and into the tiny bedroom. Bread turns up the volume on his laptop.

"Holy shit. They're talking about Frank." Kevin blurts out, watching footage from outside a jail where people have begun setting up tents. Votive candles and banners reading Free Frank! Are spread across the landscape.

Bread and Kevin give each other a knowing look.

"I'll call Chili," Bread grabs his phone.

Kevin turns off the oven and grabs a backpack, throwing clothes into the overnight bag. The pot roast will have to wait.

Jonathan has seen the news. He's getting impatient checking InkSword for the release of his interview. Tired of watching as Francesco is inflated, like a saint, to all these people who didn't even know him.

I knew him.

Jonathan tosses a tennis ball to Bella, assuming she must like the game because she continues to retrieve the ball and rush it back to him. He doesn't know she's only humoring him. Believing it's a game he looks forward to because it's the only one he knows how to play.

"It's not fair, Bella," he speaks the words aloud. She looks at him, knowingly, and drops the ball. He tosses it again and she runs near the trees at the edge of the park to find it.

This is where he and Francesco used to smoke and get drunk in middle school. It's where they used to meet up after class. Before he abandoned his friends, his family, and his whole life.

"He even abandoned you, ya know," Jonathan tells Bella as she runs the ball back to him. She drops it on the ground at his feet. It rolls and clinks against the bottle he's leaned against the foot of the bench. Jonathan reaches for the bottle and Bella lunges at him, licking his face to distract him.

When she finally settles down, he's forgotten the bottle, but only for a moment. He grabs the ball and throws it again.

He reaches for the bottle again when his phone vibrates.

"Jesus fucking Christ," he looks at the number, then clears his throat and sits up straight.

"Hello?" he answers as a question, but he knows who is calling. Bella prances toward him, squishing the green ball in her mouth. She drops it at his feet and sits, panting.

"Jonathan? This is Pat Bernardoni," the older man begins.

"Hi," Jonathan isn't sure what to say. He tries to make his voice sound upbeat. Professional. Not drunk in the afternoon.

"I hope I'm not interrupting anything important. Just wanted to talk to you about a little proposition. You just graduated, right? Bet you could use something a little more substantial than a summer job."

Jonathan can't believe what he's hearing. He jumps to his feet and his head pounds.

"Sure."

"Good, when is a good time to schedule a little onboarding meeting and I can bring you up to speed on the work I have in mind."

Jonathan eyes the bottle on the ground, "Um, tomorrow? Afternoon."

"Stop by the office at one tomorrow. And don't bring that dog."

"Of course. Thank you."

One would give him plenty of time to sleep it off, he thinks. Best to quit now. As his mind tells him this, his hand reaches down, grabs the bottle, and raises it to his mouth.

I really shouldn't...

Before he can finish the thought, the bottle is empty.

CHAPTER 94

Frank

A CO bangs on Frank's cell, jolting him awake. "Your fucking groupies are blocking up the parking lot. I had to push through the filth to get in today."

"What are you talking about?" Frank rubs his forehead, a headache following a night of restless sleep and nightmares.

"Those freaks. Antifa and whoever else you got out there. Bunch of animals."

Frank recalls his dream from the night before. If people have begun to gather, as his dream showed, then things were moving faster than he realized.

"My house is in ruins. You must restore it." The Chorus told him amid the nightmare.

"Make me an instrument of your will," He replies.

The CO grumbled something Frank couldn't hear as he walked down the hall.

It seems like days passed but it may have only been a few hours. His visitor returned. This time with a friend. Frank thought the woman looked familiar. He studied her face but sensed this was making her uncomfortable. He focused on Tabitha as they sat in the meeting room under the watchful eye of an even more disgruntled guard. Frank heard another earful of complaints as the guard walked him to the meeting room. "Must be a hundred people. Bet you think you're hot shit, but you're nothing."

"True." Frank agreed, "I am no one. I have no expectations, and I am never disappointed."

The guard shoved Frank, and unable to brace himself, he turned his face to avoid breaking his nose when he hit the floor. The man then wrenched him back to a standing position by pulling on his handcuffs.

"You need to be more careful, son. You trip a lot."

Frank laughed.

Now, sitting with Tabitha and the woman she introduced as Tania, Frank is eager to learn how far into the process they are.

"My friend here," he motions his head toward the CO, "tells me people are outside. What's going on?"

"It's massive," Tabitha's eyes widen as she leans forward and describes the scene. "The Young Turks are out there filming, and Democracy Now and a bunch of others. There are, what, two hundred people?" Tabitha turns to her friend to confirm.

"I would say, at least that," Tania replies.

Her voice vibrates in Frank's head. He turns to her again. Sees an image of a child playing the piano. Then talking about a horse. And riding. Needing new boots. His head hurts as he tries to put the pieces together.

"Are you okay?" she asks.

He closes his eyes.

"Are you okay?" He hears her voice in the memory. Sees his younger self, Bella as a puppy, and the woman called Tania. In the memory, Tania is younger, she resembled his father then, her eyes and hair only. And her name was Carmen.

"Mom's okay. She's back from the hospital. It was just dad being an asshole again." Carmen tells him in the memory.

He opens his eyes and now he sees her.

"Your sister doesn't want to be part of this family anymore." He remembers Pat Bernardoni telling his younger self as their mother sat on the floor, hands over her eyes, crying.

Recalls his father casually lying to the police. Then at the press conference.

And he sees her eyes. Her face is stoic.

What else had he lied about?

"You look familiar."

She nods. "I've been around. But my work brings me here now. I'm sure you've seen me before." She leans in confidentially, "I'm certain of it."

He senses they didn't come for a family reunion. He has work to do.

"They're here for you," Tabitha adds, "the people outside. They've got banners with your name on them. You've become a hero. They're camping out, demanding your release."

Frank furrows his eyebrows at this news. They're getting it all wrong.

"Are you going to run another story?"

"The first one isn't published yet. Just putting some final touches on it."

"Then skip ahead. I need you to send out a communique."

Tabitha looks bewildered. She eyes Tania who gives her a reassuring look.

"Um, ok. Sure. What do you want us to convey? I mean it will have to go through my editor and that takes some time…"

"No time." Frank interrupts. "You send it out personally then. On TikTok," he begins then adds, "or Facebook, no offense I don't know how old you are."

Tabitha smiles. "I have a lot of socials, so sure, what do you want to share with the public," She holds the pen to paper as Frank closes his eyes and leans back in the folding metal chair.

"There are no gods. No masters. No heroes. Do not make me a martyr, I am only an instrument. An instrument of revolution. There will be peace but first, there will be chaos. There is no avoiding it. We are at the apex. Time is running out."

Tabitha scribbles the words and Frank pauses for a moment then continues.

"The world is falling. We must rebuild it. This is what is asked of us by the Earth and all nature. There is a cost to rebuilding. The wealthy must give up their fortunes, for all fortune is stolen.

Property is theft, and so it is not theft to return to the people that which is ours in common. And to Pat Bernardoni: I demand you empty your accounts, dig deep into your pockets and return what you've stolen. You and those like you are now called to cease your destruction and rampant theft. This is your final warning. We will not ask again before we take back what belongs only to the Earth."

"Are you making threats?" the CO interjects.

Frank opens his eyes, remaining calm, he answers, "I'm reciting poetry. I have many poems to share. Be sure to come again?"

Tabitha nods. Tania leans forward, she stretches her hand to try to hold his hands, cuffed together and resting on the table. The CO bellows out again, "No contact with inmates!" and Tania jerks back in her seat.

"Right, forgot."

"I would like to send you some of my poems. When you return." He pauses and looks into Tania's eyes. "I always knew you would return."

She smiles.

"Please share my poem with those who are gathered. And then with the world." Frank asks as his guests are ushered out the door by a different guard. The man hovering above Frank laughs.

"You call that poetry? That's bullshit."

"Yes," Frank replies, "and just like bullshit, many things grow from my poetry."

The guard stops laughing and knocks Frank to the ground again.

CHAPTER 95

Truck Transporting Prison Jumpsuits Hijacked on I-95
Mid-Atlantic Weekly
July 26, 2023
Chris Fellows
Authorities are still searching for a group responsible for one of the most bizarre hijacking cases they've seen. A truck transporting prison jumpsuits was stopped at a rest stop along I-95 yesterday morning, the driver was forced out at gunpoint, and the group drove off with the truck.

"It's bizarre, but we got people desperate, maybe they wanted it for parts, maybe they thought the driver had money? But they seem to have disappeared."

Police Chief Leo Conroy gave a statement. Police are asking anyone with any leads as to the whereabouts of the truck or the gang responsible to contact officers immediately.

CHAPTER 96

Tabitha

Even when Tabitha told her people were beginning to assemble outside the jail, she wasn't prepared for what she saw. What began as a few people huddled around a portable heater overnight spread to encompass more than a hundred people.

Tania stopped at the rooming house long enough to retrieve Emma Goldman and a bag with a few nights' change of clothes and a first aid kit, then headed back to the correctional facility.

The crowd grew in size since her visit this morning. Local news crews huddled on the outskirts, avoiding the crowd but close enough to be spectators.

She walks through the encampment now, Emma Goldman wrapped laying lazily around her neck. Occasionally, she reaches one hand up to steady the cat's body and pet her head.

"Aww, it's the sabocat!" a young person with a nose ring and bright pink hair smiles as they walk by. Tania waves to them and smiles back. She surveys the scene. People are lining up at a table, a nearby sign drawn on cardboard indicates the meal is courtesy of Food Not Bombs.

Right on.

Others wear bright red tape in a cross on their forearms, their bodies and faces covered in black clothing. She recognizes their uniform as a universal indication of street medics. A medic walks past, speaking into a walkie-talkie.

Tania knows she won't be incognito with a cat on her shoulder, but she wants to scope out the surroundings before people approach and ask questions.

Around a small campfire, a group gathers, one person playing a canjo, others singing. She recognizes the melody from an old Warren Zevon song, but instead of singing about Roland the Headless Thompson Gunner, they're singing about her brother.

Some wander around handing out leaflets to attract like-minded people to their group. Others are chanting "Abolish prisons!" and "We are all Frank!"

On the perimeter near the jail, she can see lines of police forming in riot gear. There is enough media here now to keep them in line, she thinks. But when the sun sets, that may be a different story. Still, if everyone here remains through the night, the cops are far outnumbered.

A line of protestors forms facing down the police. They're dressed in black. On the sidelines, people gather, aiming phones at the cops, reminding them they are being live-streamed.

The scene is surreal. It reminds her of the old days.

But it's Frank.

She hasn't even processed seeing her brother again, in light of everything else transpiring before her eyes.

Interest will fade. The masses will return home, and the police will beat anyone remaining into submission. She's seen it a hundred times at least.

But maybe this will be different.

She sees a woman standing to her right, speaking to another woman holding a professional camera. As she passes by, she catches part of the woman's statement.

"We're here outside of Pompton Lakes Correctional where one of dozens of solidarity encampments are happening across the nation tonight..."

Was it true? She hasn't looked at the news since the trip here. She knew Frank's name was being used to agitate nationwide, maybe even worldwide. But there's a difference between what people talk about on social media and what they do in real life.

The banners are eclectic. Freedom for Palestine, The Guillotine Society, and Extinction Rebellion are among the names she's heard before.

Amidst the clamoring crowd, she hears a familiar chant. She turns to see a group entering a vacant spot and setting up a tent. On their flag, a black cat stands, back arched. The banner of the IWW.

"Communiques! Hot off the press, direct from Frank!" A man walks by, announcing into a megaphone. People stream from all directions as he hands out pamphlets with a logo she now recognizes as InkSword.

She looks up again at the line of officers standing shoulder to shoulder, clubs in hands, shields at their sides.

As she scans the growing encampment, a familiar figure stands out. Long red and black shirt, beard, and round face in a constant blush. And behind them, she recognizes Bread and Kevin.

When she reaches Chili, their back is to her. But the others see her. It's been years, but she can tell by the look on Kevin's face, he recognizes her. Chili is in the middle of a story, but Bread puts out an arm to gently turn his friend to the side.

As Chili complies, they look confused at first, until they meet her gaze.

For a moment the world is still.

"You're here."

Emma Goldman jumps down from Tania's shoulders in time for her human transport and Chili to enfold each other in an embrace.

CHAPTER 97

Tania and Emma Goldman camped with the crew from the Cabin. To her relief, the crowd remained overnight. News crews from all over the state arrived. From the top of a fence post, a raven watches the scene. She's been watching the buzz of excitement grow. Soon it will be time.

CHAPTER 98

The next day, Tania wakes to messages on her phone from Tabitha.

"Heading for the jail now, see you soon."

She's about to reply to the message when something catches her eye. A group dressed anachronistically even by conventional standards and way vintage by comparison to the assembled anarchists and radicals of every stripe.

"What's with them?" she asks Chili.

They study the conservative dress and long beards before shaking their head, "Quakers, looks like."

"Shit, even the Quakers are here?" Kevin laughs.

The one in the lead holds a Bible, or she assumes that's what it is. She can't hold back her curiosity.

"I'll be back," she tells Chili, and then wanders through the crowd, trailing the religious group.

CHAPTER 99

Tania endures the line, the scan, metal detectors, and intrusive questions. Once inside the jail, she waits for a CO to bring her to her brother. The Quakers passed through security ahead of her and huddle in the corner of the room, speaking in hushed voices.

A guard enters the room. "He can only have three people per visit," the man grumbles.

"I'm with the press. Are you sure you want to bar the press from having access to an inmate with all the attention you're getting now?" Tania adds.

He folds his arms and grunts but beckons the group forward. She follows the guard and the Quakers to the common area for their visit.

Frank sits at a table surrounded by other inmates.

"Grant," the young man says as they approach, "when you have the serenity of spirit, you are free. Accept that what you thought you could not change is only the manipulation of the powerful. We must all fight to take our power back," he preaches, oblivious to the visitors approaching.

Tania stands to the side, not wanting to interfere. She watches as the room fills with inmates. Some walking two or three to a guard.

Something is off.

The lead Quaker approaches her brother. She hears him say, "Frank, we are your brothers and sisters. We are here to administer the word of God."

The Quaker hands something to Frank. A Bible.

"Just a minute," A nearby guard cuts in, grabbing for the book.

The scene becomes surreal. She can't believe what she's seeing. The lead Quaker turns and punches the guard square in the face, knocking him to the ground. The Quakers rip off their clothes, revealing orange jumpsuits.

As if on cue, visitors throughout the room stand up and rip their clothes off. Each wears an orange jumpsuit under their clothes.

"Sweet Jesus," Tania gasps, a smile growing on her face. She has a moment to savor the scene before the guards, she can see four of them, snap out of their disbelief and begin tackling people to the ground.

"Not the civilians!" One guard shouts. Confusion- and then a brawl- erupts. Two of the remaining Quakers extend their hands to Frank, one pulls a makeshift key from a false bottom in the Bible.

"Come with us," A Quaker woman implores him.

"No, not yet. There are those here who are in more danger than me. Free my comrades first. Then I will follow."

Frank speaks to the man next to him, Grant she heard him call the man, and the man nods his understanding and runs, with the key, toward a group of Quakers who shield him from the guards. Inmates flee cells, some stay and fight, but most head for the exits, shielded and guided by protesters distracting the guards and police.

Frank remains seated, his face calm. Serene. Tania moves to block him. She pulls tables and chairs together in a barricade keeping Frank sectioned off from the melee.

Tania scans the crowd and recognizes a familiar face, one of the few now in the room not wearing a jumpsuit or guard uniform. She motions for Tabitha to join her at the barricade. A few others in jumpsuits stand before the barricade, using their bodies to shield Frank from the melee.

Tabitha runs along the side of the room, narrowly missing a chair flung against the wall as she passes.

"What's going on?" she yells, barely audible over the din.

Before Tania can answer, a voice calls out from behind them. They turn to see Frank, now ascending the pile of tables, chairs, and rubble.

"Comrades, liberate the people. Do not protect me. I am no hero. I am just a Fool. Free yourselves. Free each other.!"

The fighting continues, save for the few who stand around Frank, in awkward silence.

"Go!" He gestures to them to flee, "Don't worry about me, open the cells, free the prisoners."

They run toward the exit only to be met at the door by police running in, German Shepherds at their sides. Instinctively, those tussling in the doorway steps back, giving Tania a clear view.

The officers shout. Some of the brawlers in jumpsuits freeze, facing the door.

It's over. Holy shit. It's over. We're all dead.

One of the cops gives a command she can't hear. A German Shepherd stands taut, then turns, powerful jaws closing around the man's arm. The other dogs follow suit.

A half dozen officers crowded in the doorway and scream as the German Shepherds wrench themselves loose from their leashes and attack. One pounces on an officer, knocking him to the ground, and grabs his face, shaking him in a bloody muzzle.

Excellent praxis, her last thought before something knocks her to the ground.

* * *

Officer Dimples

The man Frank thinks of as Officer Dimples has been stationed outside the encampment all night. When the urgent call for backup first comes in, he's certain he misheard.

"The prison is being overrun…. Outsiders are rioting in the D wing."

His mind, foggy from lack of sleep, tries to comprehend who has gotten into the prison.

"We need help in here now! We have inmates attacking! Dogs attacking!"

The second message rouses him to action. His mind alert with a rush of adrenaline, he calls to the other officers in line.

"We've got a problem on the inside! Let's go, they need backup."

"What about the problem out here?" Another officer gestures to the encampment.

"They're sitting on their asses chanting and drumming. We got a prison riot inside, now move!"

Dimples leads the charge. He rushes for the main entrance as a crowd of people in jumpsuits, and some in prison guard uniforms, run toward them, fleeing the building. He's stunned, and, his delay makes their escape easier. An officer behind him tries to grab a man in a jumpsuit, but they are outnumbered.

"Forget them! Come on! We'll deal with them later," Dimples redirects his crew. The lobby to the jail is a mess with overturned chairs, papers torn and scattered, littering the floor.

They run for wing D, past cells open and emptied out.

What the fuck?

Dimples hears cries of agony as he approaches the open doors. He recognizes Officer Hurst on the floor, half his face chewed off. Blood smeared down his uniform, pooling on the ground beside him.

He turns and vomits on the hallway floor, spraying the shoe of an officer behind him.

He wipes his mouth and stands, steadying himself.

"Someone move this body outta the way!" he yells.

Two men behind him grab Hurst by the ankles and drag him to the side, leaving a smear of blood which they then try to step around.

Dimples sees the other bodies first. On the floor, some he presumes dead. Others groaning. Some are cops. Others are COs.

In a far corner, he sees two women. He recognizes one. She used to be on the news.

Fuck. The reporters saw this.

The thought barely registers as he recognizes the young man standing on a table between them. At his feet, six German Shepherds in police vests sit like sentinels.

His stomach turns. For a moment the room is silent. Then he hears it. A faint sound of chewing. He looks back to Frank, but the young man's mouth is set firm, neutral. The women beside him are still.

The German Shepherd's muzzles are all closed, motionless.

His heart races as he follows the sound.

And that's when he sees it.

The Warden's body, was recognizable only by his hat, his stout belly, and the ring on his finger. Blood and gore ooze from his face, neck, and chest.

Hovering over his corpse, a grey wolf chews on the Warden's flesh.

The officers file into the room, Volker, a rookie, stops short when he sees the wolf, causing a collision with the men behind him.

"Don't just stand there, shoot it!" someone shouts.

CHAPTER 100

Tabitha

The scene dissolves into chaos before she can process what is happening. Tabitha hovers beneath a table, shielding her eyes with one arm. She gives up on the plan to take notes by hand and instead retrieves a recorder from her pocket.

"I'm inside Pompton Correctional… Hundreds remain encamped outside. I'm watching a riot. It appears saboteurs entered the jail as visitors, they've taken their clothes off revealing orange jumpsuits…"

The shouting and crashing of tables, chairs, and bodies drown out her voice. She pauses, ducking low, as an officer's gun slides across the floor. No one notices it. She waits for a clearing and extends her hand far enough to grab the weapon and pull it close, partially concealing it.

You have no idea how to shoot a gun, she reminds herself.

She switches the recorder to her dominant hand, but keeps the gun within reach, continuing to narrate as the events grow more bizarre.

"Cops have responded to a call for help, they're crowding the entrance. They've brought in the dogs and it looks like …. Oh, Oh my GOD!"

Screams of shock and pain eclipse her voice. She begins gagging back vomit, and turns away, trying to maintain control of her senses.

"The dogs are attacking the police. People are escaping the jail and others from outside are coming in and everybody's wearing jumpsuits. An officer is calling for backup. The dogs have abandoned the officers and are... they're coming toward,... they're walking toward us," she hates the fear audible in her shaking voice.

She cowers under the table, looking for Frank and Tania. Both are above her, standing on top of the barricade. In lunging distance of the dogs.

Her heart pounds faster. The dogs sniff the ground as they approach, and the remaining guards left alive slide their injured bodies out of the way, clearing a path for the beasts.

One of the German Shepherds takes the lead, licking her lips as she approaches. She eyes Tabitha, then raises her head, facing Frank's direction.

She sits, then bows her head, and the others follow.

"What in the actual fuck is going on?" Tabitha asks her recorder.

CHAPTER 101

Frank

By the time the wolf arrives, the room has mostly cleared out. Only the reporter, he forgot her name, and his sister and one other guard remain. Bodies are strewn across the floor, some dead, others severely injured.

The guard faces Frank. He doesn't see the grey wolf slinking through the door behind him. Ignores the low growl that Frank feels through the room. Or maybe he doesn't hear it? Humans are used to ignoring the voices of nature.

The guard draws his gun and aims it at Frank. Tania leaps on him, knocking him to the floor as a bullet flies past him. He hears it. Feels the explosion from the gun. Feels the metal lodge into the wall behind where his head was moments ago.

Carmen, Tania, he reminds himself, pulls him back up to his feet. She's about to say something when a cry of agony causes them both to turn toward the guard who is now being devoured beneath the muzzle of the wolf.

CHAPTER 102

Officer Dimples reaches for his gun, aims at the wolf, and at the last minute, his hand jerks up, the bullet hitting the ceiling instead. He registers the pain moments after the first puncture. Something is hanging from his shin.

"It's a fucking rat!" Someone yells.

He looks down, a mass of grey fur stuck to him. Teeth like nails. What the fuck is this?

"Not a rat, a fucking possum,"

He kicks his foot, but Popcorn holds firm both with his paws and his teeth. Dimples tries to balance on one foot, but in doing so falls to the floor, landing hard on his other knee. Popcorn scrambles up the man's body to his head, using his paws to gauge the officer's eyes.

CHAPTER 103

Tania

Would you believe at that moment I thought of George Orwell and Animal Farm? Reunited with my baby brother for less than a day and as all hell is breaking loose, I'm thinking of Animal Farm.

In fairness, I thought of Frank first. And if I had to throw myself between my brother and the cops, I would. Second, I thought of Orwell. And third, Chili, I thought of you.

What did any of that petty bullshit matter now? This is what we hoped for. This is what we worked for. This is what our comrades died for.

The first time, I threw myself on him. We were safe.

Then the animals started pouring in. Not just the German Shepherds turning on the cops, that was cool.

But also, a wolf.

Then a possum.

Then raccoons, skunks. All rushing in. I could hear them in the hallways. And other cops came but some of them got freaked out and ran.

Running from a skunk, can you believe it?

Even Emma G., naughty girl that she is, found her way in. I saw her side eye the possum, but she understood the assignment. Jumped on a guard's back and clawed his eyes. That's my girl.

And then the windows far overhead crashed open. Birds flew in. When the officers ran for us, the birds flew in their faces. Like Alfred Hitchcock.

Crazy, right?

I can't believe the last thing I said to you was "Wait right here," before I went after those Quakers. I wish I had gotten to say more. To Frank, and to you.

But there was no time.

An officer pushed a bird off his head. Ran for us. His mouth opens in a sneer. Drool on his chin. His eyes were wild. He pointed the gun. And I didn't have time to say goodbye.

CHAPTER 104

Frank

Tania sinks to the floor, and Frank sees her blood spill out at the base of the barricade. He thinks of Mallory but only for a moment. He is no longer in his body. His roots stretch farther than they ever have. He feels the pulse of drums as people gather outside the walls of the jail, dancing. He drinks minerals from the earth. Feels Comrade Sun, the walls no longer a barrier.

Chaos surrounds him- This is his tower year- but he is at peace. He feels his sister's spirit rise, joining with Mallory and countless others whose hearts are now one drumbeat. is He has no mind to lose this time.

Make me an instrument of your will.

He walks toward the guards, now swarming into the room, fending off animals who bite at their feet and fly at their faces.

An officer lunges at Frank. A gun explodes behind him. The bullet passes somewhere over Frank's shoulder. He hears it whistle as time stands still. The man in uniform, he recognizes in a fleeting moment, is Dimples.

Officer Dimples' face contorts first in surprise, then pain as he collapses on the ground.

CHAPTER 105

Roxie

By the time Roxie runs ahead of the crowd storming the jail, darting between and around a wave of people in jumpsuits fleeing the building, the building is a mess. She enters the lobby and steps around bodies haphazardly strewn on the ground. Something scurries past the periphery of her sight. She turns her head and eyes adjusting, she recognizes Popcorn.

She follows him up a flight of stairs and across corridors, through a door marked D Wing. No one tries to stop them. Only the corpses are in uniform as far as she can tell. But she knows it won't be long before reinforcements come. Maybe even the National Guard.

Popcorn stops short in the center of a room she presumes was used not too long ago for inmate visits. Tables are shoved in a pile in one corner of the room. Officers and one civilian- a woman- lay in pools of blood on the ground.

There is no sign of Frank.

"Where is he?" she asks Popcorn, impatient. Knowing Frank was the only one who could understand him. The possum glances toward the pile of tables and then back at her. Roxie runs to the corner, trying not to vomit as the smell catches up with her. She tries to sidestep the bodies, considers sliding them to the side, and then changes her mind.

We don't have time.

Instead, she yanks the tables apart, her guts churning as the leg of one table hits one of the bodies with a dull thud. She refuses to look. Whoever it is, they are dead. No sense in slowing down. She topples the tables and chairs until she can see the bare floor.

Empty.

"What the fuck?" she yells at Popcorn. He stares at her, his expression revealing nothing.

She is about to scream something else when a voice breaks through the silence.

"Are you okay?"

Roxie turns to see a face vaguely familiar. From somewhere. The news, or a commercial on television, the moment becomes surreal as she recognizes Tabitha from InkSword.

"I'm looking for Frank."

The woman walks toward her, looking nervously over her shoulder.

"He was here. But he's gone. I didn't see where he went. But no one else is here. At least, not now. Come on, we have to get out of here."

"What about Frank?" Roxie tries to keep her voice from cracking.

"Come on. He's survived a lot. I think he'll be okay."

Tabitha takes the younger woman by the arm and leads her toward the exit. Popcorn crawls along the rubble in the shadows, following behind them.

CHAPTER 106

Six Months Later

Joann

Joann Bernardoni stares, detached, as Heather and Gina speak in confidential tones, side-eyeing the various couples about whom they gossip.

The gala is for Francesco, she tries to remind herself, to raise money for the new Francesco. To fund the new non-profit her husband started, Francesco's Fund. She reminds herself to focus. To be present. But she can't get the dream out of her mind.

"And the DiNanti's, over there, don't look…. Don't *look*," Heather implores her, putting a hand on her arm, and motioning conspicuously with her other hand, spilling a tiny splash of wine in the process, "I heard John is under investigation for embezzling from his company."

Heather's smirk reveals schadenfreude, she eyes the couple across the room. Gina leans close, speaking every word with exaggerated arched brows and an index finger pointing into the air, "And you can believe they're going to find it. Everything comes out in the wash, I always tell Marty …"

Her voice fades, as if she is speaking through a tunnel. Joann doesn't care about the DiNanti's, doesn't care about the fundraiser. Her mind is on the dream, and the unshakeable feeling that her oldest child, Carmen, is dead.

"Something wrong, Joann? You look like you've seen a ghost." Heather leans back, eyeing Joann as she asks.

Before she can answer, Gina comes to the rescue, "Heather! Don't be ridiculous. All her family's been through? Of course, she isn't okay. That's why she needs our support."

Joann tries to play along. Nodding her head, giving her friends a weak half-smile.

She did see a ghost. She's sure of it. But she can't say a word about it. Not even to her friends. She often dreamt of Carmen in the years since the fight, when her daughter left home....

Was kicked out. By your husband...

A voice in the back of her mind reminds her.

The dreams were often confusing, and vague, but reassuring. Even one dream, in which her daughter was held in some kind of prison, alarmed her. But in that dream, Carmen reassured her.

"Mom, I'm okay. You'll see me again."

But the recent dream was different. Carmen came to her door, late at night. Everything was hazy, surreal. Around her shoulders, she carried a cat with a woman's name. She remembered thinking it was a formal-sounding name, but the detail escapes her now.

The rest of the dream was as clear as if it really happened. Her daughter, all grown up and confident in a way Joann never dared to be, sat in her living room. Carmen leaned forward on the couch, hands held together as if preparing for a prayer. She looked Joann in the eyes and said, "Mom, enough is enough. You have to think of Connie."

"I am thinking of Connie. This is the best chance she has ..." Joann protested but didn't believe her own words.

Pack now. While he's not here. I have people who can help you. Bring Connie. You can do this."

It made sense in the dream. Joann stood, turning toward the stairs, "I'll think about it. For real this time. I'll think about it and I'll call you…"

But when she turned toward the couch again, her daughter was gone. And by the following evening, she knew her daughter Carmen was dead.

"Don't you worry Joann," Heather's voice returns her attention to the gala, the room filling now with friends, acquaintances, and various frenemies, "I found a great deal on a cruise, I think the three of us should get away. My treat, you just say when you've had enough and you want to get away."

Joann feels tears well in her eyes. She has had enough. She nods slowly, then leaned in close to her friends, eyes darting side to side to make sure Pat is not around, "I've actually been thinking…I mean, you know, all of this with Francesco, it's been a lot."

"Sure, honey, we know it. We're here for you," Gina rubs her shoulder as she speaks.

Joann sighs, but still treads lightly. Pat is a powerful man with many friends who love him and just as many people who fear him. "I was thinking, with everything that's happened…. I wonder sometimes… if maybe I need to get away… from Pat."

"Oh, yes, you've both been under so much stress, some time away from each other was great for my marriage, I'm sure it's all you both need," Gina chimes in.

"No, I mean… I mean getting away. Starting over? Like, on my own?" She regrets the words as soon as she speaks them.

Her friends' expressions turn from concerned to patronizing.

"Oh, honey, you've been through this before, remember? And it always works out," Gina's face is sincere, masking an authority that tells Joann there is no use arguing.

"And besides, with Francesco gone, you've got to think of what's best for Connie. You can't start over now. You need Pat. How else can you be sure Connie will be taken care of? She's all you have left now."

Joann nods, her gaze wanders as her friends revert back to gossip. Pat stands near the front of the room, his face light and radiant as he shakes hands with men she barely recognizes from the Chamber of Commerce and the Country Club. Standing by his side, she recognizes Francesco's best friend since childhood, Jonathan, the president of the Francesco Foundation.

CHAPTER 107

Narrator

Frank's story is open to interpretation, and interpret it, people did.

Some say when reinforcements finally came, the jail was empty. Void of all life, that is. Bodies littered the floor and there was detritus from the various beasts who intervened.

The woman named Tabitha was already outside, walking amongst the crowd. Rumor has it she secreted a recording device to a trusted comrade among the encampment.

As for the man who came to be known as Frank from Jersey, his body was never found. Some say he was apprehended, tortured, killed, and disposed of. Others say he turned into a wolf and ran off into the woods. Some even suggest a pack of wolves carried him away.

Word of his disappearance and possible murder took him from saint to martyr.

And we know a certain man who can't abide that.

Pat Bernardoni devoted the rest of his life to suppressing, bending, and manipulating his son's message.

He painted Frank as a fool, a zealot, or at best a hopeless idealist who wanted peace and pacifism, not revolution.

But someone made sure the truth got out....

CHAPTER 107

Tabitha

Tabitha listens to the podcasters recount the latest rash of uprisings that are now ubiquitous. They no longer mention Frank by name, but she knows he wouldn't mind.

There are no gods, no masters, no heroes, she hears him say.

She was lucky to make it out that day with her recorder, and a new friend. She scratches Emma G.'s head and her new charge jumps into her lap, circles, and then curls into a ball, purring.

She pets Emma for a moment, before leaning close to the laptop on her desk. Her hands shake as she uploads the attachment of her manuscript compiling all of her research into the Bernardoni empire. Once this email is sent, every major and independent news outlet in the world will know the story of Pat Bernardoni and Frank from Jersey.

Another of the young man's phrases passes through her mind, "make me an instrument of your will," she murmurs it as a prayer and hits send.

CHAPTER 108

Narrator

We once lived for what seemed an eternity. Not anymore. Our lives are cut short. But if there is one thing I am grateful for, as I await my death, it is that I was able to share with you this story.

Now you must repeat it. Change the names. It doesn't matter. Just tell the story.

Those who have sat sentinel on my limbs understand. They heard the call and listened. My defenders are being pulled down now by officers. Their hands cuffed and zip tied. Others gather at my trunk, but not for long. One by one they are dragged away.

My time is short.

My roots feel the ground shaking as the trucks close in. Last night was the last I will see Sister Moon. These are my final moments warmed by Comrade Sun.

Squirrels and birds flee from my branches in a panic as the chainsaws scream.

It's too late for me, but not for you.

ABOUT THE AUTHOR

Diogenes Kaufman, formerly Angela Kaufman, is an author, writer, LCSW, tarot reader, and astrologer whose novels published by Trash Panda Press include Siskiyou Prize in Environmental Literal Finalist *Quiet Man* (2020), *Golden Apple* (2021), *Murder in the Gilded City* (2022). Nonfiction books include *Queen Up! Reclaim Your Crown When Life Knocks You Down-Unleash the Power of Your Inner Queen* (Conari, 2018).